TRILOGY NO. 111:
SPEAK ITS NAME

CHARLIE COCHRANE
LEE ROWAN
ERASTES

TRILOGY NO. 111: SPEAK ITS NAME
Aftermath
Copyright © CHARLIE COCHRANE, 2008
Gentleman's Gentleman
Copyright © LEE ROWAN, 2008
Hard and Fast
Copyright © ERASTES, 2008
Cover art by BEVERLY MAXWELL
ISBN Trade paperback: 978-1-60202-124-2
ISBN MS Reader (LIT): 978-1-60202-125-9
Other available formats (no ISBNs are assigned):
PDF, PRC & HTML

Linden Bay Romance, LLC
Palm Harbor, Florida 34684
www.lindenbayromance.com

First Linden Bay Romance publication: June 2008

AFTERMATH
CHARLIE COCHRANE

Chapter One

"Mr. Easterby. Mr. Easterby, sir!" The porter's voice cut through the cold morning as piercingly as the creak from the college gate had done. Early March, 1920, and spring seemed to be taking forever to arrive, as if it, too, still mourned for the flowers of manhood that had been trampled into the mud of Flanders Field.

Edward Easterby turned to see Cranmer College's newest porter waving something at him. "Can I help you, Mr. Marsh?" he enquired in his usual polite tone. One of the few engaging qualities about this young student was the way that he treated everyone—porters, scouts, shopkeepers—with the same degree of respect as he would do a fellow Oxford undergraduate. It made him, if not popular with them all, at least respected, something that wouldn't have naturally occurred given his generally brooding and anti-social nature.

"I believe that this is yours, sir." Marsh held out an engraved silver cigarette case, handsomely made but not of the very highest quality. "Someone found it by the lodge."

Easterby smiled, a genuine, happy smile, not like the ones he produced when he had to make an effort to entertain people. "Well, it is and it isn't, Mr. Marsh. It belongs to my grandfather; our initials are the same. He must have dropped it when he was visiting yesterday. I'll take it and return it to him."

The porter smiled, too, which unsettled Edward. The college usually discouraged such familiarity but Marsh seemed determined to make a point. "I hope that he hasn't missed it, I wouldn't like the gentleman to be without something so precious." This was more forward than was acceptable in a college employee, and Edward grimaced at the familiarity. He didn't appreciate this boldness and suspected that the inhabitants of the porters' lodge had been gossiping about the meaning of the message engraved on the case, a seemingly insignificant phrase that was full of importance to the family.

Easterby would make no allowance for Marsh being relatively new and not having had all the rough edges rubbed off him yet. Like many another place, Cranmer College had lost of a number of its finest men—students, fellows, scouts, and porters alike—during the harsh middle years of the decade, when first war and then disease had cut through their ranks. New men had come in as replacements and the college hadn't yet put her stamp on all of them, but this was intolerable.

"I'm afraid that my grandfather wouldn't wish for his private property to be interfered with." Edward turned on his heels and left.

If he'd known what the porters usually said about him, he'd have been even more annoyed. *Seems like an overgrown boy* was one of the more generous opinions. *All fancy thoughts and no common sense* was another view, especially among those who'd served with similar men in the war.

The few women who were allowed into Cranmer saw things differently. They found Edward rather handsome— he had melancholy eyes that seemed full of strange emotions and dark curls that never could be restrained by brush or macassar oil. He possessed a studious face, firmly masculine in its lines, and they were sure he worked hard at his studies. *Bit of a dreamer, though.*

It wouldn't have surprised anyone to find that Easterby certainly didn't possess the common sense he'd been born with, not enough to survive happily in the maelstrom that passed for undergraduate life in Cranmer. He couldn't even avoid getting totally plastered at the hands of his so-called friends.

If asked to tell the truth, Edward would have said that he'd never really possessed a friend in his life. He had acquaintances with whom he would work through difficult problems or discuss esoteric theories—but he had no one whom he'd allowed to get close, not even in his childhood days. Perhaps he was destined to be one of life's recluses, a man designed only for the cloister, whether it be in a monastery or an Oxford college. Or the madhouse.

When one of the young men on his staircase invited him for drinks in his set, he'd been surprised—less so when he saw that all the occupants of the staircase were there. He'd made his best efforts to indulge in small talk, but gradually folk had drifted away and he'd been left to contemplate the bookcase, alone again, as he often found himself. Somebody suggested moving on to the college bar, most of those present agreed, and Easterby was swept along by the human current, in the flow of what seemed to be a river of drunkenness.

One of those who'd egged him on began spiking his drinks at the bar with increasing amounts of alcohol. Edward took them in all innocence, keeping—he'd thought—to a sensible quantity, unaware of the strength of the brew; by the time he realized what was going on, it was far too late to act. His head spun, all speech and sound around him dulled, his stomach churned, and all he sought was fresh air. Easterby wanted to be outside more than he'd ever wanted anything in the world.

He instantly regretted that he'd ever made such a wish once he hit the cold air. The universe spun like a mad thing and the reeling that came with it made his stomach contents rise up through his throat. He leant over in the quad, hoping to find some flower bed that might hide his disgrace, but all he found were a pair of well made shoes, and those he retched over without delay. Edward wasn't sure whether it was the shock of realizing what he'd done or just getting rid of what was distressing him, but he felt immediately more sober. Wiping his mouth on his sleeve and beginning to mumble an apology, he looked up to see a face that filled him with shame. Hugo Lamont. He had spewed up over Hugo Lamont's shoes.

The man was a legend within the college. He was twice a rugby blue; maybe not the finest mind in the History department, but at least expected to pass all his exams with flying colors. And he was as popular with his fellow undergraduates as Edward was out of favor. What made it so annoying was the fact that he was nice with it, not some arrogant bastard who thought himself above the rest. They held Lamont up as a shining example of all that the students of Cranmer should aspire to, and he never seemed to take advantage of that fact. There had been plenty of times when Easterby had looked at the bloke and simply hated him. There had been other times he'd looked at the bloke and wanted to strip all the clothes off his back.

"I'm so very sorry." Edward couldn't look the other man in the eye. They were already a world apart; they'd hardly had any contact in the five months that Easterby had been up, he being a humble, antisocial first year and hardly aspirant to Hugo's assured position in his second year. Indeed, it was almost as if someone had designed Lamont to be the man's direct opposite. Smiling where Edward was surly, an old Etonian to Easterby's middle class background and schooling; even their looks were a direct contrast of dark and light. Edward was tall, slimly built and seemed a mass of chocolate brown and ebony tones. Hugo was red gold and piercing blue, a stocky heap of muscle.

There had been no reason for their paths to cross directly, up until now. Edward had only seen this man from afar and admired with envy his easy manner and popularity; it was so unfair that when they did collide it should be in so embarrassing a manner. He mumbled an apology.

"Think you've had a touch too much, young man. If you can't handle it, you shouldn't take it." Lamont's eyes flickered like sparks arcing. "Suggest you take yourself back to your room before you cause any more damage." He turned on his rather stained heels, returning five minutes later in clean shoes and socks, only to find Easterby in the place he had left him, still standing and staring into vacancy.

"Are you ever going to move, or do you propose to puke on all the shoes that pass by?"

The rising anger in his voice made Edward flinch. "I'm sorry." It was all he could say. He didn't just feel humiliated, he burned with self-reproach at having offended the only person he'd ever found attractive.

"You've said that already—do something about it now. Just go away and leave decent people to get on with their lives." Lamont stormed off, leaving Easterby alone—a stranger in a society he failed to understand at times. Only one thing he was sure of; he wanted to be Hugo Lamont and not himself. But what was the point of wanting something when there was never any chance of getting it?

Any man at Cranmer would have told you that Easterby and Lamont were direct opposites, but the two men had much more in common than anyone could have guessed. A student of human nature might have concluded that Edward disliked himself and that was part of the reason he cut himself off from the world, becoming immersed in his books and experiments, unwilling to expose his weaknesses to public view. Some of those who had been just too young to enlist had a degree of self hatred, unhappy with the good fortune that had enabled them to survive while older brothers or friends had been hung on the barbed wire like washing on a thorn bush. No one knew whether Easterby had lost anyone close or if he would have been the same way irrespective of the Great War. None of them would have guessed that part of the problem was the unnatural—he'd always heard it said it was unnatural—desire he felt for other men.

A degree of self-hatred; no one said the same of Lamont. He was a popular bon vivant, the life and soul of plenty of parties, but it was true of him, also. He kept his self-repugnance hidden below a veneer of bonhomie and heartiness, a public face that smiled while his private one wept. No one guessed, given that he often had a girl on his arm, the root of Hugo's unease—no one saw the girls being given a peck on the cheek and sent off with their hopes dashed. Just like Edward, Hugo fancied men, and they both burned with shame about it.

Lamont had known this startling fact from childhood, and no amount of self-persuasion as he'd grown up had moved him. In his first year at Cranmer, wet behind the ears and with no understanding of his own ignorance, he'd even been desperate enough to pick up a hostess from a London club and take her out in his car, the novelty of a ride in such a swanky motor impressing her greatly. His sole determination had been to seduce her, or at least pay her for the privilege of letting him do so. Hugo felt that it might cure him, but every kiss they shared simply made him feel sick at the whole process. He had stopped her short, when things had hardly begun, thrust money into her hand, and left her to find a cab and make her own way home. The cry that followed him up the street, *You some kind of a bleedin' Nancy boy, then?* had added to his misery.

He hadn't gone home. He'd gone to a different club, one he'd heard guarded mention of. Here he'd picked up a young man and driven out to somewhere secluded. Lamont had his money's worth that time—it was the first and last occasion he'd indulged in this particular pleasure, and he remembered it with very little joy but plenty of guilt.

Afterwards he took the decision just to repress all his desires, to cultivate an image of cheerfulness and laughter, papering over the cracks of his unhappiness. And he'd succeeded, living an asexual life, disgusted with any desire for contact that he might feel. He particularly disgusted himself with the feelings he nurtured for the dark haired, first year chemistry student who'd appeared in the college the previous October.

Lamont had watched Easterby from the very first time he saw him at dinner in hall. He'd admired his dignity and bearing, his shyness and solemnity, and he'd wanted to kiss him, hold him, and do the sort of disgraceful things that he'd done just the once in his car in a dark lane near Hampstead Heath. It had even made him begin to hate the man, a feeling that spilled out over the shoes incident much as Edward's stomach contents had.

The man's an idiot Hugo had thought. *Just the sort of little toad that should never be allowed through the college gates. I know that the war affected us all, but why must Cranmer let its standards drop so very low?*

Ironically, he might have detested him even more if he'd known that Edward felt exactly the same about his own sex, except that *he'd* never given in, never put his desires into any sort of practice. Hugo would have been mortified to know that Easterby had been observing him at that same college dinner and had fallen for the shining crop of hair and the dizzy laugh wafting over the table from five places down—just too far to talk, just too close to ignore. He'd watched Lamont often since but had been too shy to chat, didn't dare make any sort of advance, despised himself for even thinking such things.

The last thing Hugo Lamont needed was a temptation that might let itself be given into.

The morning after Edward had ended up so slaughtered, the whole college was woken by great crashes of thunder and forks of lightning slashing through the sky. The noise drummed into Lamont's head and he found he couldn't return to his slumbers. He contented himself with a pot of tea, a novel, and trying to forget about the day before. When the rain had subsided enough to let him venture out, he sauntered to the porters' lodge to look for his post. Marsh nodded to him, passing the time of day and regretting that the inclement weather had done the unforgivable thing of delaying the mail delivery. Despite that, a single letter was nestled in Lamont's pigeon hole. He took it back to his set, alight with curiosity.

Hugo opened the correspondence carefully—he didn't recognize the hand nor the style of paper. He lifted the envelope to his face and tried to detect if there was any faint hint of perfume or other odor. Defeated, he drew out the sheets and began to read. The immediate anger he felt when, as he always did, he looked at the signature first, dissolved as he read the words. They were stiff, proper, laden with regret and formality. He could imagine the younger man sitting and drawing every word out as if it were a recalcitrant tooth.

He guessed right. Easterby had indeed drafted and redrafted this letter to so many times that his wastepaper basket had overflowed, his pen needed refilling time and again, and his fingers had ended up a mass of black ink.

Lamont was greatly touched by the strong emotion that seemed to pour out of the carefully chosen words. The letter began with profuse apologies—*I should have known better, not fit behaviour for a gentleman*—followed by gallantry—*I'd be pleased to pay for a replacement pair*. Hugo smiled at this, well aware that Easterby couldn't have the foggiest idea of how much those brogues had cost. Then there was contrition—*I hope for forgiveness, but I'd understand if this could not be found*—finally, hopelessness—*I'd understand if you wished to have no further communication. The matter of the new shoes could be negotiated by a go-between.*

Hugo put down the letter with a sigh. If it had been just

about anyone else in the college, then he could have forgiven him easily enough, with a laugh and a drink. With Easterby, this seemed impossible. To approach the man, even in reply to this painful letter, would be inviting danger. Were they to be alone together, Hugo might find that he couldn't control his emotions. He'd managed to do so before, in some fairly strained circumstances, with other people he'd found attractive, but the intense desire he felt for this young man, desire that was strangely ignited again by this letter, might be beyond his ability to keep in check.

His conscience pricked him; why should this Easterby have to pay for his, Lamont's, faults? Why, because of his own perverted nature, shouldn't they be able to resolve this matter like gentlemen? Edward wouldn't ever find him attractive anyway. Hugo could not convince himself that there'd be any chance of the other man returning his affection if he offered it, so it would be safe to invite the man for tea and cakes at least. He considered the matter again, briefly, but once he made his mind up he became precipitate. *Today—it should be today.* He found a stiff piece of card, drafted an invitation and delivered it to Easterby's pigeon hole. *All forgiven—tea and a scone at four o'clock should you wish to confirm this fact.*

Lamont was absolutely amazed when on the stroke of four a tentative knock struck his door. He opened it to find a still shamefaced Easterby who seemed like he wanted to talk to a spot that lay beyond Hugo's right ear. "I hope I got the right time, I..."

Lamont stopped him in painful mid flow; he couldn't bear to listen to such an embarrassed introduction. "Come in, please. The kettle is boiling and it won't do to keep the brew waiting."

Edward entered, all awkward corners and shyness. He perched on the edge of a chair and looked pained. "Your shoes, I've brought my check book..." he reached for his pocket.

"Oh, for goodness sake, there is absolutely no need. I

9

managed to rescue the shoes, with help from my scout. There is no more to be said." Lamont busied himself with the rituals of tea making, trying not to look at Easterby's long, elegant fingers or his dark, feminine lashes. All the things that added to his allure. The man had turned himself out well, although his clothes had seen better days and Hugo knew that he'd guessed correctly that a new pair of brogues would have made a severe strain on Easterby's bank balance. He'd expected that the gap in their social and financial standing would help him to keep his distance but it didn't—again and again his gaze drifted towards his visitor's handsome and shy face.

Hugo had put together a plan to get him through, to let him enjoy the time spent with this attractive young man without disgracing himself. In the first place he wouldn't use Christian names. He hadn't known the real name of the young man he had picked up in London.

They call me Domino, for obvious reasons. One nudge in the right direction and I'm flat on my stomach.

Hugo hadn't shared his own name at all, making the boy refer to him as "sir" throughout. It was cold and impersonal, and while part of him had wanted the lack of involvement, the absolute anonymity, part of him had despised it. It kept reminding Lamont that it had just been a sordid business transaction—no love or affection, not even friendship.

The second point was simple. He wouldn't let Easterby touch him, not even for a handshake. There had been plenty of touching in Lamont's car with Domino; he hadn't left a bit of that lad's body unexplored.

I don't mind what my gentlemen get up to—do whatever you like, sir.

But the whole thing had been curiously unmoving— fun, of course, and he'd had a final burst of unbelievable pleasure, but the whole thing was just unsatisfactory. Perhaps it was because any trust, any friendship, any love, had been missing, and that had meant Hugo found it empty of all meaning. He wasn't like other men seemed to be, he could not disconnect the physical sexual act from the mental experience that accompanied it, and that created a stalemate. If he wouldn't let himself get close to someone—for fear of rejection, denouncement, violence—then he might never find the ultimate communion. The ultimate in pleasure.

So he and his visitor simply drank tea and talked. Easterby began to act less like a naughty boy called to the Headmaster's study to explain his conduct, and Lamont felt less like a lecherous satyr on the hunt for an innocent to debauch. They found some common ground—an interest in the stories about Sherlock Holmes, a fondness for stodgy traditional English puddings, an affection for the music of Gilbert and Sullivan. They even found things to laugh over in the exploits of an obnoxious physics student who'd come a cropper on the river in a crew of little ability but plenty of swagger. Easterby brought the laughter to a sudden end by leaping up, making a hurried apology and saying that he had to leave immediately. *Another engagement,* he pleaded, *so sorry.*

This proposed departure was so abrupt and unexpected that it spurred Lamont into action. "But you'll come again? I was planning a picnic on Saturday—can't just take myself. Will you meet me here and we can go down to the river?"

"What time?" Edward ventured, after a long pause in which he seemed to be mulling things over.

"One o'clock would be splendid." Lamont bit his lip, knowing the danger he was putting himself in. He'd held out well this afternoon; how would he fare on some secluded river bank?

"Then one o'clock it is." Easterby bowed slightly and left.

Lamont watched him go, fairly certain that the excuse had been a false one, not knowing why he'd been so rash as to extend the invitation to meet again. He went over to the still warm chair and ran his fingers along the back, where Easterby's head had at last rested while he had been relaxed and laughing. He sat down in the same seat and entertained his old thoughts—joy combined with guilt and self loathing.

Edward almost ran to his room; there hadn't ever been another appointment of course, he just wanted to get out of a place in which he was feeling far too much at home. He needed to be away from company in which he was feeling uncharacteristically at ease. Separate from the temptation to touch another man.

Easterby had found the last half an hour to be one of the best of his life. He'd found someone he could talk to and who seemed to like talking to him, and quite unbelievably that person had been Hugo Lamont. But to have accepted an invitation to a picnic on the river—to be risking an intimately close encounter—he wasn't sure he was ready. Perhaps he'd never be ready.

Chapter Two

"Quails' eggs?" Edward looked puzzled at the elegant little ovals, unsure whether he should eat them or merely admire them.

"Indeed, Mr. Easterby," Lamont grinned. "I can be quite a glutton for them."

"Please, call me Edward, if that would be acceptable." Easterby was uncertain whether this was a touch too forward, but the champagne had put a boldness in him that he hadn't felt since he had first come up to Oxford. He'd never been invited to a picnic by the river in all those months, even when October had brought a splendid Indian summer and everyone else seemed to be making the most of the sunshine. He would never in a million years have expected being asked along by such a man as Hugo Lamont, who had his free choice of companions and would hardly be likely to choose an unpopular and introverted guest. But chosen he had, and Edward was very grateful. He attempted a little smile.

"If I'm to call you Edward, then you must call me Hugo." Lamont smiled, but Easterby thought it was forced. "I absolutely insist. You can't be my guest and then not address me as my equal."

Easterby hesitated over the use of first names, happy to invite, reluctant to accept, but felt obliged to comply. "Hugo," once he had used it, the name tasted as sweet as honey on his tongue, "I feel quite speechless at the spread you've produced for me. I've never seen half these things before, though I dare say I'd recognize the names."

"You'll have heard of this, Edward." Lamont dipped a little spoon into a small jar of tiny black pearls. He motioned for Easterby to put out his hand and dabbed a sample of the stuff on his fingertip. "Caviar—try it."

He did. He grimaced. "So that's what the stuff is like—seems an awful lot of fuss about nothing."

Hugo lay back and roared with laughter. "Edward, you are such a breath of fresh air. So many people I know here are full of their own importance, want to show off about their knowledge or fine taste or exotic places they've been. But you are simply honest and decent, and when I'm in your company, I don't feel that I have to make any sort of effort." Except that he seemed to be making an effort not to touch Easterby in any way. He'd kept his own fingers to the very end of the caviar-laden spoon.

Easterby blushed. "You shouldn't speak like that. It's not proper." He sounded like a parlor maid who had been given "sauce" by a house guest, but his honor had been affronted. He desired Hugo beyond all reckoning and was certain that the man could never feel the same. Any sign that Lamont was being familiar would just raise his hopes unduly, and he did not want to even acknowledge the possibility that it might occur.

"Oh, why ever not? It's the truth. There are very few people I just enjoy spending time with, and when they come along, I like to make it plain to them."

Easterby watched his new found friend smile and laugh, transfixed by Lamont's beauty—his red-gold hair that shimmered in the sunlight, the blue eyes that rivaled the sky for brilliance. He wondered what it would be like if Hugo let him touch that hair, how it would feel beneath his fingers, whether it would smell of lavender soap.

"Should we go and watch the cricket one day? I like nothing more than watching the lads getting themselves

14

covered in grass stains. The sound of leather on willow, nothing like it."

Edward nodded his head. "I agree with you entirely—an outing to a match would be delightful." He smiled and fell quiet, unsure of where this conversation was going, apart from an invitation to watch sport. He knew that he was enjoying this time with Hugo more than anything he'd experienced in Oxford. He yearned to spend as long as possible in the man's company; he was just not ready to admit it to him, in case he was answered with a rebuff. *Lamont was kind; he was just being pleasant.* There was no deeper meaning and there was no point in getting his own hopes up.

Edward was thinking as intensely as if he were solving a chemistry puzzle. At some point he had to know whether he was simply tolerated or if there was more to the friendship of the glorious creature beside him. Except this wasn't a matter of science; there was no yardstick to measure his conduct against, no previous encounter to be compared with. He was a total innocent, and while he despised himself for what he felt—*unnatural* did not begin to cover it—he felt drawn to Hugo like a moth to a flame or a child whose determination to approach the fire is only reinforced every time they are told not to touch. But he wasn't ready to touch just yet.

So they ate, they drank, they chatted and Edward found the afternoon wore on pleasantly enough.

The plates were bare, the bottle of wine empty and the two young men on the river bank were too full to attempt another morsel. Hugo lay back on the mossy bank and stared at the blue sky. "Today has certainly turned unseasonably warm for March, Edward, but we won't complain in case someone hears and does something to rectify it." Hugo was at last comfortable about using his friend's Christian name. He'd worried about it all morning, aware that they could not continue with *Lamont* and *Easterby*, but knowing it would mean the first level of the defenses that he'd constructed for that first meeting would be breached. There were other walls, other ditches and towers, but the curtain had been broken. He wasn't sure if he was pleased or not, this was unknown territory.

He looked up. "Come here...no, right next to me so that I can see both you and the sky at the same time." He'd spoken his innermost thoughts and he was cross at himself for making so bold a suggestion. Words once spoken can't be recalled and he shivered as his guest moved closer. Hugo had been very careful, when offering the caviar, not to allow even a cat's whisker of contact. It had been his next line of defense, along with not mentioning anything personal or too close to the heart. If he could keep this as friendship, then he'd be fine—at least that's what he kept telling himself.

It would have been terribly easy to simply reach up and draw a line down Edward's spine. That would have been an undeniable invitation, a statement of intent. Yet Hugo still had no idea whether he wanted to go so far or whether he would want Easterby to accept the invitation if he did. This situation was unique—for once in Lamont's life desire and friendship had coincided. Perhaps this was even the budding of love, a precious bud that could easily be nipped by the frosts of a rejected pass. The risk of making a move and having it turned down, of then losing a precious acquaintance, was far too great a one for him to take it lightly.

He'd been aware all afternoon that he was being scrutinized, in the same way that he'd been casting glances at his companion. Surely he couldn't expect Easterby to be having the same fantasies that he was trying so hard not to indulge; fantasies about reaching out and touching another man? Lamont shivered at the thought that Edward might have had the same dreams, that he wouldn't necessarily reject a pass.

That could be even worse, being able to kiss Easterby,

to touch him. Would Hugo end up hating the man as much as he hated himself, just for letting him exercise his unnatural desires? Would a kiss ever be enough? Could they leave it there—wouldn't it naturally end up with them moving towards a bed or the back seat of a car or any one of a dozen squalid places that his mind could run to? And then they would both loathe each other and curse themselves.

Hugo stared at the sky, stared at Easterby's back, tried very hard not to look at the man, failed, and got angry with himself. Quite unexpectedly, Edward moved even closer to him, sitting so near that Lamont could feel the warmth of the man's body through his shirt. He realized that he was being given a clear signal that he was liked—more than liked. It was beyond all his hopes and filled him with fear that he'd give in and disgrace himself. He could reach out and pull Edward to him—that's how it would start, and it would end in tears.

Very slowly, Easterby began to lean down and nestle against Hugo, laying his dark head on the man's chest. Lamont didn't reject the movement, although he felt himself become noticeably tenser and his breathing wasn't as relaxed as it had been. He relished the warmth created by muscle and flesh meeting, and as he felt Edward tentatively nuzzle against the open buttons of his shirt, he enjoyed the way the hairs on his chest brushed against his friend's smooth cheeks. Guilty pleasures, all of them; Lamont felt as if he'd ceased breathing altogether, but still he didn't pushed Edward away.

"This is idyllic, Hugo, I wouldn't be anywhere else or doing any other thing at this time. You have no concept of how rare it is for me to find myself so content. Like being a child again."

Lamont couldn't speak. His second line of defense had come down and he had no idea of either what to do or what he really wanted. The whole situation was impossible. Slowly he put his arm around Edward's shoulders and held him lightly. All he could concentrate on was to keep his face, his lips, away from any part of this beautiful young man. It would be terribly easy to just move slightly, rest his chin on Easterby's head, smell his hair, kiss his brow. There had been no tenderness like this with Domino, things had been wild and frenzied that night.

You seem like you're in a proper hurry, sir. I like to meet a gentleman that knows what he wants and sets his store by getting it.

Every time Hugo thought of what he'd said and done, he hated himself even more for having sullied himself so readily with an unknown man. Especially when he found it so hard to find intimacy with someone he knew and liked. They lay together, Edward trying hard to get closer and Hugo keeping him at a distance, until the unseasonably warm day started to cool and they had to leave the riverside and go back to college.

They parted at the porters' lodge, having barely said a word during their return. Easterby had been too enraptured and Lamont too scared that he would invite Edward to meet him again.

"Will you take coffee with me tomorrow after chapel? I can't produce a picnic like you managed today, but I pride myself on the quality of the coffee I make." Easterby's eyes held such a pleading look, like a child desperate for another piece of cake, that all Lamont's resolve disappeared, like the heat had totally vanished from the day.

"I will. Most kind, thank you." And not trusting himself to utter another word, Hugo turned and lugged the hamper and rug back to his room.

As the evening drew on, he was glad he'd had the foresight to fill a bottle to warm his bed, despite the turmoil that his mind was in. It was going to be hard enough slipping into cold sheets, ready for a night of nothing but thinking, without being cold as well. That afternoon he'd broken all the rules he'd made. He'd called Edward by name, they had touched and held each other close—and while they hadn't kissed, if they met again it was merely a matter of time.

If they met again. He suddenly decided that he should write Edward a note, push it under his door, say the afternoon had all been an awful mistake, call off their meeting for coffee, and prevent any other occasion of meeting. He should do just that. He couldn't.

Clear skies that had been a blue banner all day, letting the sun warm the air, had left a cloudless night that threatened to be cold enough to even produce a sharp frost. Easterby lay in bed unsleeping, shivering slightly as his body met the cold sheets, feeling a strange mixture of excitement and dread. Hugo had let him touch him, had allowed him to lie with his head on his chest, hadn't rejected or teased him. It was a gift beyond price. But Edward had no idea whether this was right or wrong. He couldn't tell one from the other anymore, being too blinded by the brightness of a golden smile. He had been told often enough that to love another man in anything other than a fraternal way was immoral. He'd heard awful stories of what had gone on between some officers and their batmen in the trenches, when the strain of conflict had led to what the tellers of the tales referred to as *sins almost beyond forgiveness.*

This had always puzzled him. Easterby knew that they were always told in chapel to value loving kindness above all other virtues, and he'd naturally concluded this meant that any unnatural affection between men had to be full of cruelty and animal lust, emotions that soiled and marred any spark of true love. But he'd felt no such thing that afternoon with Lamont—just a tender affection for each other, a delight in their mutual company and a need for gentle contact. Such things hardly seemed sinful.

He reflected again on the day ahead. They would meet again and who could tell what joys the meeting would bring. Perhaps a kiss? Edward debated to himself whether that would feel as wonderful as lying in Hugo's arms had done. He'd no experience of kissing, and the thought of it both intrigued and disturbed him. And after making such intimate contact, would he feel as confused as he felt now? His thoughts churned full of Hugo Lamont until he fell into a fitful sleep and then the man invaded his dreams as well.

Easterby opened the door to his friend's knock, wearing the broadest smile that Lamont had ever seen displayed on his handsome face. In the room there was coffee waiting, with little biscuits and cakes that looked like Edward had arranged and rearranged them fifty times for perfection of display. Hugo took a seat, picked up his cup and a tiny sweetmeat, but said very little. The careless conversation of their first meetings had dissipated, leaving a hollow awkwardness that came mainly from the older man this time, not the younger.

Edward looked like he could stand the tension no longer. "You don't want to be here, do you? You want to say that this is all an awful mistake; that we should never meet again. I know that what I did yesterday stepped outside the bounds of decency. I'm sorry, I've made a terrible error." Tears began to well in Easterby's eyes and he wiped them on his sleeve like a little boy.

Hugo could have borne shouting, he'd half expected insults or argument, but to see his friend cry unmanned him completely. The sight of such a handsome face wracked by pain and tears overwhelmed him. "No, no. It's not like that at all." He left his chair, moved across to Easterby, took the man's face in his hands, let the last walls of defense go down. He gently kissed Edward's brow again and again, working down his face, cheeks. The skin felt softer than he'd expected when he'd only kissed it in his imagination. "I didn't mind a bit what happened yesterday, but you don't understand what all this is about, truly." He had reached his friend's lips and their mouths met.

The intimacy of the act shattered them both. Moist, soft, tender, frightened lips meeting for a fleeting moment and then again for a longer congress. Neither had ever known so profound an act. The sweet taste of their mouths, the darting tongues that pushed against lips and made them lose all ability to think clearly. Lamont had done this just the once before, kissing that nameless boy in the back of a car, but kissing Easterby was more stimulating, more thrilling, than anything he had done with Domino. Now he was close to someone for whom he had great affection mingled with desire, and now Hugo was more frightened than words could possibly describe.

He pulled away from the by now frenzied kissing, holding Easterby's face between his hands and breathing hard. "You have no idea where this might lead, Edward. I swear that I didn't hear a word of the sermon in chapel this morning. I just spent the whole time praying not to be led into temptation this day, and in your room temptation comes in droves. If I kiss you again, I'll want to touch you, and if I touch you, I'll want to take you to my bed. Do you understand that? Do you understand what would happen there? And afterwards there wouldn't be any happiness left, just hatred of each other and what we let happen here. I don't ever want to hate you, Edward." Hugo shook with emotion.

"But couldn't we stay with this?" Easterby's fingers traced the lines of Lamont's mouth—Hugo shut his eyes and breathed in the smells of coffee and cake that arose from those hands. "I'd be content with kisses, with lying in your arms."

"You might be, but I can't trust myself, Edward. Not to stop at just a kiss."

"Then what are we to do?" Easterby's fingers left Lamont's mouth, moved down over chin and neck, rested over his heart. "I can't lose you, not now."

Hugo shook his head, ruefully. "Could you be content with just my friendship, Edward? Would you come to that

21

cricket match and just drink champagne and talk with me? If all kissing were forbidden, would you still want not to lose me?"

Easterby thought for a long while, his face etched with pain and worry and looking ten years older than it had by the river. "If the choice was that or not to have you at all, I would settle for it." He tightened his grip on Lamont's jacket, as if he would never let it go.

"And would you still be saying that in a year's time? In five years?" Hugo lightly caressed Easterby's hand, trying to memorize how it felt, in case he was never able to repeat the experience.

Edward moved his hand up from Hugo's chest, found his face again, and looked into his eyes for what seemed an eternity. "I don't know, but then I can't predict whether in a year's time we would still even like each other. Maybe by then we'll have ceased all contact, or perhaps you might even be in my bed and happy with it. I've only known you for a few days Hugo, that's all, and if it takes another year to reach another kiss, then so be it. I've waited all my life, I have patience enough."

Lamont smiled, a real smile this time, a surge of relief filling his heart. "You might need all that patience, Edward. I have no idea when or even if I'll lose these feelings."

Easterby took his hand, squeezed it gently, let it fall. "All I ask is to have the chance of being with you when you do." They sat together, hardly touching and didn't speak again until the college clock struck one, although all thoughts of lunch had flown away. Hugo took his leave—he really did have work to do—with a fond ruffle of Easterby's dark locks and a promise to meet at hall that evening.

Edward closed the door behind him, then rested his brow against the cool wood, pretending it was resting against Hugo's head. At last he understood. His family bred dogs, and he'd known all the mechanics of the breeding process since he was a lad, but the whining of the bitches in heat, the near uncontrollable behavior of the dogs who came to serve them, had been an absolute mystery. Now he knew what it all meant. He burned with desire for Lamont, and it was too cruel to have found such a fondness within his grasp and then have it snatched away. He'd have to wait what seemed an age until the man would let him come near again. Assuming that he was ever given another chance.

Chapter Three

The Easter vacation was looming on the horizon, horribly near for Easterby, who preferred even his lonely life in college to the tense and repressive atmosphere of home. He met Lamont every day between the time they'd sat down to coffee, cakes and guilty kisses, and the end of the Easter term. Sometimes they walked, or sat together in hall—it was just friendship on the surface, but all the time the undercurrent of attraction wouldn't go away.

On the last but one day of term, Easterby stood in Hugo's rooms, watching the man pack, desperately keeping his hands pinned behind his back so that he couldn't reach out and touch him. "I suppose you'll be having a big family gathering to welcome you home?"

"I guess so." Lamont didn't look up from his packing. Edward wondered why the man looked so uncomfortable; he hoped it was at the thought of their being apart for weeks on end. "I dare say all the family will turn up in Hampshire at some point, they usually do, although it won't be as mad as when I was a boy. Not so many Lamonts now—what the war didn't take, the flu did, but Mama will make sure we keep up the traditional family festivities."

Easterby always felt jealous of Hugo's family—not just because they had first claim on the man. "I don't suppose we'll be particularly festive, we've never been great ones for partying." He swallowed hard. "I'm dreading going home, really."

Hugo put down a book he was putting in a box and looked straight at his friend for the first time that morning. "I'm sorry, truly. If I could do anything..." Lamont trailed off; there was no point in even beginning the conversation. "You'll write?"

"I will." Edward felt the tears welling, turned on his heels and returned to his own rooms, where he started drafting what would be the first letter.

It arrived in Hampshire only a couple of days into the break, a very stiff and proper letter full of formality, but awash, to Lamont's eyes, with a million hidden meanings. He pored over it time and again, wondering whether *last term was a very interesting and instructive one* referred simply to the chemistry lectures Edward had sat through or if *I look forward very much to my return to Cranmer* meant that he was as desperate as Hugo was for them to meet again.

Lamont wished he'd had the nerve to ask Edward to come and visit, but he didn't have the moral courage for it yet. His mother would have been delighted that one of his friends was paying them a call as her son rarely invited any of his acquaintances home. But it wasn't any inconvenience to his parents that was the important issue; it was the temptation that his hands and lips would be feeling that was crucial. Having Edward Easterby halfway across the college, sleeping in his little bed, breathing softly into the night, was a clear and present danger. Having the same man three doors away, down a carpeted and quiet corridor, in a large and warm guest bed, would have been the height of peril.

His letter of reply was slightly less cautious, although still within the most strict bounds of decency, and the to and froing of letters continued to the brink of their return to college and the chance of saying aloud what they'd only been able to write for the previous month. By the time the last letter appeared at Easterby's breakfast table, Lamont's style of writing had become like his conversation that day by the river—light and full of laughter, warm and generous, speaking of a love that was burgeoning without ever using the word itself. Whatever Lamont had said over coffee and cakes, the day he had both awakened Edward's soul and almost broken his heart, the words he used on paper told a very different tale. Perhaps their separation was making the man's heart grow fonder, as the old saying had it.

"Mr. Easterby. Mr. Easterby, sir!" Edward turned around, half expecting to see Marsh again, but delighted to see Lamont, who was grinning to himself at his impersonation of the porter's fierce voice.

"Hugo! Did you have a good Easter?" Easterby resisted the temptation to embrace his friend, settling for a handshake.

"We did indeed."

Easterby noted the "we" and felt a pang of jealousy at the other man's obvious delight at time spent with his nearest and dearest. "You look well."

"Did you expect me to be a mass of spots or something, like my poor nephew with German measles?" Lamont cuffed his friend's arm. "And you look as if the break has done you the power of good."

It was a lie. Edward knew that. He was paler than he'd been, as if he'd hardly ventured out the last four weeks, and when he caught himself in the mirror, a tired face looked out. "It did," Edward lied in return, "but I'm pleased to be back here. More than pleased." He held Hugo's eye for a just a moment too long, then immediately regretted it. It had been so very easy to write long letters that were filled with hidden meaning, spending happy hours in his bedroom carefully constructing them line by line, filling each word and phrase with veiled allusions. It had been an intellectual

26

as well as a romantic exercise, satisfying on many levels. And it had been safe. With seventy miles between them, he couldn't lead Lamont astray, there could be no touches to regret, no kisses to feel guilty about.

Now a yard of courtyard separated them and the danger of the situation became clear again. Edward had made extravagant promises to Hugo in good faith—*I'll wait a year for another kiss*—like he was some poor hero in a storybook, and these had all been easy to keep during the back end of the previous term. Now a combination of separation and correspondence had made both hearts grow fonder, and they couldn't bear the thought of being no more than friends. The hero's promise seemed like some miraculous quest now, hardly to be attempted, let alone achievable.

"Will you be in hall tonight?" Hugo broke the awkward silence with a stupid question. Of course every member of Cranmer would be expected to come to hall tonight unless he was in the sick bay. The Warden of Cranmer would be addressing the college and would as usual be reflecting on the sacrifices made by the students of past years, a favorite theme and one which had become increasingly poignant in the last few years.

"Indeed. Would you...?" Edward left the question unfinished, suddenly unsure of his words, wanting simply to say *sit next to me* but feeling too shy to utter the phrase.

"Join you at table?" Hugo seemed to be struggling to wrest his words out. "I would. If the Warden is going to wax lyrical, I would appreciate your comments on his speech afterwards."

Edward looked keenly at his friend, as if he was expecting some sign that Hugo was making fun of him, but the remark seemed genuine enough. "Perhaps we could have a drink beforehand? I have a bottle or two in my room."

"I'm sorry, I can't. Time's on short commons today. We'll meet at dinner." Hugo held out his hand for it to be

27

shaken, to agree the arrangements, turned, and departed, leaving Easterby to wonder whether he'd ever have to open the bottle of sherry and port he'd lugged up to his rooms. He heaved a huge sigh and set off for his desk and a book about inorganic chemistry he would find comfort in until dinner time.

Hugo almost ran back to his rooms, a great gobbet of guilt stuck in his throat. It was plain that the time Edward had spent with his family hadn't benefited him. He'd have been far better off spending the holiday, or at least part of it, in Hampshire. He cursed, again, the moral cowardice that wrapped him up in such chains of guilt and fear that he couldn't have offered this friend some simple hospitality. And now he couldn't even accept an invitation to a drink because it brought such danger. They hadn't been alone in a private place together, after dark, since they had kissed, and Hugo didn't feel confident enough in his own powers of self-control to risk it now.

Lamont knew that Edward would have seen his blatant lie about lack of time for what it was and suspected he would guess the reason behind it. It was all a bloody mess, and if he had to be at hall, then perhaps the best he could do was to avoid Easterby entirely.

When the time came, he dressed for dinner and reluctantly wandered over to hall, where the Warden of Cranmer was preparing to speak. Doctor Phillip De Banzie was a handsome man, erect, silver haired, and with a patrician air. His students admired and feared him in equal measure, as did the members of his Senior Common Room. He began each term by addressing the entire college after dinner, and the theme, whatever its nominal title, always veered in the direction of sacrifice. The recent events in Europe had added enormously to his scope for elaborating on this. He had good right: he'd lost a nephew at Ypres and a young cousin a mile further along the line. For him the loss of the flower of English manhood was a real and present tragedy.

Lamont and Easterby sat side by side, not intentionally, their having ended up among a crowd of Hugo's friends who had swept them into hall and given them no choice of seat. They listened intently to the head of their college, even though they had heard much the same stuff before.

De Banzie mentioned those who had sacrificed their social life in the pursuit of pure academic excellence, *giving up the chance of wife and family so that they could make great strides in medical or scientific research that would benefit many people.* The Warden then turned to men who had given their lives in many a conflict down the years *so that England could remain free and unsullied from the foreign touch. Cranmer men have always done their duty— they sailed with Collingwood's squadron into the French line at Trafalgar one hundred and twenty years ago and they were trodden into the mud of Picardy within the last few.*

Suddenly a new theme emerged, one that Hugo had heard before but that first year students like Edward had yet to encounter. It concerned the sacrifice of desire and self-will, the sublimation of the cravings of the flesh in order to allow for the perfection of study or the living of a perfect life. Of course, the main target of these barbed words was the small number of undergraduates who were heavy drinkers or clients of the painted ladies of Oxford and who were on a final warning as to their conduct. But Hugo felt them pierce him to the soul, as if De Banzie had a telescope that could peer into the heart of a man and pinpoint all the sinful inclinations.

He sneaked a sidelong glance at Easterby, but the man's face told nothing. Perhaps he felt the words as keenly as Hugo did but could hide his emotions more successfully. Perhaps the only thing they meant to him was that he must not overindulge in port or loose women if he wished to graduate with a shining first. Lamont could not even begin to guess which of his guesses was nearer the truth.

The speech ended, the listeners all applauded, and the fellows of the college took their leave to enjoy port and fruit in their common room. Easterby turned, a hopeful look on his handsome face. "Will you take a glass of port with me, Hugo? I can't offer you sweetmeats such as our betters no doubt will be enjoying," there was an unfamiliar air of light-heartedness in the man's voice, "but I think the vintage is acceptable. Dr. De Banzie would have been proud of the sacrifices I made to obtain it."

Lamont stammered, for once entirely uncertain in front of his peers. It should have been the easiest thing to say either *yes* or *no*, the sort of social decision that was taken every day, but now he was paralyzed by his guilt. His desperate longing to see Edward again, that had eaten at him all the holidays and been communicated in every line of his letters, was counteracted by the harsh words the Warden had spoken—*set not your desires above the demands of your college*—and the lingering disgust he felt at his own nature.

One of his more hearty rowing friends took the decision out of his hands, slapping him on the back with a vigorous, "See you tomorrow, then, Hugo. We're back off to Alistair's set for a game of bridge. I know that pastime bores you rigid," and then leaving the man, still dumbstruck, alongside Easterby.

"Is that a *yes,* then?" It seemed like the wine and candlelight had made Edward bolder.

Lamont, tortured on the rack of his own indecision, merely shook his head, looked at his friend with an entirely hopeless expression, turned, and made his way out into the dark quad.

"Hugo!" Easterby's deep voice split the still sharp air of the April evening. Lamont didn't turn, nor was he steering a course for his own rooms. Edward kept up a pursuit, eventually abandoning words and grabbing his friend's arm. "Hugo, I only asked you to come and take a glass with me.

Can't we do that, like any two civilized human beings?"

Lamont turned, hot tears welling in his eyes. "But we're not civilized human beings, are we? I told you before that a lost legion of temptations lies in your room, and I haven't the armor to fight any of them. Don't tempt me, Edward. Please."

Easterby looked stunned. "I never meant to tempt you. I..."

Hugo laid a hand on his friend's arm, equally quickly removed it. "I know, you're innocence itself, honestly. But can't you see that I'm burning?"

"But your letters...I thought that you were perhaps warming to the thought of being *close friends*. There was so very much affection in each line. Or so I thought. Perhaps I simply imagined it all; wishful thinking on my part again." Edward turned away, gulping as though swallowed pride had stuck in his craw.

"Letters were safe, Edward. It was easy to pour myself into them, and like a fool I succumbed to the temptation to do so. I could kiss your letters and not be tainted. Having the same feelings while being so close to you is agony." He reached out again, merely brushed the wool of Easterby's jacket and shook his head sadly.

"Will you meet me tomorrow, then?" Easterby's voice was full of defeat and sadness. "Not in my room if you can't bear it. At a café or in the bar. Anywhere. I need to talk to you." He raised his hand, let it stop within a hair's breadth of Lamont's face. "I've missed you so much."

Hugo nodded. He didn't dare say anything—his treacherous tongue would betray him. He gently grazed his own hand along Edward's, resisting clasping the fingers.

"At *The Bath Bun,* then? At eleven?" It was unlike Easterby to be so forceful. Even with such a man as Lamont.

Hugo nodded again, shook Edward's hand and made off for his rooms, mind whirring and confused.

31

Easterby half expected that Lamont wouldn't come. He'd been having second thoughts himself, tossing and turning in his bed, mind full of guilt—not for his feelings for Hugo, he believed that they were above reproach—but for the obvious strains that their affection was putting on his friend. He'd gone though in his mind every conversation they'd ever had, but the more he analyzed, the more he was puzzled; this wasn't some compound that would give up its secrets to solvent or litmus paper. All that Edward could really make out was that Lamont felt shame at being attracted to another man, that was understood, but there was something else, something deeper and more painful that he couldn't even guess at. Something that was eating into Hugo's heart like a worm in an apple and making the center rotten.

But Hugo did come to *The Bath Bun* that next morning. On the dot of eleven he appeared at the café door, gave Edward a sheepish smile and made his way to the table where he ordered coffee and cakes.

"I was afraid…"

"That I wouldn't come?" Lamont grinned slightly, obviously not fully at ease. "I couldn't be so rude. Again." He looked Easterby in the eye for the first time since before the Warden had started speaking the night before. "I'm sorry about last evening. I feel that you deserve a full explanation, and I've screwed my courage to the sticking place in order to deliver it. But not here."

Edward felt puzzled but nodded his agreement. They ate and drank in almost total silence, passing stilted pleasantries but unable to really communicate until they'd cleared the air between them. They'd paid their bill and walked half the length of the street before Hugo began to speak in earnest. "Edward, you must think I am the most inconsistent of creatures, and I apologize for it most profusely. All that I told you in your room the day we," he cast a quick glance around to ensure they wouldn't be overheard, "kissed was

32

true. I can't trust myself when I am alone with you."

"We're alone now," Edward said and immediately regretted it.

"I mean in circumstances where we could do what we liked. I don't think that we could kiss here and now, walking along the main road." Lamont grinned and part of his old spark of mischief, sadly missing since last term, flared again. "What you don't understand, because I've never told you, is the intense regret I feel about something I did. Something that happened before I met you." Lamont suddenly found the pavement to be enormously interesting. Edward couldn't begin to guess what thoughts were going through his friend's mind. "Do you want to tell me what it was? Is it so bad that I would turn on my heel and leave?"

Hugo looked up, then along his shoulder at his friend, his face a picture of uncertainty. "I honestly don't know. Tell me," Lamont stopped, looked the other man uneasily in the eye, "was there ever anyone before me? Some lucky man or girl who stole your heart?"

The words seemed light, almost frivolous, but Edward recognized that they hid a wealth of feeling. He drew a long breath. "There's never been anyone who's even looked at me twice, until you invited me to that picnic. So the answer is a resounding *no*."

"It's not the same for me, I'm afraid." If Hugo saw the brief look of distress that appeared on Edward's face and was quickly hidden, he didn't acknowledge it. "I know that you're going to be disappointed in me, but we've got to thrash this out. I have to tell you the truth." He sighed. "I went to a club in London. Picked up this girl and took her out in my car."

"Girl..." Easterby couldn't stop the word from escaping his lips, nor the obvious surprise in his voice.

Lamont seemed deliberately to ignore the remark, as if he'd started his confession now and was afraid that any distraction might make it impossible to finish. "I wanted to prove to myself that I was normal, that I could feel and do

33

as other men did. I suspect I hoped that if I tried *it* the accepted way, that it might make me want to carry on doing the same. Stop wanting to do *it* any other way." He looked by turns embarrassed or on the verge of laughter.

Even Edward saw the comical side; Hugo sounded like a convent girl trying to discuss intimate matters without ever letting a dirty word pass her lips. "And did it?" Edward's training in analytical chemistry might not have been a great preparation for life, but it had given him the skill of cutting through to the crux of any matter.

"I never found out. Trying to embrace her was bad enough. Have you ever tried to kiss anyone while the act made you feel physically sick?"

Easterby shook his head in answer to his friend's question. He'd known no such thing, but he thought again of their own first meeting, because of the association with being sick. Strange how the memory of that time was full of happiness for both of them, although it had been such an unpleasant experience.

"I had to get rid of her with a handful of cash and a lift to a cab rank. It wasn't something I would ever want to repeat." Lamont's cheeks burned as he spoke.

Edward waited for the story to continue, wondering what could have happened to make his friend so flushed. When they'd gone a good hundred yards and Hugo was still silent, Easterby knew he had to speak. "So why do you feel guilty about that? You seemed to act like a gentleman, in the end."

"There's more to tell, Edward, I just needed to find the right words to make it appear less tawdry than it was. I know I behaved like a gentleman but it didn't stop her calling me *A bleedin' Nancy boy*. That was all too close to the truth. You see, I went off to another club straightaway afterwards. It wasn't the sort of place that respectable men, certainly those who wish to keep their reputations, visit." He cast a sideways glance at his friend. "I picked someone else up there—a young man, not yet twenty I'd have said. I took him out in my car as well."

"What did he look like?" Edward kept his questions clinical. He was a man used to analysis, taking and sifting facts to form theories about them and he had to apply those skills now. It was the only way he could cope with such painful revelations.

Lamont considered the query. "He was pretty enough, although not really handsome like you, and I suspect that within a few years his looks will be long gone, especially if he keeps to his present way of living."

"What was his name?"

"I never knew. They called him Domino, because..." Lamont seemed reluctant to explain further and Edward guessed there was some dim-witted joke behind the name, "of some stupid thing or other. That's what he wanted me to call him, and so I did." They'd reached the road along to the river, so kept walking in the direction of the bridge.

"Where did you take him?" It was surprisingly easy just to ask simple questions, to ease the story along. Edward expected a candid answer and Hugo was obliging him.

"Out to the back of Hampstead Heath. You can see the lights of the city there, but it feels like the deepest countryside to me. I used to go flying my kite on the Heath with my nanny. I think I'll never go there again."

"Was what happened there so bad? Why has it ruined the place for you forever?"

They'd reached the bridge and Lamont stopped to lean on the balustrade. "I think that it's ruined everything." He looked down into the swiftly running water. "I wish that somehow this river would carry my sins away as easily as it takes the silt from the fields. Take them down to the sea and lose them."

"What on earth did you do?" Easterby was stunned at his friend's words. What could they have done, Lamont and this strange boy, to have left such a legacy of guilt? "Did you couple with him? Is that it?"

They stared down at the river again. Ducks were

dabbling, their tails sticking up and looking ridiculous, and a little grebe was diving into the fast running current and hunting for fish. This was all evidence that life was going on, even if their hearts had frozen in the telling of this tale.

Edward lightly touched Lamont's arm, indicating that he'd stayed silent too long. "Tell me, Hugo. Please."

"I paid him to…I want to say *perform certain acts,* but that's just a euphemism, and it's not fair to you to be less than honest. We had sex. There was no affection in it, not as you and I shared when we kissed. For him it was just a matter of making a profit, a handful of money earned to spend on who knows what. It's the only time in my life I have done such…*things*, and I'm angry that I did them there and with him. There are times that I feel I never want to do anything like that again."

"Even if it were with someone you loved?"

Lamont rubbed his hand over his face. "It was pleasant, Edward, I can't deny that it was the most exhilarating thing. To go the rest of my life and not know that ecstasy again would be hard. But I'd rather that than pile another burden of guilt on my back. What I did was wrong, and wanting to do it with you is wrong, too." He slapped his hands on the stone of the balustrade, not seeming to notice the sting the action must have caused his palms.

"Even if it wasn't about money? Even if you loved me and I loved you?"

"Edward, my dearest Edward." Lamont spoke to his friend as if he were a child. "You're so wonderfully innocent, it's breathtaking. You sound as if you believe all those storybooks where love makes everything right."

"Perhaps it does…"

"What about guilt, though? What about remorse? I know you can't find them in your books on inorganic chemistry, but they're real and they consume you." Lamont looked sidelong at his friend, who was still studying the Isis. "I've fallen in love with you, Edward; I knew it from the moment you laid your precious head on my *manly chest*,

36

that day by this same river. And I'm guessing, from the letters we exchanged and the flush on your handsome cheeks now, that you're quite possibly in love with me. I'm not sure if that fact makes things better or fifty times worse."

Easterby didn't know the answer to that, of course he didn't. Hugo had been right to say that he'd no knowledge of feelings. He was in uncharted territory, and he wanted to be guided through it step by step. The only man who could do it was Lamont. "You've still not answered my question. About love making all things right."

"I'm sorry. That's because I have no answer. I told you once that if we slept together, we would end up hating ourselves and each other. As I hate both that boy and myself for having used him. I simply can't see any other outcome. The ruin of a life, two lives, for the sake of a few minutes pleasure." Tears came welling up in Hugo's eyes. He wiped his face on his sleeve, like a schoolboy might, and for the first time Edward saw not the great Hugo Lamont of Cranmer College, but someone young, vulnerable, and as always, beyond adorable.

Easterby laid his hand on Hugo's shoulder, not knowing any words that he could share. He felt that he should be making some wise pronouncement either to offer comfort or to persuade Lamont that all his guilt and distaste was stupid, but he'd no idea what would work in either case. By accident he hit upon exactly what Hugo required; not gabbling words or advice, pious or otherwise, but a quiet companionship. All the comfort that Hugo needed, he found in that light touch upon his back; all the counsel that he sought was in the gentle breath playing upon his cheek. After a moment or two, he looked up at Edward and smiled wanly as if he was broken in heart and spirit. "I know it's a simple choice, but it's one I can't make. Part of me says I should say farewell here and now, taking myself away from you and all the temptation you bring. And the other half says you're the thing I treasure most in all the world and I should just stay with you and risk everything." He shrugged and merely patted Easterby's back. "I'm sorry. It's me. I'm hopeless and that's all there is to it."

Edward remembered all the college stories about Lamont that he'd heard when he first come up to Cranmer—Lamont being held up as the shining example, the man that all other men should aspire to. Seeing him so distraught, so lacking in any confidence in his own powers, was untenable. "You're not hopeless. Far from it." He tried to catch Hugo's eye. "It'll be all right. It will." The words sounded so vapid, so utterly useless, but somehow they sparked a slightly happier smile from Lamont.

"Whoever would have thought, when you so kindly christened my shoes with the contents of your stomach, that you would have been the one giving me the pep talk a few months down the line? You're too good to be wasting your time on an idiot like me. Go and find yourself some nice chap who's pure and unsullied and would make love to you without a second thought. You can discover the pleasures of the flesh together." Lamont laid his hand on Easterby's shoulder, his hand trembling with emotion.

"You are a bloody idiot if you think that's what I want. I've never felt the slightest inclination towards anything approximating romantic activity..."

Lamont looked like he was repressing a smile and Edward realized that long words were beginning to pepper his speech again. It was a sure sign that he was becoming emotional, he knew that his letters had been full of them, but he couldn't stop himself.

"And, therefore, I would not be liable to be going off with anyone else." Edward's face flushed and he looked so pompous that Hugo's urge to kiss him was almost irresistible.

Lamont began to laugh, a sound that Easterby had been sure he would never hear again. "I said I was hopeless, and I am. I've been standing here racked with torment these last few minutes, telling myself to be brave and good and *repress the desires of the flesh* like my dear old nanny used to tell me. Then you make a pompous speech and I lose all my resolve. Don't you dare go and find yourself anyone, do you hear? We'll grow old together like two monks from some order that encourages laughter and happiness rather than silence and solemnity. Perhaps I'll embrace chastity and be happy. All it needs is for you to smile and it'll seem possible." He tapped Edward's shoulder, then linked his arm and they set off back to Cranmer, Lamont suddenly talkative, full of ridicule at the ridiculous ducks on the Isis and the even more ridiculous people in rowboats. Easterby was happy to see his friend suddenly in his proper spirits again, but deeply concerned about the words spoken about chastity and references to monasteries. If Hugo really did intend to remain chaste all his life, he wasn't sure he'd survive.

Chapter Four

Lamont had lugged his picnic blanket and basket to the first cricket match of the season at The Parks and there was not a speck of caviar in it. He refused to touch the stuff since Easterby had been so scathing about it. There was champagne, though, and a fine veal and ham pie, salad, cakes and tiny tomatoes that were as sweet as a kiss. Edward had contributed a box of candied fruits, sharp and succulent, making the fingers of the diners even stickier than the cakes had made them

"He needs to watch that spinner." Hugo licked his fingers and pointed airily in the direction of the batsman who was about to face. "There's a fair amount of rough at this end and he'll be turning them through ninety degrees in no time."

Easterby nodded, but not in a convincing manner.

Hugo studied him closely. "Shall I say that all again in English?"

Edward grinned sheepishly. "I can't help it, we were never a great cricketing family. Golf, that's what the Easterbys play, summer or winter. I could wax lyrical about mashie niblicks and spoons, but the art of the off spinner is beyond me. You might as well be spouting Russian for all that it means to me."

"Then we'll need to attend lots of matches and you'll have to listen very carefully. I shall ask questions afterwards to make sure that you were paying attention." A tender smile lit up Hugo's face. He adored exchanging banter with his friend, just as he loved the man himself. There could be no denying it now. For all he was never more than arm in arm or lying side by side with Edward as they were now, their association had passed beyond friendship. They both knew it, although nothing had been said outright—looks and nuances of speech spoke much more loudly than declarations of undying affection might ever have done. They were inseparable at hall, they went to concerts and watched the oafs in eights flailing down the river. Everyone at Cranmer recognized that Lamont and Easterby went together like lamb and mint sauce.

Even the porters had recognized the blossoming alliance, although they firmly believed that it was no more than platonic, the sort of thing that they'd seen in the trenches where lifelong friendships had been forged and withstood the fire of conflict. Most of them had served in France or Belgium, most of them had known many an officer come close to a fellow combatant who'd ended up meaning more to him than the wife or sweetheart left at home. Comradeship in the face of adversity, perhaps. It was no wonder that some men had come home from the war almost as strangers to their families, feeling lost in a world they'd once known but which now had no color or depth for them.

There were some old soldiers at the cricket match, swapping stories, delighting in being able to relive the past. Perhaps regretting the way their lives had turned out. Edward watched and listened to them, deep in thought. In the end he began to clear lunch away. "Let's go back to my rooms, Hugo. There's something rather special I want to show you." They strolled back to Cranmer, where they'd barely been in Easterby's room a moment before he thrust a silver object into his friend's hands.

"I didn't know you smoked." Hugo admired the handsome cigarette case as he turned it over in his hands.

"I don't, that case was my grandfather's. He's given up the things as being bad for his lungs and left it with me, in case I took up the filthy habit." He smiled ruefully. "This nearly fell into the hands of those ogres down at the porters' lodge. I had to tell a lie or two to get it back."

Lamont had noted the strange tone in his friend's voice. "I don't understand."

"The old gentleman was visiting last term. As he left he presented it to me and then held me in a huge embrace. It was the first time I can ever remember him showing such affection. I was so overcome that I didn't realize we'd dropped this," he fingered the case lovingly, "until Marsh caught me the next day to return it. I was rather abrupt with him."

"Why? Surely he was just doing his duty? The initials on the outside would guide him to you." Hugo traced the outline of the E. "Is your grandfather an Edward, as well?"

"No, he's an Edwin. The name suits him much more than it would me. Anyway, it wasn't so much the snapping up of lost trifles I minded, I trust them not to try to steal things, it was the thought that they may have been snooping around." He opened the case to reveal an inscription. "Grandfather was very particular about pointing this out to me."

Lamont took the case and inspected the handsome copperplate writing. *To thine own self be true.* "It's from Hamlet, isn't it?"

"Indeed. Polonius' advice to his son, I believe. I didn't want Marsh and his colleagues speculating about its meaning." Easterby fell quiet, still considering the case. "It was given to him—my grandfather, I mean—when he was twenty one, by a maiden aunt. He says that she was particularly perceptive." He turned the thing over again.

"There's a story here, isn't there? Don't feel obliged to share it with me if you feel that it would break your grandfather's confidence."

"No, I feel that it's important that you know. We should

have no secrets." Edward looked deadly serious, an expression that always melted his friend's heart. Just like a schoolboy explaining something to a teacher or making a report to the Headmaster about why a window had been broken, Easterby seemed very young and vulnerable. "When he was younger, Edwin Easterby fell in love with a girl. His parents felt that the match was totally unsuitable; she was only a servant and him the son of the house. They intervened, sending grandfather away to join the army and her to service with a family in Scotland."

Lamont shook his head. "I know that it goes against the grain, that there are norms of society and unspoken rules that everyone expects to be obeyed, but this seems ridiculous. I can't understand why two people who love each other should not be allowed to do so." If he appreciated the irony in what he said, he didn't show it.

"My family wouldn't hold with that point of view. As far as they're concerned, one has to do one's duty in terms of finding a suitable partner. So my grandfather married a pleasant young lady of his own standing. There was no great love between them, but an agreeable friendship—and my father was produced. He was an only child, against a family tradition on both sides of large families." Edward looked shrewdly, surprisingly shrewdly, at Lamont. "I think that speaks volumes, doesn't it?"

"It appears to. Is your grandmother still alive?" Hugo sat down next to his friend, closer than they'd been since the morning they'd kissed.

"No, she died two years ago. What I never realized, as he'd never told any of us, was that my grandfather immediately set out to locate his old love. He traced her via the family she had been sent to. Their identity had never been divulged to him by his parents, but he found an old servant who had kept in touch." Easterby didn't look at his friend. "Hugo, I've never believed that I could really open my heart to anyone before now, but I've kept this secret too long."

"And did he find her? Is there a happy ending to this?" Lamont kept his eyes fixed on Edward's face, even though the man could not seem to tear his gaze from the cigarette case. His friend was unbelievably beautiful, and when he was solemn, as now, it added greatly to his allure. Hugo couldn't, in all conscience, resist touching his hand.

"He did, or rather he found her grave. She, too, had married, been mother to five children and had died in childbed with the sixth." Easterby acknowledged the touch with a movement of his fingers. "Grandfather met her husband, and the man was happy to talk about his *bonny Rosie* as he called her. My grandfather said that it was obvious that this chap had loved her very much and that their marriage had been extremely happy. Much more so than his own had turned out to be."

"And his aunt had known? That the family hadn't let him to be true to himself?" Hugo was beginning to understand why Edward was sharing this tale with him. He caressed his friend's hand again.

Edward nodded. "I was very surprised that he chose to tell me this story, of all the family, but perhaps he shared that lady's insight." He began to study his shoes, a signal that meant he was talking about things that mattered very deeply to him, but he kept a grip on Hugo's hand. "I don't want to have the same misgivings as he has. He told me very plainly he regretted that he'd not simply defied his family, followed the girl, and married her himself. Perhaps I wouldn't be here, then; it's an interesting philosophical point, but I sympathize with him entirely. To live your whole life wishing that events had gone otherwise must be mortal hard."

"It's a feeling many folk must share after these last few years."

"But that's different, entirely. Serving one's country is a question of duty, and it would override personal considerations. That would be a question of protecting the innocent, seeing that the aggressor doesn't go unopposed.

But no one was at risk in my grandfather's case—all that was at stake was our family's sense of their honor, their ridiculous concept of the importance of their name." Easterby was becoming heated, this whole affair having touched on a raw nerve.

Hugo understood for the first time why his friend hadn't wanted the porters to touch the cigarette case. It was as if they would be touching the man's heart. "Families do protect their honor. In England there is a ridiculous amount of importance put on a man's surname, his family history. The Lord alone knows that I've had to live with it all my life." Hugo's voice began to falter. "I'm not the eldest son, so there's not the pressure that there is on Gordon to marry and produce an heir. But they still try to put me in the vicinity of eligible girls and drop subtle, and in my mother's case unsubtle, hints about me settling down once I'm finished here and starting to make my way in the world."

"Do they have any idea?" Edward raised his head, looked at Lamont face to face once more. He clasped his hands tightly, as if he was trying to stop them reaching up and touching Hugo's face.

"No, there's no one in my family of your grandfather's discernment or common sense. Or if there is, they've not informed me. It's part of what makes the whole thing so very hopeless." Tears began to well in Lamont's eyes. They were exposing the deepest recesses of their souls, and it felt wonderfully liberating. "It's hard enough to live with the disapproval of the church and the world in general, but to be letting one's family down as well is just about unbearable."

Edward gently offered his handkerchief but didn't offer either advice or platitude. He squeezed his friend's hand once more.

Lamont accepted both the linen and the kind-heartedness it represented. He knew that at times like this, listening and companionship were what counted, however much he wished that Edward would take him in his arms and smother him with affection. He shook his head and tried to compose himself. "Sorry." It was the only word he could manage and he couldn't trust himself to say more.

"You need never apologize to me, Hugo. I won't have you debasing yourself."

Lamont began to laugh, tears turning into giggles, especially when Easterby looked so solemn and puzzled at what had caused the transition. "You are absolutely priceless, Edward. There are times you resemble nothing more closely than a hero from a romantic novel."

"Am I that funny?" A few months before, Easterby might have been offended at such a remark, but now they were used to teasing each other. Although they'd never been so bold as to hold hands while doing the teasing.

"No, you're absolutely wonderful. The lady who would write about you in that novel—it would be a lady, no doubt of great virtue and the highest morals—would fall in love with her creation and portray you as the absolute pinnacle of what women desire." Hugo shook his head ruefully. "I suspect that you're the pinnacle of what I desire as well, and I should just damn well kiss you here and now. If I only had the moral bravery to say that the opinion of the world and my family didn't matter a jot."

Easterby studied him carefully, still stroking his friend's hand. "I've already made that decision, back when we walked down to the bridge and you told me about that boy. I will not marry just to please my parents, nor will I turn my back on my true nature just to satisfy the expectations of my peers. I'm not a popular man; I can cope with being rejected."

"Even by your very nearest and dearest?"

"I only hold two people dear. One is my grandfather, and I believe he's given me as clear a sign as he could that he would want me to live my life as honestly as possible. The other person is you. No one else counts."

"And you would give it all up for me? Your good name in the eyes of your parents?" Lamont was finding a glimmer of hope. Somewhere in all this mess of emotions and expectations, there was a possibility that things could be all right.

"I'd rather that than lose touch with you. I've tried to imagine myself in my grandfather's place, taking a wife he didn't love just to satisfy someone else. Losing the one thing he cherished because others thought it wrong. It makes me furious on his behalf. I won't have some grandchild of mine, the product of the unwanted offspring of a loveless marriage, thinking the same of me. I'd rather go to that monastery of yours." Edward clung to his friend's hands still, and Hugo wondered whether he was trying to ensure he'd never let go of them, in case letting go of the hands meant letting go of the man.

Lamont shook his head affectionately. "To offer all that…it's like a pearl beyond price and you're casting it before a swine like me."

Edward reached up, stroked Hugo's cheek. "You are not, never have been, a swine. You're the first friend I ever had, the only person here who had sought to be truly kind to me and not take any opportunity to gull me. You're kindness itself, young man, and I will not hear you degrading yourself."

Hugo began to chuckle, letting all his hurt and nervousness dissipate into further laughter. "You sound like my great uncle giving me a lecture on losing my temper on the golf course. *Young man*, indeed." He caressed Easterby's face, savoring the feel of the smooth skin beneath his trembling fingers. "Edward, you're the pearl beyond price yourself, or the nearest equivalent I'll ever meet walking the cloisters of this college, if not the face of the entire earth."

Easterby leant forwards and gently kissed Lamont's brow before the man had a chance to pull back or react. "I can't believe this is wrong, Hugo, any of it. It doesn't hurt anyone. For goodness sake, we're pulling ourselves to pieces trying to deny it. I find it so hard to keep my hands from holding yours or my arms from enfolding you."

Lamont acknowledged how the pompous and embarrassed tone of his friend's conversation reflected his mood and felt strangely touched by the haughty words. The sweetest murmurs of affection or dripping praise couldn't have had such an effect. He tilted his face upwards, inching his nose along Edward's jaw and cheek. His lips grazed the smooth skin of his friend's temples, kissing his brow in return for the salute he'd received. It all felt wonderful. "I wish that life could be simple. I wish that it could just be you and me and no one to judge us or condemn."

Edward snuggled his head down onto Lamont's shoulder, sighing deeply. "We could remain here, you know. There's no reason you couldn't stay on to take a doctorate. You're bright and popular with everyone, and think of the influence your father could bring to bear on the college. I'd work hard and make sure I could do the same. There are plenty of old bachelors within the university, it wouldn't be looked on as out of place." He held Hugo tight, as if by clinging to him like some talisman, he could make all their wishes come true in an instant.

"Perhaps. It would certainly be easier to keep each other's company if we were colleagues here." Lamont began to laugh, making Easterby's head bounce up and down against his chest. "You might end up as Warden and you could give *the talk* every term. You'd change the subject, of course, from self-sacrifice to being true to one's lights. I could end up as the sort of crusty old fellow who scares the living daylights out of the first year students but who is adored by them by the time they leave." Maybe this was the light at the end of their tunnel, the means that they could be together, but the idea did have its ludicrous aspects.

Edward lifted his head, his eyes bright with tears that might be of laughter but could equally be relief at seeing a possible way out of their impasse. "Everyone would adore you. It's me they'd be frightened of, quite rightly, as I'm scared of De Banzie." He focused his eyes on Lamont's lips. "Hugo, please…"

Easterby didn't need to elaborate. Lamont knew what he wanted from the direction of his gaze, his flushed cheeks, the plaintive note in his voice, and he no longer had it in him to resist. He leaned down and kissed his friend, very lightly at first and then more firmly, once for friendship, once for love. Edward responded in kind with warm and affectionate, tender and shy kisses, the sort he'd been desperate to share since those first coffee flavored ones had both shattered him and shown him a world of possibilities.

Hugo ran his tongue along the gentle contours of Easterby's lips, tasting the lingering sweetness from lunch. "I love you, Edward, you big soppy idiot," Lamont's voice was hoarse with emotion, "and I promise I won't let myself be separated from you just to suit someone else's convenience. We could only ever part of our free will." He kissed Easterby powerfully, letting his tongue plunder the other man's mouth. He expected to feel tensing of muscle but not the unexpected relaxation that came as Edward probably realized that this wasn't just normal, it was lovely, and began to respond in the same way.

"I love you as well, Hugo, beyond all logic or reason. It would have to be love for us to want to risk all the disapproval, wouldn't it?" Edward looked at his friend with eyes that appeared awash with a strange mixture of fear and delight, then reached towards him for another kiss or three, the pair of them making up for all the months of unrequited desire.

"It could only be love or folly, and I don't think that either of us is stupid. Nor precipitate; we've had a long while to mull this over." Lamont drew his hand down Easterby's neck, enjoying the texture of smooth, delicate flesh that barely felt like it saw a razor. And for the first time, he felt no self-loathing at touching another man, just a simple joy and wonder at the marvels of love and how it could take all one's fears and doubts and transform them. No wonder he'd never felt this happy previously, he'd never been in love before.

Quite against all that Hugo anticipated, Edward began to take the lead, kissing and caressing—all innocence and wonder and not showing a trace of animal lust or desire. It was everything that Hugo needed to feel at ease with the situation. If there had been overt passion, he might well have felt brimful of doubts again, but the purity of Easterby's approach reassured him that things wouldn't get out of hand. Edward would probably feel they had all the time in the world and all the world of love to discover in that time.

Lamont broke from a passionate kiss and nestled down into his friend's arms, buried his face in the folds of the man's jacket. "Did we decide that quote was from Hamlet? The one on your grandfather's case?"

"We did, indeed." If Easterby was puzzled at the sudden change of tack he didn't show it.

Lamont wondered whether this man found him infuriating at times, but if Edward couldn't help being pompous, *he* couldn't help being wordy. "Then I can match it with another, if you'll excuse the adaptation. *I shall wear you in my heart of hearts*, Edward, as long as you're willing to have a place there." Hugo rubbed his fingers along his friend's jacket, caressing the material as if it were the man's skin.

"I would never ask to be removed from there. It would take a Somme or Flanders Field to wrench me from you." Easterby held Lamont close as if they really were about to be separated by bugle call or order to march. He seemed determined now that he'd never let this man go or turn his back on such pleasure as he found in Lamont's arms.

"Then we should pray God that we truly have seen the war to end them all." Hugo lifted his head, found Edward's lips once more, and as they touched was filled with joy, more than he'd ever felt in his life and the source of that elation was the man he'd got wrapped in his arms. Easterby started to explore underneath Hugo's coat with his fingers.

Lamont was taken aback by how bold his friend was turning out to be, but Edward's whole demeanor had changed now. Perhaps once they'd taken the final step over the threshold from friendship to love, he'd discovered within himself an audacity that had long been kept hidden. Hugo waited for the expected frisson of guilt to strike him now that he was lost in the pleasures of kissing and caressing. But it didn't come, and he was thankful for being spared it at last.

"Shall I take this coat off? It's mild enough." When Lamont had carelessly stripped off with Domino, it had cost him more than money. It was as if he'd bared part of his soul with each item discarded. It had been wrong then, that fact did not and would not change, but it felt absolutely right at this moment. Hugo regretfully pulled out of their embrace, slid off his dinner jacket and was pleased to see Edward perform the same maneuver. Their freshly laundered shirts were no longer as crisp as when they'd first been put on, and Easterby's bore a patch of perspiration where his friend's head had lain. Hugo gently drew his fingers down it, savoring the slick feel of the moist material in his hands.

"Can you stay a little while longer? People will think we're chatting over a cup of tea. I'll lock the door so we needn't worry." Easterby rubbed his face in Hugo's hair, enjoying the smell and taste of it.

"Leave the door, it'll only make folk suspicious. We'll hear them soon enough on the stairs." Lamont's fingers began to ease themselves into the folds of Easterby's shirt, inching nearer to a spot where they might get under the material and find Edward's skin. "I'll stay as long as common sense and our reputations will allow." Hugo could feel Easterby's hands tugging at the tail of *his* shirt, seeking to find some flesh to caress. It felt so much more exciting with Easterby's fingers just touching the small of Hugo's back than anything that Domino had done for him. Perhaps Lamont could only find true ecstasy if love were at the heart of it.

"Will you stop thinking and kiss me again, or must I wait another two months?" Edward tried to look serious, but the twinkle in his eye belied the stern voice.

"I will kiss you as often as you deserve and you may take that answer as you wish." Hugo was as good as his word, kissing his lover frantically and letting his hands work on buttons and waistbands until they were both short of breath and neither of them had a shirt on their backs.

Lamont began lightly to caress his friend's chest, drawing circles, tracing ribs, noting each line and curve and freckle until he'd memorized it entirely. Edward in his turn scanned every fraction of Hugo's back with his fingertips, mapping each square inch and defining its properties. Only the unknown could be truly fearful. Making your lover's flesh as familiar as your own eliminated all apprehension. They placed tender kisses on each other's skin and hair, Edward exploring the rough acres of Hugo's mane of a chest, Hugo enjoying the novelty of smooth flesh under his fingers and tongue.

"I must go soon." Lamont bent to kiss the tender inward of Easterby's hand, returning to kiss his mouth once more via his collarbone and neck, each touch of skin to lips being savored anew. "This is just the beginning, the start of many such afternoons and evenings, should that be what you want." He sealed the invitation with a kiss so passionate that it left the answer in no doubt.

Easterby nodded, and Lamont suspected he was too overcome to speak. He watched as Lamont slowly drew his shirt back on, secured the buttons, sought for his cufflinks. "No, let me." Edward gently inserted the little gold fastenings through their holes.

Hugo found as much delight in being dressed by his friend as he had in being undressed by him. He was pleased when Edward remembered to take the tie and make it up neatly, as he was bound to be spotted on his way back to his rooms to change for hall. They could not risk giving anyone the slightest cause for suspicion.

Lamont slowly slipped on his jacket, held Edward close and reveled in the sensation of the man's bare skin nestling against his clothing. He felt warm, secure and ridiculously alive, willing the minutes to crawl by while Easterby was next to him, fly when they were apart. "Tomorrow? After hall?"

Easterby nodded again, head against head. "Every evening after hall. All the rest of this term. Forever." The last word was little more than a shared exhalation—they both knew better than to tempt fate.

"Every evening it will be, then. For as long as we're granted." Lamont breathed into his friend's neck, drank in once more the sweet scent of sweat and exhilaration to better remember it once he was alone. "Kiss me once more, then common sense shall have to prevail." A huge smile lit up his face, one that Easterby mirrored.

The lingering sense of that final embrace of the day stayed alive for them both well into the night.

The End

GENTLEMAN'S GENTLEMAN
LEE ROWAN

Chapter One

July, 1880
Maiwand, Afghanistan

The heat was the worst of it. Major Robert Scoville gazed over the cracked earth and stark mountain range with eyes that felt baked raw. The thin air didn't help, either, clogged as it was with a fine powdery dust raised by thousands of feet and hooves.

And the waiting was almost as bad as the heat. Instead of being ready for a fight, with the normal anticipation of victory in battle against a half-civilized enemy, the men were quiet, almost nervous, preparing to meet their ends. And Scoville could say nothing to contradict that expectation without insulting his men's good sense and making himself look a fool. How was an officer supposed to put heart into his men when every scrap of intelligence numbered at least ten Afghan tribesmen to every British soldier? No amount of pride and patriotism could overcome those odds.

It was madness to attack Maiwand. They couldn't even keep Ayub Khan bottled up in the city, much less drive him from it. If a lowly major like himself could see that, what in God's name was wrong with the generals?

He nodded as his sergeant came up beside him. "Darling, are the men ready?"

"Ready as they can be, my lord," said Sgt. Jack Darling. "Waiting to get on with it and get it over."

"Ours but to do and die," Scoville said. Their eyes met for a moment, and Scoville knew that even if his sergeant had not read the poem, they were in agreement that someone had blundered.

"I'd like to get my hands on the bastard who thinks this mess is glorious." Darling wiped sweat from his forehead, leaving a dark streak of mud along his temple. "No offense meant, my lord, but I'd wager he never risked his poetic arse on a battlefield."

"No, I think Tennyson was a confirmed civilian. Ever consider a civilian life for yourself, Sergeant?"

"On days like this, my lord—constantly."

That was just the reply Scoville had been hoping for, though the timing could not have been less opportune. "When I leave the service," he said, "provided I live long enough, I shall need a man who possesses both nerve and discretion and is able to keep track of my effects—a gentleman's personal gentleman. I've been spoiled by your competence, Darling, and I couldn't dare hope for such luck a second time. Might you be interested in the position?"

He could feel Darling's gaze upon him, knew the thoughtful look that would be on his sergeant's face. "Very much, my lord," Darling said at last. "But would you give odds on our chance of seeing a peaceful life?"

"No," Scoville said. "Not really." Nor any life at all, he added silently. He caught a small movement off in the direction of General Burrows' headquarters; his spyglass revealed the General's messenger leaving the command tent, and he knew what the message would be.

"Won't be long now." Scoville put away the glass. Ten minutes of quiet remained, perhaps fifteen. Another few hours of life? It might not even be that long. "Sergeant?" He ducked into his tent with Darling on his heels.

Everything inside had been packed up; his camp-desk stood ready to throw on a pack mule. "I think we deserve a last drink, don't you?" He unscrewed the lid on his hip-flask and filled the shot-sized cap for Darling. "Here's to dying in our beds in 1950."

"Yes, my lord. I'll look forward to it."

The brandy went down elegantly. Napoleon brandy, it was; Scoville had won the bottle from a brother officer in a card game in Herat. "Have another, Sergeant. No point in wasting it. The enemy will only pour it out if they get their bloody teetotalling hands on it."

"Can't have that, my lord." Darling did his duty, handed the cap back and straightened his shoulders. "Shall I tell the men to make ready, then?"

"Yes. It's time."

Darling gave him a crisp salute. Scoville returned it, and they both went back out into the blistering sun.

The battle began slowly, as such things always did, men moving into position and advancing until the first shot unleashed the thunder. Scoville had never seen anything like it—hundreds, thousands of shrieking Afghans in their sloppy tribal attire, with their deadly efficient weapons raised high. The first row fell to British fire. The rest leapt over the bodies and kept coming, faster than the riflemen could reload. Within minutes the fight deteriorated into desperate hand-to-hand combat.

And then the battle rose up like a living thing and tore them to pieces. In no time at all Burrows' forces were outflanked, their ammunition spent, the disciplined lines splintering apart as the tribesmen came on and kept coming, a seemingly endless flow of swords and knives and fury. The heat and dust increased a hundredfold; sanity fled in the dull roar of howling attackers and screaming wounded. The only constant was Jack Darling at his side as the two of them tried to maintain enough control of their men to manage an orderly retreat, using their rifles as clubs.

Scoville caught a movement from the corner of his eye—more Afghans cutting into their squadron from the right.

"Major, behind you!"

He started to turn. Then something slammed into him, and the world went dark.

Chapter Two

May, 1891
The Continental Express, transiting Germany

The sudden clash of steel woke Lord Robert Scoville from a troubled doze. His head jerked up, and for a confused moment he looked around for the enemy. Then he realized that the sound was not the clash of arms, but merely his hired railway carriage rumbling over a switch point, the metallic rattle and rumble merely the wheels on the track and the links between cars. He was a decade and a continent away from that old horror, somewhere between Zurich and Salzburg, lounging about in a private railway car in which everything was modern and agreeable. The comfortable divan upon which he sat would, come evening, be transformed into an equally comfortable bed. His man—for not only had Darling survived, he'd accepted Scoville's offer of employment—was in an adjoining compartment, ready to supply anything his lordship might require.

The newspaper he had been reading was folded neatly beside him, and a small brocade cushion had been tucked between his face and the window against which he was leaning. Obviously, Darling had found him asleep and tidied up rather than waking him, as he occasionally did if Scoville dozed off in his study at home.

Darling was a treasure, without question. His

unobtrusive competence allowed Scoville to maintain his town home with only a housekeeper and maid who went back to their families in the evening, and additional hired help for the occasional party. The peace and solitude were balm for Scoville's soul. He no longer wished, as he had in his childhood, to be poor enough that he didn't require servants trooping through the house at all hours. One man was all he needed. The right man.

Scoville occasionally wondered about Darling's origins; he'd never been able to tease the secret out of the man himself. It sometimes seemed as though Sergeant Jack Darling had materialized from the ethers in full uniform when the regiment first assembled, but Scoville suspected an investigation would reveal his gentleman's gentleman as a gentleman in blood at least. He might be a younger son disgraced or strayed, or possibly the indiscretion of some nobleman who'd had the decency to see that the boy got a good education.

It would be possible to hire someone to investigate Darling's past, of course, but that would be a betrayal of trust. Better to wait, observe, and see if he could eventually solve the mystery on his own. He hadn't really made an effort in that direction, though. There weren't many clues.

Darling had made the transition to civilian life without so much as a blink. His careful attention to uniform regulations and placement of insignia was transformed into a scrupulous exactitude regarding what a self-respecting gentleman was required to wear, enforcing his dictates with a deference that held a touch of gentle mockery. Always inclined to comfort rather than fashion, Scoville allowed himself to be bullied in matters of haberdashery. Darling's taste in such matters was impeccable.

Darling himself was no chore to look at, either— strongly built without being bulky, thick dark hair neatly trimmed, eyes a surprisingly dark blue, a pleasantly shaped mouth in a pleasantly arranged face, and throughout it all a spark of intelligence and humor that belied the man's less than lofty occupation. He moved with the grace of a dancer or an athlete; he would have looked perfectly at home sitting in Parliament or at the head of his own firm. Why he chose to devote his considerable talents to making Lord Robert Scoville's life comfortable was another minor mystery, but his lordship was content to let that one lie. A pity he couldn't just marry the man—Darling would have made a splendid life's companion, without the trouble of children or feminine vapors.

Scoville warned himself off that line of thought. Discreet Darling might be, a pleasure to gaze upon, loyal as a bulldog, even willing to turn a blind eye to his master's occasional male guest who stayed the night and shared His Lordship's bed. That was more than a man of Scoville's unconventional sexual habits could reasonably expect, and Darling had never given any hint that he might be willing to consider a more personal sort of service.

And that was just as well, wasn't it? If that particular question were ever raised, it would forever affect their relationship, might even destroy it. The principle that Scoville always followed in the army, *A good officer keeps his hands off his privates*, was just as sensible a maxim in civilian life. One did not make advances to an employee whose livelihood depended on pleasing his employer.

Lord Robert had an ingrained awareness of his own privilege—not a sense of entitlement, but the sure knowledge that he'd done nothing to earn the good fortune that was his by birth. He had seen too many working-class heroes to think that his title made him better than the soldiers who had fought and died beside him, and he abhorred slavery, whatever its disguise. He might have paid for sexual services on occasion, but only in fair trade; he had never bedded an unwilling companion and never intended to.

Particularly not someone whose friendship he valued. If he looked at the matter squarely, Darling was perhaps the best friend he'd ever had. He could think of no one he trusted more or would rather have at his side in a tight spot. If he asked Darling for more than the man was willing or able to give, he'd lose him, certain sure—and he did not want to lose Jack Darling. How could one replace the irreplaceable?

This would all have been so different if they had met as equals. He could give the man a look, say, "Well, Jack, how about it?" and go from there—or go nowhere at all.

But at least that way he would know. As it was, the forces of social convention could be a straightjacket for a man with principles.

Still, there were things one couldn't alter, so any invitation would have to come from Darling himself, and Scoville wasn't about to hold his breath waiting. Darling had never given the slightest indication that he might dance on that side of the ballroom; he always seemed to have a flirtation going with some pretty housemaid or shop-girl, and he came home very late on his nights off.

Scoville couldn't name the girl, but he knew there must be one. Sooner or later, his comfortable existence would have to make allowances for a Mrs. Darling, and possibly a brood of little Darlings as well. It was a daunting prospect, but he could hardly deny the man a chance for a normal life. Perhaps a detached cottage in the back garden would suffice to quarantine wedded bliss away from bachelor comforts.

At any rate, Darling's hypothetical love life and possible future were far afield from where Scoville needed to focus his thoughts. Although he was a gentleman of leisure, noblesse did require him to oblige at times by combining his genuine love of travel with the odd errand on Her Majesty's behalf. These were usually minor chores, no real inconvenience, and this trip was no exception. Scoville had already intended to visit the newly opened conservatory at the University of Vienna. Years in the building, it was said to be the finest botanical conservatory on the Continent, and if it was true that they'd acquired tropical plants that no one in England had ever seen, he wanted to be among the first to lay eyes on them.

Half his duty to his country would be discharged when he had assured an unreliable member of a foreign court that England very much supported him even though the political climate required that the Queen's public attitude was one of disapproval. Of course the Baron knew perfectly well that Her Majesty would chuck him under the train if necessary. Everyone knew their steps in this little dance, but the steps must be performed nonetheless. He could attend to that in a single afternoon.

It was the second part of his mission that was likely to produce complications. Mr. Smythe—of course that wasn't his name, Scoville knew the gentleman's name perfectly well, as did any Englishman who read the *Times*—had gently hinted that one of Scoville's old acquaintances had been gathering useful information in Paris and would pass it along to his former army chum in a little cafe in Vienna. The missive would be nothing much, only a few pages, small enough to tuck into a book or magazine. Not worth mentioning to any border guards, of course.

It would have been nice to know the chum's name. "You'll recognize him from your days in the Service." Lovely. Scoville had known a number of men when he'd worn the uniform of the British Empire. Many of them were dead. And some of those still among the living were not men he wanted to see again. "Smythe" claimed he could not reveal the contact's identity because he did not know it; Scoville translated that to mean that he himself was not to know who he was meeting until they were face to face.

That secrecy told him something about his current errand. Whatever this was about, it went well beyond what he had been led to believe would be expected of him back when he'd agreed to act as a messenger without portfolio. This was not just a matter of passing along "unofficial" official messages. When he started acting as a courier of secret materials gathered in foreign countries, presumably without the permission of the countries' governments—that, however delicately one phrased it, was espionage. Espionage was not a healthful activity for a gentleman who preferred the quiet life.

The connecting door to Darling's compartment opened with a discreet click. "Good afternoon, my lord," his man said. "A pleasant nap, I trust?"

"Yes, thanks. All the better for it."

"Would your lordship prefer to go to the dining car, or shall I procure a menu?"

Scoville yawned, considering, and decided he should be up and about. "The dining car, by all means. I need the exercise. You go on ahead and find a table for us, please. I'll only be a minute."

"Very good, my lord."

Scoville rose and stretched. It had been a pleasant, uneventful trip and the scenery was interesting, a trip backwards in time. France had been charming in her springtime dress, but as they ascended into the Alps the land went back to winter's drab white and brown. Now, with the train circling north of the highest elevations, spring was returning. He could see patches of land showing the first touches of green where the snow was beginning to melt away.

But it was all just pictures from here inside the car as it rolled steadily across the countryside. Scoville was looking forward to standing on a floor that wasn't swaying. He loved walking outdoors, especially in this season, with the scent of warm earth and spring rain.

It did look fine outside, good weather for a postprandial cigar on the dining car's rear platform. He patted his pockets, realized his cigar case was in his trunk in Darling's compartment, and made a detour through the connecting door to fetch it. If the cuisine in the dining car was any portent of things to come, it wasn't espionage that would put him at risk. The only danger he was certain to face was the tightening of his waistcoat if he lingered too long in the coffeehouses indulging in the fine flaky Viennese pastry.

When he awoke some time later with a blinding headache, that idiot optimism was the last thing he remembered.

As he made his way to the dining car, Jack Darling noted that two more passenger cars had been added during their stop in Munich, shortly after breakfast. All to the good, that. The additional corridors provided a few dozen yards more exercise to whet the appetite for a meal as good or better than what they'd find at home. A word with the maitre d' on their first afternoon aboard, with a sovereign tucked into the parting handshake, had ensured them a good table and prompt service. And, just as he'd expected, their usual table was ready and waiting.

Jack perused the menu briefly. How the devil had they managed to make sauerbraten in a dining car's cramped kitchen? Did some restaurant along the route marinate a tub of beef for them? No matter. He'd lay odds on that being his Lordship's choice. Always eat the local dishes, Lord Robert said, otherwise what's the point of travel?

But what was keeping him? If Lord Robert said he'd be a minute, that was generally what he meant. It had been— Jack checked his watch—nearly ten minutes. That was not just unusual, it was unprecedented. And worrisome.

Something was wrong. He'd known from the start, when Scoville returned from his meeting in Whitehall, that there was something different about this trip, something shady or dangerous. Jack had known Lord Robert far too long to miss the little signs that something was afoot.

We're on a train, he reminded himself as he stood and headed for the exit. *What could possibly happen on a train?*

A train with two more carloads of strangers aboard.

A lot could happen, and much of it bad. Jack managed to walk in a calm and composed manner to the end of the dining car and through the door to the next. Then he ran.

Scoville took careful inventory of himself before attempting to open his eyes. His head throbbed, his face was pressed against something rough and slightly musty-smelling. And the floor rumbled. He needed to get himself up.

But not just yet. He couldn't even force his eyelids open, could not find the strength to move at all.

The door squeaked a bit. Why had he not noticed that the door squeaked?

"My lor—Dear God!"

Nought to fear, Darling's here. Scoville tried to say hello, but for some reason even that was too much for him.

A hand touched his face very gently, sought the pulse at his throat. "Major— my lord, can you hear me?" The tone of Darling's voice hardened. "Find a doctor—now! And bring me some ice!"

Ah. Sergeant Darling had matters in hand. Somebody would be going for a doctor, double-quick, and hell to pay if one could not be found. Scoville swallowed and summoned resources enough to say, "At ease, Sergeant."

"My lord—what happened?"

"Help—help me up, would you?" He opened his eyes, squinting at the brightness of the light, and raised a hand, heavy as lead, expecting Darling to pull him to his feet.

Darling took his hand, but merely held on to it. "Best stay where you are, my lord," he said firmly. "I'm told there's a physician aboard, and he should be here shortly."

"Darling, don't be an ass." Scoville rolled onto his side, but a wave of pain and dizziness kept him there. "God *damn.*" Whoever had hit him might not have meant him to survive—or had not cared if the blow killed him. "I don't know what happened. Didn't see anyone. Help me up, damn it."

"I don't believe you're entirely yourself, my lord. And your head is bleeding. If you'll just lie back, I'll fetch a compress."

"I'm not a bloody invalid." He felt like one, though. He wouldn't swear that his skull hadn't been split, but it was beyond embarrassing to admit that someone had been able to creep up on him.

"No, my lord."

It was impossible to argue with Darling when he went all deferential, therefore equally impossible to win an argument. "Very well, I'll keep still. Bring on the bandages and barley-water."

"Yes, my lord. If you would lie back on this handkerchief—yes, thank you."

Scoville lay back with ill-expressed gratitude and let himself drift while Darling returned with a cool compress, which did reduce the throbbing pain and made the short wait for medical assistance more bearable.

When he finally appeared, the doctor, a sensible Belgian, put three stitches in Lord Robert's scalp, diagnosed mild concussion, prescribed a day of bed rest, and advised him to find a physician in Vienna if he was not much improved the following morning.

The doctor had barely left when the train stopped in Salzburg, and an Austrian Customs officer came through to inspect their passports. When the Customs man learned that Lord Robert had not even seen his assailant, he offered his regrets that he could not hold all departing passengers on suspicion. Darling assured him that the intruder had fled without taking anything. On that inconclusive note, they were left alone.

His lordship, denied the luxuries of the dining car, supped on tea, crackers, and boiled chicken in broth, with Darling hovering in solicitous attendance. Even that light meal was more than he could finish. Pushing away the half-empty bowl, he found a reclining position that kept the sore spot on his head clear of the pillows. "Well, Darling?"

"My lord?"

"That's enough coddling for now, thank you. What I need is information. You said nothing had been taken—I assume that was to get Customs on his way as quickly as possible." At Darling's nod, he continued, "Then what was he after? Is anything missing?"

Darling raised a hand. He stepped silently to the door, eased the lock back, and suddenly yanked it open. The corridor outside was empty. He peered out, looking both ways, then relocked the door. "Forgive the dramatics, my lord, but I'd rather be certain we don't have eavesdroppers."

"The train does make a fair amount of covering noise," Lord Robert said, matching his low tone. "So what did you find?"

"Nothing was stolen, but we seem to have acquired this." He held out an old-fashioned snuffbox. "It was in your trunk, tucked under your unmentionables."

Lord Robert took the box, a handsome item. Something of an antique, it had a tiny ivory panel set into the chased silver, the British lion rampant carved upon its surface. "He didn't need to brain me to present this."

He started to flip open the catch with his thumb, but Darling quickly touched the box lid. "Best not, my lord. It's full of cocaine."

"I could do with an analgesic," he protested, but left it closed. "What the devil do you suppose this is in aid of?" The stuff was legal enough in England, but Scoville did not know, offhand, what the laws might be in the various countries they would be passing through, and he did not want to find out by running afoul of them.

"If your assailant was a madman, I suppose it might be seen as an apology."

"What, he meant to make amends for braining me by leaving a painkiller?" Lord Robert would have laughed, but he had a feeling that would make the headache even worse. "I can't believe we're dealing with a lunatic."

Darling shook his head. "Nor can I. It might have been left by mistake—a delivery intended for someone else."

That was possible, of course, but it seemed unlikely. "For whom? I don't believe there's another private car on this train. And why knock me unconscious, then leave the item in my trunk? You weren't gone long enough for him to have had time to put it there before he hit me. That was deliberate."

"Yes. Deliberate and foolish, my lord, and that's what I don't understand. He was able to enter my compartment undetected, from the corridor. Why didn't he simply wait until you had also gone to dinner and the coast was clear— or at least step back into the corridor when you opened the connecting door?"

Lord Robert sighed, letting his face rest against the cool linen of the pillow case. "Excellent questions, Darling. Would that I had an answer."

"Are you missing anything from your pockets?"

Since his pockets, as well as his clothing, had been confiscated when Darling helped him into his pajamas, Lord Robert could only shrug. "You'd know that better than I."

Darling nodded and returned with the little tray on which he kept the pockets' contents. A few mixed coins of assorted nationality, a nail file, a comb, a Swiss soldier's knife. And one wallet.

"Contents intact," he reported after checking, "including cash. This is making less sense by the moment."

Darling frowned at the tray. "Another possibility is that he expected to be searched at some point and wanted to let you smuggle that object for him, since your luggage isn't likely to be bothered. We might simply put it back and wait to see who comes looking now that we've passed the border."

"Mm." There might be other possible explanations, but Scoville couldn't gather his wits enough to define them, even to himself. He handed the snuffbox back. "I think we've had enough excitement for one evening. Lock the blasted thing in the briefcase and let's get some sleep."

"Yes, my lord."

Darling disappeared into his compartment; Scoville heard some thumps and dragging noises. Darling popped back in, announced that he'd put their trunk in front of the door in the other cubicle, and blew out the lantern sconce on the wall beside the door. Then he returned to his compartment. Scoville reached over to turn out the light mounted beside his bed, but before he could do that Darling reappeared, carrying the mattress from his own cot.

Scoville frowned. When Darling tossed the pallet onto the floor in front of the door to Scoville's own compartment, his lordship saw that as absolutely unnecessary, and said as much.

"I expect you're right, my lord," Darling answered. "But on the slim chance you're mistaken, I'll be comfortable enough here. Good padding and a nice thick carpet, as well—we've both slept rougher on campaign." He added pillow and blanket to the makeshift bed and arranged himself upon it. With his body alongside the door to this compartment and his feet extending through the doorway to his own quarters, there was no way anyone would be traversing the space undetected—especially not in the dark. Before lying down, he added, "You will let me know if you require anything?"

"I hardly think I'll have the opportunity," Scoville said, not bothering to hide his annoyance. "I'm sure you will anticipate my every need."

"I do my best, my lord," Darling said with a grin.

Scoville wanted to heave a pillow at him. "Damn it, Darling, I don't like this at all. You're not a dog, to be sleeping at my feet."

"No, my lord." He raised up on one elbow, his eyes even darker than usual, the cheerful expression wiped away. "I'm not a dog, or I'd sniff the bastard out. I'm just a man who's damned angry at that swine slipping past my guard. If he comes back, I want first crack at him, and if I'm right here, I know I'll get it."

"That's my prerogative, wouldn't you say?" Scoville hated the petulant tone of his voice—almost as much as he hated being managed. And he knew better. He knew he was in no shape to fight his own battles. That only made it worse.

Darling didn't answer his question. "The doctor did say that you might be out of sorts, my lord. From the concussion."

Scoville sighed. He didn't have the energy to argue, and it was a stupid argument anyway, grossly unfair to berate a man for his loyalty. Darling was only doing his best, and wouldn't he do the same if their positions were reversed? "Yes, and he's right, damn him. Sorry, Sergeant."

"For what, my lord?"

"Being an ass." He turned the wick all the way down; the light wavered and went out. "Good night, Jack."

"Pleasant dreams, my lord."

"Same to you."

Jack settled himself in unexpected comfort on the well-padded mattress, waiting while Lord Robert's breathing slowed and eventually shifted into a light, intermittent snore. He had nearly forgotten himself for a moment there. It would've been beyond bad form to confess that the incident had frightened him worse than an attempt on his own life would have.

What would he have done if he'd returned to the car and found a dead body? To lose him without ever—

No. That didn't bear thinking about. That way lay nothing but frustration and distress. Better to think about pleasanter things, such as the day years before, in the steam and stink of a railway station in India, where Sergeant Darling had been sent to meet his new commanding officer, summoned in haste to replace an incompetent bully who'd had the good grace to take himself off in a fit of apoplexy. Darling had been prepared for another commander of the same sort—there were so many of the type in the upper echelons. He had learned to deal with them by being efficient, correct, and opaque. He was prepared for any stupidity.

He had not been prepared for Major Scoville. In the first place, the man barely looked old enough to be wearing the uniform, much less experienced enough to take command. Slender and fair, with keen, sky-blue eyes, a longish face, and a strong chin, he was the most beautiful thing Darling had ever set eyes on. When Scoville saw the sergeant's Army uniform, he smiled, and his face lit up like a sunrise.

Darling curbed his reaction—he'd had plenty of practice at that—and presented himself to Major Scoville with all due formality. Over the next few months they found that they worked very well together, particularly after the young officer proved himself under fire.

Despite his quiet manner, Scoville had a presence that his men responded to almost instinctively. He never blustered; he didn't need to. He gave no quarter to insubordination or sloppiness, and when he had a soldier hanged for raping an Indian woman, the men knew he was deadly serious about discipline. The Major seldom raised his voice unless it was necessary to be heard above the sound of battle—but he faced battle unflinchingly, and he was one of those rare officers who never ordered a man to do something he would not do himself. They'd have followed him into Hell—and before their tour of duty was over, they had done just that.

Darling was smitten from the start.

But he was not stupid. Even when he perceived a slight irregularity in Major Scoville's friendship with one or two other officers, he kept his own counsel and made certain that the Major's private affairs remained absolutely private. Jack knew that it would be career suicide to make an improper advance toward his commanding officer without at least a hint, some indication that it would be welcomed. The invitation never came. Issuing one himself was something that could never be undone, and so he had not done it.

He had hoped that the offer of employment after they

mustered out had been a veiled invitation for something more, but he'd been disappointed. In ten years' time, Lord Robert had not precisely made a secret of his preference for men, but he had never given the slightest hint that his interest extended to men outside his own class.

Had it not been for a slight irregularity of birth, Darling might have met that qualification. His sire had provided generously for Mrs. Darling, had seen to it that Jack had a comfortable home and respectable schooling, but due to the unfortunate situation of his being already married to someone else, that gentleman could give the mother of his son neither his name nor the benefit of his social standing. So instead of being the younger son of a man well-placed in the nobility, Jack Darling was raised as the son of a widowed officer's wife... a widow who had never actually been married. Her lover had influence and money enough to arrange for her to move to London with a new name and a carefully constructed history; Mrs. Darling raised her son under a mantle of genteel respectability.

It wasn't until Jack had actually joined the army that his distraught mother revealed any of this. Up to that point, he'd believed what she had told him, that his father had been a captain in the cavalry and had been killed in action just before his only child was born. In the few minutes it took her to explain, he was transformed from hero's son to bastard.

So much for illusion. He had already enlisted, though; it was too late to do anything about that. "At least let your father get you a commission!" his mother had wailed.

Anger made him snap, "My father's dead. You told me so yourself," before making his escape. It had been a dramatic exit line, but he could have kicked himself afterwards for the missed opportunity. He'd had plenty of time to regret his rash decision, even though he had made amends with his mother.

Luckily, his army-mad boyhood had prompted him to learn all he could about the job, and he proved to be good at it. It was not until he met his Waterloo at Maiwand, and knew that he would follow Lord Robert Scoville to the ends of the earth, that he realized just how comprehensively stupid he had been. What might have happened if he could have met Lord Robert as a fellow officer?

As the years passed and hope died, Jack learned to make the best of things. He enjoyed the travel that was part of his job. He expanded his mind in museums and his soul at concerts and the theater. He lived in comfort and ate the best foods, becoming something of a chef along the way. He enjoyed the intimacy of those shared meals, prepared and eaten without the bother of a cook or other domestics. When the physical frustration became unbearable, he would indulge in a casual *pas de deux* with another man who shared his inclinations—not infrequently those who worked for Lord Robert's acquaintances. There had never been anyone special, though, and he never allowed the indulgence to become habitual.

Lord Robert had once made a mild joke about Darling's dallying with housemaids, and Jack had cultivated that inaccuracy. He might not be deemed worthy of his lordship's attention, but his pride would not allow him to let it look as though he might want it.

By now, Jack felt that his position as indispensable manager of Lord Robert's household was fairly secure. He was relieved that his employer had never made any effort toward acquiring a wife to keep up appearances, and was equally grateful that his lordship lacked any interest in the aesthetic set that circulated around the flamboyant Mr. Wilde.

Taken altogether, Jack's life was a pleasant one. If he had the occasional pang of longing as he'd had this evening, a wish that he could slide into bed beside that strong, slender body and gather it into his arms... Well, how many men really got everything they wanted?

It helped that he could remind himself that Lord Robert was far from constant in his affections. He had gone through a string of temporary, occasional lovers. Jack had seen them all—and he had seen them leave. It was better to be the one who stayed. Not perfect, perhaps. Not his heart's desire. But better.

The gentle rocking of the car eventually lulled him into a dreamless sleep that was disturbed, much too soon, by a faint but insistent tapping. Jack opened his eyes in pitch darkness, which at this time of year meant well before five a.m. And the porter wasn't supposed to wake them until a quarter past six.

The tapping stopped. Ten seconds later, it resumed.

As quietly as he could, Jack extracted himself from his bedroll and went through the connecting door to his own compartment. Pistol? No, the noise would bring unwanted company. But he did snatch up Lord Robert's ebony walking-stick with its heavy silver handle. The rumble of the train's movement muffled the slight sounds as he pulled the trunk aside and cautiously opened the second compartment's door into the corridor.

A short, well-dressed man was standing, slightly hunched, outside the door to Lord Robert's compartment. Darling could not see his face beneath the brim of a dark homburg, but as the man raised his hand to tap on the door once again, he closed the other door behind him. "May I assist you?"

The inconsiderate visitor jumped at the sound, and looked up; it was Jack's turn to be surprised. The last time he'd seen this gentleman, they both had been in uniform. "Captain McDonald?"

"No names, if you please." He took a few steps toward Darling. "I must speak to Lord Robert immediately. It's a matter of greatest urgency."

He was speaking in a low tone, which suited Darling perfectly. "That will not be possible. His lordship is unwell." Even if Lord Robert had been in perfect fettle, Darling would have discouraged this particular visitor.

But McDonald was a man accustomed to getting his

own way; he didn't budge. "His lordship could be a damned sight worse than unwell if he's not careful. There's a man aboard this train who's a danger to all three of us. Will you open this door?"

"No, sir, I will not. In any case, I believe your warning may be several hours too late."

Alarm flickered across McDonald's handsome but peevish face. "Unwell, you said—was he attacked? Injured?"

"Not seriously. However, the doctor prescribed a good night's sleep, and I intend to see that his orders are carried out. If you would care to return at seven a.m., or perhaps join his lordship in the dining car for breakfast?"

"No. We mustn't be seen together. That's why I came by at this ungodly hour."

"If you would be so good as to entrust me with the particulars, I will convey the information to his lordship when he awakens. The name and description of—"

"Stuffy as ever, aren't you, Darling?" McDonald smirked, looking him up and down with a more than casual eye. "You really should have stayed in uniform—it lent you a certain air of authority."

Jack said nothing. Cecil McDonald had been one of those officers who stayed overnight at Major Scoville's quarters. The association had been short, to Darling's relief, and the break had been complete. He did not know what had caused it, nor did he care.

The army captain's uniform McDonald wore back then had lent him a certain air, too, but he had been slimmer then, and better looking. What once was youthful charm had deteriorated into a petulant childishness, and his insults were no more clever now than then. The only thing to do was ignore them and wait him out.

"Oh, very well," McDonald said, when it became apparent that Jack was neither going to let him in nor respond to his gibe. "I'll return at seven—and you'd better drop those airs, if you know what's good for you."

"As I told you once before, sir, I answer to Lord Robert, not to you. You may discuss my behavior with his lordship at any time you choose."

For a moment Jack thought—hoped—that McDonald might be about to strike him, but he was cheated of the opportunity to defend himself when the other man whirled and stormed off down the corridor. Jack waited for several minutes to be sure McDonald was well and truly gone before returning to his compartment. So that was the familiar face that his lordship had hinted they might see. Damn. So many good men they'd known, and it had to be that arrogant bastard.

Jack found his watch where he'd left it, and by the light of a match he saw that it was twenty minutes shy of four in the morning. He might yet salvage a couple of hours' rest; best to get back under the covers before a brass band and a troupe of acrobats paraded down the corridor. Snug in his blankets, he ordered himself to go to sleep and not think about this new turn of events.

Easier said than done. He could remember the first encounter with McDonald as though it were yesterday. The regiment had been stationed in India at an established outpost, which meant actual barracks instead of tents, cisterns that held rainwater, some rudiments of civilization. If one took care to avoid the cobras and nastier vermin, one could achieve a minimal degree of comfort.

Then Captain Cecil McDonald had ridden through on his way to a new posting. Major Scoville had greeted him in a friendly manner—a *very* friendly manner—and told Darling to put McDonald in the room beside his own, after he got him a bath and saw to his comfort.

McDonald jumped to a conclusion that took far too much for granted. "Darling, is it?" he said as he followed the sergeant into his quarters, then laughed in a way that made Jack want to knock him flat. "Well, then, Darling, I could use a bit of comfort—" He began to undo his uniform trousers, and Darling stepped back.

"Captain, I fear you have come to an erroneous conclusion." He slapped the tin washbasin down on the rattan table and placed the heavy pitcher of water beside it. "Here is your washwater; I will see to it that food is brought to you."

McDonald grinned and tilted his head. It was clear that he thought himself irresistibly charming. "Come, now, Darling—what a perfect name!—I've seen the way you look at him. Surely you don't expect me to believe it's all platonic!"

"What you believe is not my concern," Jack had shot back, mortified that his feelings were so obvious to this oaf. "I take my orders from Major Scoville, and he has never given me an illegal order. Nor do I expect him to. You are, of course, free to report any dereliction on my part." He turned on his heel and left, and made arrangements to have McDonald's meal taken to him by an elderly servant afflicted with broken teeth and boils.

He'd spent the night wound up in a knot of anxiety, wondering what sort of report Major Scoville would hear. Should he have put his aversion to one side and acquiesced? A bad report from an officer could ruin a soldier's career, and he had not served with Major Scoville long enough to guess what his reaction might be to McDonald's complaint.

As it turned out, there'd been no reaction at all. Jack had never dared ask whether a complaint had been lodged, and of course he had held his peace regarding McDonald's imposition. Scoville's only comment, when his fellow-officer left the following morning, had been to the effect that people could change in ways one would never expect. Jack guessed from the customary neatness of Major Scoville's bed that if McDonald had expected to spend the night there he had been disappointed, which would account for his poisonous attitude at the breakfast table.

Why had McDonald survived the war, when so many good men were dead?

And here he was back again, ruining what was left of

another night's rest. Jack sat up and flipped his pillow over, seeking a more comfortable position. He could not find one, and finally gave up on the prospect of getting to sleep. He wasn't going to relax until he knew why Cecil McDonald was here and what he was up to.

"McDonald!"

"I'm afraid so, my lord."

"Damn." Scoville closed his eyes again. He'd awakened feeling quite well, much better than he'd expected to, but Darling's announcement was a headache all by itself. "Didn't he tell you anything?"

"Only that he believes there to be a man on board who is a danger to us all. I could not determine whether that was all he knew, or simply all he would tell me."

Scoville rubbed his forehead. "If we're in danger, it's stupid to play guessing games. What if he were killed before he told us?"

"Well, my lord, should that happen, I suppose we would at least know that he was telling the truth."

"He's a damned fool."

"I would certainly never contradict your lordship's assessment of the gentleman's character," Darling said with an ironic look. "Ready for a shave, my lord? I've heated the water on the spirit lamp."

"Very well, Darling. I suppose if he's going to inflict himself upon us I'd better be prepared. Seven, you said?"

"That was the hour I suggested. I have no idea whether or not he will appear."

It was true that reliability had never been one of Cecil's virtues. Hard to remember, now, whether he had actually been possessed of any, apart from a willingness to engage in bedroom sport. That was all Scoville himself had been interested in when they were at Oxford, but he should have put the youthful indiscretion aside when he'd graduated. Allowing it to continue when they'd both entered the service had been a mistake.

"Let's make ourselves presentable, then. Or, rather, I must let you make me presentable—you are never anything less."

Their conversation ceased while Darling shaved him—sensible in any case, more so when the train's movement made the ordinary task just a bit hazardous. If anyone else had been wielding the razor, Scoville would have postponed the shave until they reached their hotel. He considered being shaved a silly ritual—he could have done the job himself—but Darling did it better, his sure, deft hands scraping away the stubble with a surgeon's skill. And the hot towel he drew across Scoville's freshly-shaved face felt wonderful, easing the lingering headache from yesterday's misadventure. By the time Darling patted on the bay rum, Scoville was feeling ready to take on the world.

But seven a.m. came and went with no sign of a visitor. After they'd waited for half an hour, Darling went off to locate breakfast while his lordship gazed out the window at the scenery speeding by and mused on the night's peculiar visitation.

Cecil the ever-unreliable. Why the devil had he appeared on the train, instead of the café in Vienna in two days' time? Why hadn't he simply handed his parcel, whatever it was, to Darling? Surely he had to know that passing the information to Darling was every bit as secure as—

No. Scoville's thoughts hit a bump just as the train did, going over switchpoints. Perhaps he should consider the event in a different light. What if Cecil were not the courier?

Well, if and when he appeared, that would be easy to ascertain; back in Whitehall, Smythe had given him coded countersigns. But McDonald might be playing some other game altogether, and if so it probably had nothing to do with their current errand. When they reached glorious Vienna, their first destination would be a telegraph counter, where he could wire a carefully worded query to Mr. Bloody Secretive Smythe. Something along the lines of, "Damn your eyes (stop) This is urgent (stop) Who is contact (query)."

Scoville's head still ached; he knew it was making him irritable. The doctor had left tablets for him to take, but they had to be taken with food.

What a nuisance! There stood the Alps off to the south, the morning sun dazzling white on their mantle of snow, but he couldn't let his attention wander. He couldn't even doze. He had to sit here with pistol to hand, on the off-chance that his assailant might return to finish the job while Darling was away.

What was taking Darling so long, anyway? Scoville looked at his watch and realized that his man had been gone for only ten minutes. Nothing was likely to happen to him in broad daylight, in the public rail cars. He'd be back soon enough.

There was nothing to do but puzzle over the situation. Why had McDonald come by at four in the morning? That was an insane hour for a social visit. If he had been on urgent business, why had he refused to deal with Darling?

And why did Darling have such an antipathy toward McDonald? In Scoville's own case, he had simply realized that his boyhood acquaintance had grown into a man with an ugly imagination and no tact. Was Jack Darling simply a better judge of character, or did his attitude spring from some other source? Scoville didn't want to pry, but if their lives were in danger, he might have to. Just another headache to add to the growing list.

Why couldn't this infernal train get to Vienna?

At least one of his questions was answered in a few minutes' time. Darling appeared with a coffeepot in his hand, followed by a waiter bearing a heavy covered tray. His first words were, "No visitors, my lord?"

"None. And he'd better not show up until I've got outside some of that coffee. It smells delicious."

Darling nodded, tipped the waiter, and locked the door after he left. "I hope you were not inconvenienced by the delay, my lord. I thought it best to fetch our food directly from the kitchen, so no one else would have a chance to tamper with it."

"Good thinking. What have you brought for us?"

"Nothing elaborate," he said, pouring the coffee. "Fine coffee, for a start."

It might not have been elaborate, but Scoville was not in the mood for a fussy meal. The coffee was perfectly brewed, and he found that the crusty rolls, buttered eggs and bacon, still piping hot under the silver cover, were exactly what he needed. After several minutes of determined ingestion, he swallowed a last morsel of jam-covered bread and sat back, replete. "Darling, I thank God every day that you remember Bonaparte's maxim."

"My lord?"

"An army marches on its stomach."

"I have always considered that a very undignified position, my lord." He raised an eyebrow. "And damned uncomfortable."

Scoville laughed. "Perhaps so, but I never feel more optimistic than I do just after breakfast." He poured himself a last splash of coffee so Darling could finish his own meal uninterrupted. "I don't suppose you saw any sign of McDonald?"

"No, my lord. I did mention to the conductor that I thought I had heard someone outside our room during the wee hours, but he swore that no one was about."

"Lovely." Scoville smiled wryly. "This is not shaping up as the pleasure trip I was hoping for. Once we complete our errand, I have half a mind to get on the train, report back, then turn around and have ourselves a real holiday. Do the job and be done with it, get it off our hands."

"The visit with the Baron, my lord?" Darling asked.

"Yes, that ..." He hesitated for a moment, then made up his mind. "Darling, I expect you're well ahead of me on this one. The fact is, we've got two jobs to do in Vienna, and the second is to meet some sort of courier who will give us something that we must take back to England in secret."

"You're not referring to the snuffbox, my lord?"

"I—" That stopped him short; he rubbed his chin reflectively. "You know, Darling, that's a notion. Though why a courier would knock me over the head—no, we're supposed to receive a small packet of papers from an old Army chum of mine at the café in the Sacher House. And that's not until the day after tomorrow."

"And Captain McDonald, is he—?"

"I don't know. I was a fool not to insist on that bit of information, but they wouldn't give me the courier's name."

"Balls!" Darling looked instantly abashed at his own crudeness, but Scoville had to smile.

"That about sums it up, Sergeant. Someone has blundered."

"Philharmonikerstrasse 4, *bitte*," Scoville told the cabman. While planning the trip he had considered stopping at the Imperial Hotel, but had decided upon the Sacher, instead. The Baron was certain to be in residence at the Imperial, and this was one time he preferred to keep business and pleasure—or more accurately, one business and another—as clearly separate as possible.

Besides, he liked the Sacher. It was a hairsbreadth less grand than the Imperial, its vaulted ceilings perhaps not quite so high and gilt-encrusted, its paintings worth only a duke's ransom, not a king's. It had never been a royal residence as the Imperial had, but what the Sacher's chef could do with coffee and chocolate was sheer genius. And it was directly across from the Opera House, a building that Scoville could gaze at for hours without tiring of the elegant balance of its architecture.

Lord Robert would never be so disloyal to London as to make an unfavorable comparison between the city of his birth and any other in the world. But Vienna, with its wide, open thoroughfares, had a bright, gay charm unlike any other city he'd ever seen, the hybrid vigor of a cultural crossroads. He could spend a month here just visiting museums and galleries, and not reach the end of them. Ever-changing music, new ideas in art, the finest opera, and the food! The Viennese even had legends about their coffee, and it deserved them. He could smell the aroma here in the street, wafting out from the cafes.

The cab driver clucked to his horse and drove them quickly to the hotel. While Darling saw to the luggage, Scoville found a quiet corner of the lobby where he could sit and compose a telegraph message that would convey sufficient urgency without attracting any undue attention. He finally decided upon "Dear Uncle John, suffered minor injury on the train, urgent you send name of doctor you mentioned last week." If that didn't do the job, he'd have to talk to someone at the Embassy and hope that they were *au courant*.

He took his message to the concierge and arranged to have it sent; by the time he was finished, Darling was at his elbow with the key to their suite.

"I've taken the liberty of having our briefcase locked up in the hotel safe, my lord."

"Excellent, Darling. Glad you thought of it. Does it still contain the antique item we acquired on the train?"

"Of course, my lord. If our visitor wanted the item smuggled across the border, this ought to make it impossible for him to take it back the same way he left it."

"My thought exactly. Well done. Let's nip upstairs and have a wash, then find a bite to eat. Did they give us a suite with a view?"

"Second floor front, my lord." Darling grinned; he was aware of Scoville's infatuation with the Opera House. "I shall place a chair directly opposite the window, for your ease of viewing."

He really was indecently attractive when he smiled.

"Don't tease, Darling," Scoville grumbled, giving his baser instincts a mental thump.

"Of course not, my lord. I was merely admiring your lordship's appreciation of fine architecture."

"And that's two 'lords' in one sentence. For heaven's sake, man, have mercy!"

"Yes, my lord."

Scoville and his man were in the café, working their respective ways through plates of weinerschnitzel and chicken-and-leek strudel when a bellboy brought the return telegram from Smythe. Scoville unfolded the message while Darling tipped the messenger.

"Interesting," he said as soon as the boy was out of earshot. "We are to visit the British Embassy at our earliest convenience, and take care for our personal safety."

"A pity they didn't consider our personal safety from the first."

"Quite. Well, marching down to the British Embassy should make us as inconspicuous as the changing of the Guard, so I can only assume that a cat somewhere has escaped the bag. We must go—this wire names no names."

Darling took a thoughtful sip of his wine. "Therefore it either is McDonald and they want to avoid naming him in a telegram, or it is not, and—"

"And they don't want to name the real contact. Or it was McDonald, and he's met with foul play and all hell's about to break loose, in a most clandestine way. Sorry, Darling, I really had not expected this."

Darling shrugged. "No one's shooting at us, my lord—not yet, at least. It could be worse."

"I expect it will be, before we're done. It's not so much that I mind, it's that if we'd known what to expect I wouldn't have this Belgian lacework decorating my scalp."

"Are you certain you're well enough to go out in the night air, my lord?"

"Oh, yes. Itches like the devil, but I believe that's a good sign. And for heaven's sake, it's coming on to summer." He folded the telegram and placed it in an inner pocket. "Our earliest convenience will be after dinner. I refuse to be hurried through a good meal. Here, try some of this *erdäpfelsalat*—they've given me far too much for one."

Darling nodded, his mouth being too full to reply.

"I'm glad of this, actually," Scoville said. "I'll have the chance to ask for a hint as to what's going on in the larger scene before I smooth the Baron's ruffled feathers. And perhaps the Embassy will have some notion of what's become of McDonald."

"If they know, my lord." Darling said, scooping a small portion of the tangy potato salad onto his plate. "It was late and I was not at my best, but he seemed very anxious to avoid being seen. If I erred in sending him away—"

"No, Darling. I appreciate your taking the role of dragon at the gate. If he had to insist on waking me up only to tell me who knocked me on the head, he wasn't half anxious enough. Cecil's wily. It's just as possible he was being pursued by someone he'd loved and left and was looking for a place to lie low. He has an amazing talent for giving offense." That was not the sort of remark he ought to have made, but he could rely on Darling's discretion. "We can't assume he's our contact, after all. Half my club knew we were traveling to Vienna. Anyone might have told him."

At Darling's frown, he added, "Yes, that would be stretching coincidence very thin, but it is possible." He'd sooner believe McDonald was an annoying complication than imagine he'd been entrusted with important State documents. If he was their contact, the man who recruited him must not have known him very well.

Scoville banned any further business discussion and ordered himself a slice of sachertorte and a cup of coffee. Darling had the same. When the meal came to a satisfactory close, they sought the concierge once again and asked that gentleman to summon a cab.

Jack dismissed his worries about Lord Robert's health as soon as they stepped out into the lingering twilight. The sun was down, but it was May, after all, and the day's warmth still lingered. The fresh air would do them both good.

Since the cabdriver was Viennese, it was reasonable to guess that he would have at least a smattering of many languages, English among them. Further discussion of their current affair would have been out of the question even if they had anything left to say. At this point it was useless to speculate.

His lordship was always able to find something to talk about, of course, and turned to a familiar topic that alternately amused and annoyed him. His grandmama had written his mother about his obligations, and his mama had relayed the message as she always did. The letter had arrived just before they departed for the Continent.

"Apparently being a kind and generous uncle to my elder siblings' spawn is not sufficient proof of my devotion to family. Grandmama is renewing her campaign to see that I secure a wife and kiddies as quickly as possible."

"She is a very determined woman, my lord." Darling liked the old lady, in small doses. He would not have wanted to work for her, though. She was the sort of crusty individual best admired at a short remove.

"Excellent word. Determined indeed. Much as I appreciate her fine qualities, you know as well as I that it's a hopeless case, and I'm reaching the point where I no longer find her instructions entertaining. I don't suppose you have any useful ideas for spiking her guns?"

"My lord, it is hardly my place—"

"I don't know who else's it might be, Darling. If anyone knows me, it's you. And I've never known you to give me bad advice, even when I have to pry it out of you. You have my permission to speak freely, Sergeant—there is no one else to whom I might turn."

Darling wondered whether his lordship's head for wine had been softened by that thump it had received. "My lord... May I presume so far as to postulate that you do not expect, ever, to meet a woman who would be a satisfactory wife?"

"Good heavens. Took me at my word about speaking freely, didn't you?" Lord Robert smiled in a melancholy way. "But that's the whole point, isn't it? You're the only one who could." He fell silent for a little while, then finally said, "Jack, I can't bear the idea of marrying a woman I dislike just to satisfy my family. And tying myself to an unsuspecting woman that I did like—like, not love—would make two people miserable. Three, counting yourself—"

Jack sat up in shock, not sure he had heard correctly.

"Since such a marriage would put me in a permanently rotten temper," Lord Robert finished. "And that would be bound to have an adverse effect on your peace of mind."

Jack wasn't sure whether to be relieved or disappointed.

"Therefore—yes, Darling, you may make that assumption. I can't bring myself to contemplate anything so entirely wrong for me as marriage. What I need is an unassailable reason to deny myself the wedded bliss my female relations would force me into—something to stop their pestering once and for all."

"They mean well, my lord."

"They do." He laughed ruefully. "They really do. That's why I can't simply tell them to mind their own damned business. The way they see it, I *am* their business."

They rode for a few minutes in thoughtful silence. Then Jack said, "My lord, you must invent a woman."

"What, pretend to be engaged? That wouldn't serve for long. There'd be that telltale lack of a fiancée."

"No, my lord. An unattainable woman. So long as the ladies think your heart untouched, they will be persistent as water on stone. But because they do want to see you happy, if you could convince them that the subject is painful for you, they might desist."

"Yes, that might work. I'm always tempted to go ahead and tell them the truth, but that would only make it worse. My mother would think she failed, my father would die of fury, and they'd all want to 'cure' me."

Over my dead body! Jack restrained himself. "What I'm suggesting, my lord, is that you invent a long-lost love to whom you gave your heart, who married another or suffered untimely death." He placed a hand on his heart and rolled his eyes in a tragic manner. "She is forever out of reach, but you cannot love another."

"You scheming devil!" his lordship said admiringly. "You've been reading trashy novels again, haven't you?"

"No, my lord. It was a trashy melodrama, in a theater far below your mother's standards. The story would have no effect on the matchmakers outside your family, of course."

"The husband-hunting mamas can go hang. It's mainly my mother I'd like to discourage."

"Untimely demise would be the most effective." Jack was beginning to enjoy the drama of his brain-child. "No one could attempt to discover the lady's identity in order to ask her why she chose your rival over you. Or—I hesitate to suggest this—you might tell your mother that while you were in the Army, you married unwisely—"

"What?"

"To a young lady in another country—Italy, perhaps— who has since vanished, and you do not know whether she is alive or dead."

"Oh, that would never do. Seriously, Darling, you don't suppose my mother would rest one moment until she unearthed the poor girl, do you? Alive or dead, that wouldn't stop her. Vesuvius pales by comparison. I wouldn't have a moment's peace until she had names, dates, and places."

"I see your point, my lord. Your lady mother would be indefatigable. I have only one other suggestion, but you may not appreciate it."

His lordship waved a careless hand. "Go ahead,

demolish what's left of my reputation! What is it? A secret seraglio? Loathsome disease?"

"If your lordship recollects our extremely close call at the Battle of Maiwand..."

"I almost wish I could forget it. We lost so many good men." Lord Robert leaned back in the seat, his face suddenly sober. "Overrun by those devils two minutes after the doctor sewed up my leg, and him shot too, with the bandage in his hand. If his orderly hadn't been as quick on his feet as you were, we'd both have been buried there. About the third time you saved my life, wasn't it?"

Darling shrugged. "I was considering the geography of your injury, my lord. If your mother believed that the wound was not to your leg, but higher, and slightly more central, so as to interfere with dynastic ambitions..."

His Lordship winced. "Ye gods, man, that's brutal."

"Yes, my lord, but only consider—it is one thing that you can be certain she would never share with her friends, and perhaps not even with your grandmother. You might explain to your esteemed parent that you feel you must tell her outright, since she had not been able to apprehend your subtle hints."

Lord Robert gave a most ungentlemanly snort. "So subtle as to be nonexistent."

"You are a master of subtlety, my lord. Such restraint you have, such consideration for the young lady who would, as your wife, never know the fulfillment of motherhood."

"Motherhood looks like a lot of damned hard work, from what I've seen of my sister's family. Not to mention nine months of serious discomfort to acquire the little devils." He shuddered. "Another reason to avoid marriage—I shouldn't want to be responsible for putting any woman through that!"

"I suspect your lady relatives care less about your prospective wife's discomfort than the acquisition of grandchildren, my lord. But I believe your mother would refrain from matchmaking if she has the least regard for your feelings, any sympathy for the anguish you feel when you realize you will never hear the patter of little feet—"

"Enough! Darling, I once told my mother that if I longed for the patter of little feet I would buy a spaniel." He frowned, considering. "Perhaps I should. She'd remember, I'm sure—she never forgets a thing."

"Spaniels are generally good-tempered, affectionate creatures, my lord. Considerably more so than most children."

"Or wives. Though I really shouldn't say that, life is probably as short on choices for women as it is for men like myself. I'm lucky to have you, Darling. It'd be damned lonely otherwise."

It was a very good thing that they were in an open cab, surrounded by the evening traffic from restaurants and other establishments, or Darling might have thrown his arms around his employer and lost his position. "I consider myself very fortunate, my lord."

Lord Robert laid a hand on Jack's arm. It was an unusual gesture; he seldom made any sort of physical contact. "Darling, I've been meaning to mention this for some time now." He hesitated, as though not sure how to proceed. "I want you to know that if you find yourself a girl—a special girl—that is, if you should decide matrimony is the thing for you—well, you mustn't let my misogyny stop you. We'll find a way to work things out."

You're trying to kill me, aren't you? Jack had to swallow before speaking, and he chose his words with care. "I'm quite happy with circumstances as they are, my lord. I don't believe I've ever met a woman who would entice me to renounce my bachelor status."

Was that a sigh of relief from his lordship? "Well, I'm selfish enough to be happy to hear it," he said, "even if I'm not quite selfish enough to insist on keeping you to myself." He looked around as though trying to find a distraction. "Ah, I believe we're nearly there. Enough of domestic matters, let's turn our attention to foreign affairs."

"Dead?" Scoville said. "How? Who was he?"

They hadn't been met by the Ambassador himself, but by Sir James Woodward, a member of his staff. Sir James was a square-faced, iron-haired man of vigorous middle age who was probably the Embassy's Intelligence Officer. In his large, comfortable, and extremely private office, Sir James gave them some excellent sherry and a summary of how their assignment had been intended to proceed—and how it had gone wrong when McDonald had disappeared and his contact was found murdered.

"No one you would know, my lord. He was involved in the German munitions industry, but he had the pragmatic attitude that all secrets sooner or later cease being secret, and wished to profit from accelerating the process. As to how, it appeared to be a robbery. He was struck on the head from behind, a single blow that killed him instantly."

Scoville had to restrain himself from reaching to touch his own head, where the stitches were still annoying. "That's a bit too close for comfort."

"Yes, my lord—it is suggestive. We had dealt with this fellow before—that is to say, our intelligence chaps had—and his information was generally reliable. Captain McDonald's orders were to make contact and exchange a small parcel of gemstones for a handful of very important papers."

"Gemstones being untraceable?"

"Precisely."

"Did he succeed?"

"We don't know. McDonald's whereabouts are unknown at this point. We had expected him to arrive in Vienna at least a day before you did. He seemed convinced that someone—the Prussians, or perhaps the French—were having him followed. That was why you were enlisted. A chance meeting of an old military acquaintance would be natural enough, and he would have had no obvious contact with this embassy or our staff, who are of course known to all the local agents of other powers."

"Would the papers be of use to anyone else, sir?" Darling asked.

"Oh, certainly. Anyone in France or Italy would be as interested as we are in knowing what sort of weapons the Germans are building. There are rumors of chemical weapons, poisons—these documents should confirm the rumors and might even contain a formula. The Germans will surely be trying to get them back, if they know of their loss. We hope that Captain McDonald is simply lying low, waiting to rendezvous with you tomorrow at the Sacher Café."

"So am I, Sir James."

"If he does, we're past subtlety now. Bring the documents here straightaway and we'll send 'em out in a diplomatic pouch. We appreciate your assistance, but it was never our intention to put your life at risk. If McDonald was being followed, his attempt to contact you on the train may have brought you to the attention of whoever killed his German contact. You are armed, I hope?"

"Yes, we both are. I need to ask, sir, at what point in this exercise am I supposed to visit the Baron?"

Woodward's eyes sought the heavens. "That damned— I'm sorry, my lord, please forget you heard me say that. While you were en route, the Baron managed to utter two more idiotically belligerent statements—I hope it's still only two—and for you to convey Her Majesty's warm wishes would give him altogether the wrong impression. The Ambassador will be paying the visit himself, and encouraging the Baron to express his opinions a bit more diplomatically."

"Will that help, do you think?"

"No, but you know how it is—it's the look of the thing. One never knows what seemingly insignificant comment will blow up into a storm, so we must keep on top of the matter, just in case."

"I'm sure you have it well in hand, Sir James," Scoville said. "It's a pity you diplomatic gentlemen don't get the credit you deserve."

"Ah, but that's the trick of it, my lord." Sir James permitted himself a small smile. "If we do our job properly, it appears that we've done nothing at all." He scanned the single sheet of paper before him, and said, "I think our immediate business is finished, unless you have any questions."

"None at the moment, sir. If our expedition tomorrow is successful, we'll be back here as fast as a cab can carry us. We are to meet Captain McDonald at one in the afternoon, so I hope to see you before three."

"Very good. If you require assistance, just send a messenger detailing time and place. We have guards here at the Embassy who are prepared to supply the sort of help that you might not wish to ask of the local police."

"Thank you, sir. I appreciate that, and I shall bid you good night."

"The same to you. A good and uneventful night—it would be best if you keep your man close by until this affair is concluded. "

"I will, Sir James. Until tomorrow, then."

"Good night."

When they reached their suite at the Sacher, Jack Darling was pleased to see that the hotel staff had been as thorough in its preparations as he would have been himself. The lamps in their rooms had been lit, there were fires in the grates, and the golden silk and damask of draperies and coverlets gave the rooms a warm, welcoming air. He turned the key in the lock with a tremendous feeling of relief.

Jack was looking forward to a good night's sleep, especially after the previous night's alarums. But the evening was still fairly young, and Lord Robert seemed restless. He picked up the book he'd brought along, a new novel by the American humorist Mark Twain, then put it down in what looked like annoyance and spent a minute or two gazing down at the street, only to give that up and return to his book. But after finding his place, he closed it again and was back at the window once more.

"Shall I mix a nightcap, my lord?" Jack asked after several repetitions of this exercise. "The cabinet is well-stocked with refreshments."

"Yes, thank you. A small brandy, if we have it. Fix something for yourself, if you like." He put the book down again, but stayed in his chair. "I'm sorry, Darling. You must be on your last legs. Why don't you toddle off to bed?"

Even though he'd just been thinking of sleep, Jack resisted the suggestion. "It's early, my lord," he said as he poured the drinks. "And I'm wondering if I ought to spend the night on your sofa."

"What, in here?" Lord Robert shook his head. "Nothing doing. You can't have got more than a few hours' sleep last night."

"It looks comfortable enough."

"We can put a couple of chairs in front of the doors and pile our luggage on them. No one would get past that without one of us noticing."

Jack put the drink on the small table near the window, where his lordship was seated. "I suppose you're right, my lord."

"I know I'm right. Besides, that's a fine piece of furniture, but it's too short. The only sensible alternative would be for you to sleep in here with me. The bed's big enough, but I hardly think you'd appreciate the offer. Cheers."

For one mad instant Jack wanted to say, "Yes, please!" to the offer. He forced a smile instead. "I doubt it would matter, my lord—you're a gentleman and I'm a sound sleeper." He took a sip of the whiskey and soda he'd mixed for himself, glad to have something to do.

"Well, in any event, the fellow who left the trinket in

my trunk must know you'd have found the thing when you unpacked, and the Sacher does employ a hotel detective. A stranger roaming the halls would be bound to excite suspicion."

"I suppose so, my lord. I've been wondering if we might not get that snuffbox back in the morning and see what's inside it. Cocaine, certainly—but we don't know whether that's anything but a distraction. There might be a message of some sort beneath it."

"We may as well. In fact, we should have taken it to Sir James. It's possible that little souvenir has something to do with our mission. Sit down for a moment, would you?" Lord Robert looked at his book again, lifted the cover, then flipped it shut and placed his drink on the table. "Darling, there's something I need to ask you. It's prying—damned rude, in fact—but I'm not asking out of personal curiosity."

Darling took the chair on the other side of the table. "My lord?"

"This business with McDonald—much as I hate to admit it, I'm reluctant to trust him."

"I agree, my lord—and I see nothing rude in that."

Lord Robert smiled faintly. "I haven't got to the nosey part yet. Darling, when you first met Cecil McDonald, it was pretty clear you didn't think much of him. I didn't want to press you then—none of my business, really, and he was gone the next day. But under the current circumstances I'd like to know why you dislike him. You're a perceptive chap. What put you off?"

Jack hesitated. "I meant no offense at the time, my lord. It seemed that the two of you were old friends."

"We'd known each other at Oxford," Lord Robert said "Our paths crossed occasionally after that, but by the time I arrived in India, I hadn't seen him in ages. The friendship was casual at best, we had little in common, and I found that he had changed in ways that I could not appreciate. What was your impression?"

Jack hated to resurrect the old complaint, but he

couldn't think of any other way to explain his dislike. "Captain McDonald did make an unfortunate first impression, my lord. As I recall, your orders were along the lines of seeing to his comfort, finding him a room and something to eat." He glanced at the curtains stirring lightly in the gentle spring breeze. "You might say he put an unreasonably broad interpretation on the term 'comfort.'"

Lord Robert's eyes narrowed. "What exactly do you mean by that?"

Thank God for a good vocabulary; this was definitely an occasion for euphemisms. "Captain McDonald was under the misapprehension that the scope of my service to you was of a more personal sort, and that your orders included similar service to himself. Service of what I might call an intimate nature."

A slow flush crept up Lord Robert's fair skin. "That— that smirking son of a bitch!"

"Yes, my lord. I told him that he was mistaken. He declined to believe me. I concluded the discussion by advising him to consult with you if the accommodations did not meet his needs, and I left the room. I may have judged him harshly—he made no attempt to interfere with me in any physical way."

"I should hope you'd have knocked him on his arse if he had!"

Jack released the breath he'd been holding. "Indeed, my lord."

"That explains it, then," Lord Robert said. "He made himself obnoxious that night, teasing me about my devoted, 'darling' batman and—well, suffice it to say I saw nothing amusing in his attempt at humor. Even if the fool weren't completely mistaken about you, to suggest that I would take advantage of a man under my command—!"

His face was still flushed—whether with anger or embarrassment, Jack could not tell. "It was enough to make me wish for the old days of pistols for two at dawn and coffee for one afterwards. I wanted to smash his teeth in."

Jack said nothing. He didn't dare. The truth was stirring in him like a living thing, but he simply did not know what to say. *No, he wasn't mistaken. I would love to have you take advantage of me!* That would hardly do. In fact, he was grateful for his lordship's integrity. How wretched it would have been to serve under an officer who expected sexual favors, if the attraction were not mutual.

But was it mutual? Jack could not deny what he himself felt. And hope stirred again, a tenuous thread of possibility. A man who would not take advantage might be exercising self-restraint, not indifference. Did he dare speak?

Lord Robert was still fuming, oblivious to Jack's dilemma. "He must have thought me absurdly naïve. I suppose I was. It had never occurred to me that anyone would stoop so low as to make such an assumption about me. Or about you!" He looked up, his eyes full of some unspoken emotion. Anger? Guilt? "My dear fellow, I am deeply sorry. You must believe I never intended to subject you to anything like that. I can't do a damned thing about my own nature, and I'm grateful beyond words for your tolerance. I had no idea you would be offered such an insult."

"Insult, my lord?" Jack's chest felt tight, and his heart was suddenly pounding. Here it was, then—the chance of fulfillment or the destruction of all he had come to know.

"That you were my—that I would—" Lord Robert flung a hand into the air, helplessly.

"The only insult Captain McDonald offered," Jack said carefully, "was the assumption that I would be willing to lie with *him.*"

It was Lord Robert's turn to hesitate. "I'm not certain I understand."

Their eyes met once more, and Jack could not look away. "He was not mistaken about my nature." And, since at this point there could be no going back, he added, "Nor my feelings for you."

His heart sank at the look of shock on Lord Robert's

face, and he rose hastily. "I'm sorry, my lord. I've said too much, I'll go to my—"

"No." Lord Robert caught his hand. "Jack, sit down, please. I had no idea—"

Someone knocked on the door.

They just stared at one another for a moment. The knock came again. "I'll see who it is," Jack said automatically, not moving.

"Yes. Do."

Another knock, and Jack shook himself out of his paralysis, moved to the door like a sleepwalker, and opened it.

Cecil McDonald stood outside, a carpetbag in his hand. "Don't just stand there, you fool," he said, shoving past Jack. "I've had a hell of a day."

Lord Robert was on his feet, his face a courteous blank. "So have we," he said icily. "You're making quite a habit of ill-timed visits, aren't you?"

"I needed to change our meeting tomorrow," McDonald said. "I'd have told you so last night, but your nursemaid wouldn't let me in."

"He was acting on my instructions, Cecil," Lord Robert said. "And if you came here to insult my man, you can leave now. You'd have saved us both some trouble if you'd just told him what you were about last night. Saved even more trouble if you had delivered the parcel to him while you were there." He did not seat himself, nor did he offer McDonald a chair. "And where were you at seven this morning?"

"I was in a damned Austrian police station, answering stupid questions. They took me off the train at Linz. Some fool of a French detective had mistaken me for someone else and told them I was carrying stolen goods."

"And were you?"

McDonald gave an unpleasant smirk. "You're in fine form this evening, Robert. You might offer me a drink."

"Certainly. What would you like?"

"Gin and tonic. A large gin and tonic."

Lord Robert nodded to Darling, who silently fixed the drink and handed it to their unwelcome guest.

"The police couldn't find any reason to hold me, so they finally let me go. I took the next train to Vienna and only arrived here an hour ago." McDonald threw himself into the chair Darling had just vacated. "I knew I was being followed. I didn't realize it was the police; I thought it had something to do with the parcel I have to give you."

"If you were arrested," Lord Robert said, "I presume you were searched. How is it they didn't find that parcel?"

"I wasn't stupid enough to have it in my possession. The papers are in a safe place, here in Vienna. I came straight here from the station to change the time of our meeting."

"You could have arranged that last night. Darling knows my schedule better than I do."

"My orders were to contact you, not your servant. Why should I assume he was in your confidence?"

"You didn't need to, did you? You could simply have said you wanted to meet me—somewhere—for a chat. There'd be nothing top-secret about that!"

"Well, you don't have to fly off the handle," McDonald said crossly. "Do you want the papers, or not?"

"Of course. The sooner the better. Right now would be best."

"I don't have them with me," McDonald said. "They're in a safe place—I need to go fetch them. When would you like to meet?"

"Would it be possible for you to retrieve them now and come right back here?"

"What, tonight?"

"Why ever not? If you're concerned about being seen in daylight tomorrow, why muck about?" Lord Robert pulled out his watch and consulted it. "It's not quite nine. It would be convenient if you could be back in two hours. I'm still feeling a bit rocky from being knocked on the head, and I want to see if the Turkish bath downstairs is open. Could you return at eleven p.m.? If you're worried about being out past midnight, I'm sure the Sacher can find you a room."

McDonald frowned at Lord Robert, then at Darling. "I must say you're taking a matter of national security very casually."

"Oh, I'm taking it seriously," Lord Robert said. "You have no idea how seriously. It's your Cheshire Cat behavior that fails to impress."

McDonald snorted, and tossed down the rest of his drink. "Very well. I'll see you here at eleven p.m.—if I'm not murdered by footpads. Do have a lovely time together in the bath, won't you?"

He closed the door behind himself with a little more force than necessary and once more the two of them were left to stare at one another. The moment stretched out with no end in sight, and Jack was almost afraid to speak for fear of saying the wrong thing. What more could he say? Finally he tried, "I have a suggestion, my lord."

"What's that?"

"Do you think we might let the personal matter lie for a little while? I would hate to say or do something hasty and risk making a mistake about something so important."

"But—" Lord Robert stopped, considering. "Yes," he said. "I believe you're right. And in any case, we have all the time in the world for that. We need to keep our minds on the job at hand."

"All the time—" Jack caught himself. "Then you wish me to stay in your service?"

"Jack, for God's sake—yes, of course I do. But you're right, we have two separate matters to think about. There's no point in getting them muddled. Once we have Cecil's papers in hand and deliver them to the Embassy, our time is our own. We can sort it out then."

Lord Robert held out his hand, not a gesture a man would make to a servant. "In the cab, I told you I was lucky to have you. I meant that."

The firm, warm touch was almost painfully intimate. Jack fell back on force of habit to break the mood. "Did you also mean what you said about visiting the bath?" he asked, releasing the handclasp. "If so, I should inquire immediately."

"Yes, I did. Still do."

"Very good, my lord. And—my lord, if Captain McDonald had been taken into custody this morning, doesn't it seem likely Sir James would have heard of it?"

"Yes." He shrugged as if shaking something off his shoulders. "I wonder if anything Cecil said just now was true. It's rather sad, but after being around him for even those few minutes, I feel the need for a thorough cleansing. Just ring for the bellboy, would you?"

The bath was indeed open and would be for another hour, time enough. When they stopped at the desk to drop off their room key, Scoville took a moment to send a message to Sir James at the Embassy. It wasn't likely that McDonald had let anyone else know of his arrival in Vienna, and if he went missing again, it would be Woodward's job, not theirs, to set the hounds on the trail.

It wasn't until Scoville was in the changing room of the men's bath that he felt a faint shock at the change reaching into the very core of his life. He was no longer performing a relaxing ritual of hygiene with his manservant; he was undressing beside a potential lover. He had never felt self-conscious around Darling before, but he felt naked, not merely unclothed, when they exchanged their garb for voluminous white robes of Turkish towelling. Jack was unusually silent and had turned away slightly. Scoville wondered if he, too, was feeling exposed.

They put on cloth slippers and followed the attendant through the bath's anteroom. A few other men, pink as boiled shrimp, were sitting wrapped in robes and towels, letting their bodies cool before they put their clothes back on and ventured out to the hotel proper.

Beyond that area was the low-ceilinged steam room itself. Heat and moisture swirled around them as they stepped inside. Despite being tiled in dazzling white the room was dim, since the only light came through a thick plate glass panel in the door. Two heavyset older gentlemen were sitting on the bench to the left of the doorway, so Scoville automatically turned toward the one on the right. Jack sat down beside him, a judicious foot away.

Scoville leaned back cautiously against the warmth of the tiles and took a slow, deep breath of the heated air. It was only when his body began to relax in the comfortable quiet that he realized how thoroughly tense he had been.

The chamber's other occupants were conversing quietly in German, not his best language. What little he could understand suggested that they were concerned with the quality of last year's hops, and speculating on the coming season. It was good to know that despite international intrigue, unreliable colleagues, and sudden emotional revelations, someone was still looking after life's real essentials.

He stole a glance to his left. Jack was leaning back against the wall, his eyes closed. The poor chap must be exhausted, though he never showed it. No matter where they went or what he had to contend with, Darling was always alert, always on hand with the answer a half-second before Scoville uttered the question, always ready with a neatly phrased quip to turn attention away from his deeper feelings.

Until this evening. *"He was not mistaken about my nature. Nor my feelings for you."*

Dear God. Scoville closed his own eyes. Darling had first met McDonald when, ten years ago? No, closer to twelve. It wasn't that long after he'd assumed command in India. Had Jack been carrying a torch all this time?

That would answer one of the perennial questions, though, wouldn't it—why Darling had been willing to settle for a position so far below his potential. Love could do that to a man. If Darling had been a woman, his motive would have been clear as daylight. Of course, if Darling had been a woman, the question would be moot.

Scoville knew men who could deal perfectly well with marriage. Most of the men he'd shared favors with had been married, in fact, and some even spoke affectionately of their wives. He'd envied them that ability to have a lifemate who was a friend as well as a sexual partner, though he suspected the wives would be horrified to know their husbands were stepping out on them, let alone with a man.

Or perhaps not. One of his own aunts made no secret of having ordered her husband to get himself a mistress after the birth of their sixth child. Scoville didn't pretend to understand women; they were simply outside his frame of reference. Bedding one? He didn't think he'd be able to accomplish the act.

So… marriage with a woman was impossible, marriage with a man was illegal. He had adjusted his personal expectations accordingly and avoided forming deep attachments with any of his lovers. It had been surprisingly easy; he already had a steadfast companion.

Who loved him.

Robert Scoville had not expected that anyone would ever love him, except perhaps in the physical sense. It was a rational policy for a man of his sort, and the men he consorted with had similar expectations. Except for Aurelio, that summer in Rome. Aurelio had told him he was a fool, that he could trip over treasure and never see it for what it was. Aurelio had kissed him farewell and said, "I pity you English. So clever in your heads, so blind in your hearts."

Right you are, Aurelio. Blind as a bloody bat.

He had not been paying attention to the two Germans; their quiet conversation was a kind of background murmur, and he noticed only when it stopped. They were standing now, wrapping their robes more closely around themselves and preparing to leave.

He was pleased to see them go. It meant he could look at his companion without arousing their curiosity. Jack looked terribly young asleep in that big robe, his hair ruffled, his lashes two black crescents on his cheeks, his mouth open just a little. So different from the alert, competent aide-de-camp or the impeccable gentleman's gentleman. So different, too, looking at him with the full knowledge that those parted lips were no longer forbidden fruit. That in time, maybe soon, they might become lovers.

Scoville lost track of time, just watching him sleep.

But they did have that rendezvous upstairs, and it wouldn't do to be late. The sooner those papers were in their possession and McDonald sent on his way, the sooner they could finish the job and have their lives back.

Scoville rose, tightened his belt, and glanced through the plate-glass window. Yes, the attendant was just outside, damn him. It wouldn't do to steal a kiss, much as he might want to. Instead, he put out one tentative hand and brushed the side of Darling's face with the back of his fingers.

Jack's eyes flew open. Wordlessly, he reached up and covered Scoville's hand with his own, leaning into the touch. Their fingers wove together as though they'd done this a thousand times. It was nothing that could be seen outside the room, but Scoville thought the attendant must surely hear his racing heart. He cleared his throat. "Duty calls, Sergeant."

Jack's smile flashed in the muted light. "Doesn't it always?"

It was a strange response, that of a lover, not a servant. Scoville rather liked it. "Yes, but not forever. The job's nearly done."

"Mm." Jack sighed and released his hand. "Yes, my lord."

Things were changing between them. He didn't know what was going to happen. That was unsettling, but he didn't mind. He could not imagine going to bed with Jack as a subservient partner. Or anyone, really—but especially not Jack. Their roles would have to be reconsidered, somehow.

They had already shifted; he suddenly found himself unable to think of the man beside him as "Darling." Yes, that was his name, always had been, but in the privacy of Scoville's own mind it now sounded more like an endearment. He wondered what they would call each other when they were alone.

But they were not alone yet, so they went through the rest of the bath ritual, declining a massage but submitting to being sluiced down by the shower-room attendant. At least they had the choice of warm water or cold, and Lord Robert saw no point in subjecting himself to a case of goosebumps.

He permitted himself a quick peek at Jack's nicely shaped backside while they were dressing. He'd seen it before—the Army left no secrets—but this was different, too. He was no longer just another soldier having a wash. Scoville wanted very badly to touch and had to turn his mind firmly back to their mission. His mind was obstinately resistant to such discipline, and his body wasn't doing much better. He pulled his trousers up with only seconds to spare.

Retracing their steps, they stopped at the desk for the room key and the briefcase. Scoville had his suspicions about the silver box that it contained, and he felt certain Darling shared them. He hoped to hell he was wrong. He didn't want to have to bother with any other business tonight. He wanted to sit down with Jack—better, lie down with him—and explore the future that was opening up for them. He really, most sincerely, wanted to be wrong.

Neither of them said anything on the way back to their rooms. Jack put the key in the lock, pushed the door open, and turned up the light. He froze, and turned to Scoville wordlessly, his jaw set and his eyes angry.

"Damnation." Scoville followed Jack inside, pushing the door shut behind them.

He had not been wrong.

That was clear from the devastation that greeted them.

108

The bed's pristine coverlet had been ripped away, sheets and blankets knotted in a lump on the floor, the mattress pulled half off its frame. All the dresser drawers had been yanked out—not just removed, but thrown. They lay several feet from the dressers where they belonged. The little table, the nightstands, anything light enough to lift, had been overturned and flung. Chair and sofa cushions had landed at odd angles all over the place.

"The damned fool," Darling said. "He threw a bloody tantrum."

"That's exactly what it looks like." Scoville glanced around the wreckage. The door to the adjoining room was closed. "Shall we check your quarters? I'm not about to make the same mistake twice."

"Yes, my lord." Darling fished the briefcase key out of his breast pocket and unlocked it; he handed Scoville his pistol and took the second one himself.

"The room's bound to be empty, you know," Scoville said.

"I hope so, my lord."

They moved toward the door, Scoville going left, Jack right. Interesting. In a crisis, they left the uncharted ground of what might lie ahead and slid effortlessly back into their roles of officer and noncom.

To no point, as it turned out. The intruder was long gone, but he had spent some time here; this room had been ravaged even more completely than Scoville's. A long streak of bay rum stained the carpet and spilled onto the polished floor, a shaving mug lay in shards below the marble windowsill where it had been smashed, and their luggage was tumbled everywhere.

Jack walked over to the window and picked up a curved piece of heavy porcelain, the handle of his mug. "I got this when I joined the Army," he said in a curious light tone. "It was advertised as nearly unbreakable."

"We'll find you another. And the hotel's bound to have a barber."

Jack let the handle fall; it hit the sill and cracked in two. "I could grow a beard."

They were back in terra incognita. For some reason, Jack seemed truly distressed at the loss of a bit of cheap crockery. "I'd really rather you didn't," Scoville said. "I like your face just as it is."

Jack shook himself slightly and glanced around the room as if seeing it for the first time. "Shall I ring for assistance, my lord?"

"I'd just as soon ask for different quarters," Scoville said. "But we can't leave these rooms yet. McDonald will be here in half an hour."

"This room needs a mop and bucket," Jack said. "The other doesn't, not really. Let me ring for help, and we can get that room set to rights in fifteen minutes."

"So quickly?"

"I didn't think to bring a stopwatch, my lord, but yes, if we're quick about it. Captain McDonald needn't see any disorder at all."

That last sentence had an edge to it. "Good thinking." Scoville pulled the cord for the bellboy himself. "Let's not waste time. You and I can put the mattress back on the bed and bundle my things into this room."

Jack grinned. "Not the exercise I'd been hoping for, my lord, but it's a step in the right direction."

Thank God he was back to normal. And, even better, flirting. "By the way, Sergeant, do you mind if I kiss you?"

"Not at all, my lord."

Scoville had thought it would be a difficult thing to initiate; as it turned out, the only difficulty lay in stopping. The touch and taste of lips opening under his sent a jolt through all his limbs and straight down his body; he felt like a steel splinter beside a magnet. His self-control counted for nothing. One kiss wasn't enough. A thousand wouldn't be enough. And damn two layers of clothing all to hell.

Hands slid down his back, squeezing his arse, and they rocked together as he surged forward. Why had he expected

110

Jack to be shy or diffident? He was a volcano. All that pent-up heat and power—how could he have hidden it so well? Scoville's arms went around the man as their bodies melded together—no, they couldn't do this, not now. They'd already rung for assistance. But he simply couldn't stop.

"Bellboy," Jack mumbled, turning his face away so his temple rested against Scoville's cheek. "We can't. No time."

Scoville drew back enough to look at him. Jack's mouth was reddened and soft-looking; his pupils were so wide his eyes looked almost black, and he was breathing hard.

So was Scoville. Reluctantly, he released the body pressed so sweetly against his own and took a careful step back. "You're right. Let's get to work."

The bellboy appeared just as they'd put the first sheet back on the bed, disappeared again, and came back in three minutes with Herr Krieger, the night manager. By then the bed was made, and while Jack set the furniture to rights his lordship explained the situation and showed Krieger the other room. The poor man was so shocked that he sent the bellboy off again for reinforcements and pitched in himself.

They were finished ten minutes short of the appointed hour. Herr Krieger, relieved that his lordship did not intend to call the police, was more than happy to send up a pot of coffee and arrange for a new suite. Scoville warned them that he would be expecting a visitor and would be ready to change accommodations after their meeting was finished, most probably by midnight.

"Alone at last," he said when the door clicked shut.

"But with no time to spare."

"I'd rather continue our personal affairs elsewhere." Scoville rubbed his eyes. It had been a hellishly long day, and worse for Jack. Time for them both to be in bed. He smiled wryly. No, not just yet. Best avoid that train of thought for the moment.

They would have time for a few kisses, though. At least they would have if Jack had not sensibly adjourned to his room to finish packing up their clothing and effects while Scoville waited for their visitor.

And waited. Eleven came and went. At a quarter past the hour, Scoville looked at his watch for the third time and was about to declare Cecil McDonald once more among the missing when he heard a slight movement outside the door, followed by a knock.

Jack popped in from the next room and answered it. McDonald stepped inside and looked around.

His split-second of surprise, quickly masked, told Scoville more than he wanted to know. "You have the papers?" he asked.

McDonald put a hand inside his jacket, then hesitated. "We really should exchange sign and countersign, don't you think?"

"I think we're well past that," Scoville said. "But if you feel the need to be coy, I say it's been a long time since I saw you in puttees, and you tell me I don't look two minutes older."

"That's the boy." McDonald took a chair and tossed a packet onto the table between them. "I could use a drink."

"In a moment." Scoville examined the packet. It seemed to be in order—a few sheets of paper, folded as a letter would be. They were tucked in an unsealed envelope, but the papers themselves were sealed with red wax and the ornate signet "V" that he'd been instructed to look for.

"These are the same papers you obtained in Paris?" he asked.

"Well, of course," McDonald said. "What do you take me for?"

"A fairly clumsy burglar."

McDonald turned beet-red. "What's that supposed to mean?"

Scoville put the packet in his own pocket. "Cecil, no one but you knew that we'd be away, or how long we would be gone. Ransacking the room was stupid. I'd had my suspicions, and that confirmed them. Especially the jealousy. Cruel as the grave, they say."

"You always were good at cryptic utterances."

"The mess in Darling's room. That wasn't just a reckless search. That was anger. Jealous anger, I think. You might as well have signed your name. But you didn't find it, did you?"

"Find what? Robert, you and your little Darling are becoming delusional. I don't know what you're—"

"Were you looking for this, Captain?" Standing slightly behind McDonald, Jack held the snuffbox out, just a bit too far away for him to snatch it. His fingers twitched as Jack handed it to Scoville.

"I—where did you find that?"

"In my underclothes," Scoville said. "It's all right—I wasn't wearing them at the time." He could see by the avid look in Cecil's eyes that he wanted that box, and by now he could guess what was in it. "I was sorry to see the cocaine, Cecil. It's a dangerous habit. Rots a man's self-control. Is that what happened to you?"

"I'm not using cocaine," McDonald said indignantly.

"Then why? And how do you explain it getting into my trunk?"

"It—it was him—the man on the train. He stole it from me, picked my pocket—"

"That invisible fellow you warned me against?" Jack put in. "Or the French policeman who was following you?"

McDonald ignored him. "Robert, you really need to discipline your valet—he's getting quite above himself."

"That's my business, don't you think?" Scoville exchanged a look with Darling, not even caring if Cecil saw the warmth in his gaze. "I'm quite pleased with him, actually. But let's not get off the subject of your snuffbox. A stranger stole it from you. On the train, I presume?" He turned the box over in his hands, his eyes never leaving McDonald's face. "And then he filled it with cocaine and gave it to me. What a strange thing to do. Or was there some other reason? You knew I'd never touch the drug

113

myself, didn't you, that I'd never do something like—this."

Before McDonald could say or do anything, he flicked the lid open and let the white powder spill onto the tabletop.

"No!"

He blocked McDonald's hand. It wasn't just powder lying on the linen cloth. There in the crystalline heap were five much larger crystals—glittering, faceted diamonds.

"Why don't you just tell me the truth?" Scoville suggested. "What are these—payment for the papers?"

"No—" McDonald caught himself and nodded. Scoville could almost see the gears whirring in his brain, making up a new story. "Yes. Robert, you don't understand. My contact—he was getting greedy, he was afraid he'd overreached himself this time, and he wanted more money. He meant to leave Germany for good. When I gave him the diamonds, he said, he said he would only give me half the papers until I brought him more money. I shouted at him, lost my temper—"

"You killed him." It wasn't even a question.

"It was self-defense, I swear! His life or mine! But after that—what good would the diamonds have done him? I need to get out of the game, Robert—I know they suspect me, I'm no good as an operative any more, I needed the money…"

"And you had a buyer for the stones here in Vienna, didn't you?" Darling interjected. "You used us to smuggle them over the border for you."

"Is that true?" Scoville asked. McDonald's guilty face gave him the answer. "You damned fool! Didn't you realize you could have simply given me the parcel and asked me to carry it through for you? I'd have thought it was part of the mission. And what was the point of hitting me—from behind, damn you! Are you going to tell me that was self-defense?"

McDonald licked his lips nervously. "I…I wasn't sure I could still trust you, Robert. It's been a long time. What if you'd asked me questions about it? What if you looked in the package? I couldn't risk that."

Scoville said nothing.

"I didn't hit you very hard, did I?" McDonald wheedled. "You seem to be just fine—"

"No thanks to you," Darling said. "Shall I send for the police, my lord?"

Scoville shifted his attention for only a moment, but in that instant McDonald had a gun out, aimed at Jack. "I'm leaving, Robert." He reached over and scooped up the gems. "You've got the papers. They're genuine enough. Give my regards to Sir James, would you—and tender my resignation."

He rose, motioning with the gun to make Darling get out of his way. Jack didn't move.

"It's all right," Scoville said. "Let him go."

"My lord—"

"No. It's all right." As Jack wavered, he snapped, "That's an order, Sergeant."

Darling stepped out of the path to the door. McDonald backed slowly away from the table, then suddenly seized his chair and threw it at Darling, who knocked it aside. But the distraction bought the fugitive the seconds he needed.

As the door slammed, Jack pulled his gun out. But when he started after McDonald, Scoville called, "Jack. Don't bother. It's all right."

Darling whirled, furious. "All right? He's a murderer, a traitor—I could stop him!"

Scoville closed the space between them and pushed the door shut. "Yes, I know you could." Standing so close, he could see that Jack was practically vibrating with anger. "But he wasn't always like this. When we were at school, he was the only living soul who knew what I was. The only one who accepted me."

"But—" Jack looked at the door once more, incredulous. "He could have killed you, on the train. And you're letting him go for old times' sake?"

"No! No, of course not." It was hard to admit, even to

115

himself, that a part of him still wished he could have done just that. "As you say, he's a murderer. But he was my friend once, Jack. I don't want his blood on your hands. It's already on mine."

"What do you mean?"

"I sent a message to Sir James when we went down to the baths. There were guards from the Embassy waiting for him downstairs. Look." He strode over to the window, pushing the drapery aside. Darling leaned close, looking over his shoulder.

An elegant closed carriage with the royal coat of arms, an embassy vehicle, waited before the entrance. While they watched, two men escorted a third to the street. They couldn't make out faces in the dim light of the streetlamps, but as the three climbed into the carriage it was clear that the man between them was handcuffed to one of the guards.

Scoville dropped his hand; the drape fell back into place. "Even if he were to escape," he said, "where would he go? Not back to England. And he's wanted in France for murder. He isn't important enough for any country to give him sanctuary—he can only hope that England will keep him safe from the guillotine because they're afraid he might tell France what little he knows about the errands he's done."

"Safe?" Jack raised a skeptical eyebrow. "My lord, wouldn't stealing government property and murdering one of Her Majesty's informants be considered treason?"

"Yes." Scoville closed his eyes, trying not to think about the reckless, playful lover of his younger days. "I think it would. If he knows too much, he may not even reach England alive. But he did give us the documents, and that might save his neck. I have no idea if it will."

"I'm sorry, my lord."

Scoville shook his head. "No. I could have warned him off. I very nearly did. But when he pointed that gun at you, he lost any hope of mercy."

"I'm still sorry you had to make the decision." Jack

touched him on the arm, tentatively. "My lord—would you mind if I kiss you?"

"I would be delighted." As the painful memories were eclipsed by the warm, living present, Scoville decided they really would have to do something about Jack's formality— at least in private.

The way the evening had been going, he shouldn't have been surprised by the knock at the door. They sprang apart. Jack reached up and smoothed his own hair, then smiled faintly and did the same for Scoville, his fingers lingering on his lordship's face for just a moment.

Scoville raised his voice. "Who's there?" Bad manners, but he wasn't about to have Darling shot down for the sake of courtesy if Cecil had come back nursing a grudge.

"Woodward."

Darling immediately leapt to the door. "Sir James! Please come in."

"I was still at the Embassy when your message arrived, my lord," Woodward said, shaking Scoville's hand. "It seemed best for me to be in at the finish of this affair."

"Thank you, sir. I wish your trip had not been necessary." Scoville handed over the packet that had caused all this trouble, glad to be rid of it. "Two lives wasted for such a small thing."

The packet disappeared into an inner pocket. "Not wasted, my lord. If this contains the information we're hoping for, it could save thousands of lives. I'll leave you now—you've had a long day." He rose, then turned. "I know McDonald was a friend of yours. I am sorry."

"So am I, Sir James." The words were inadequate, but it was kind of him to offer them. "More than I can say."

Jack escorted their distinguished visitor to the door, closed it behind him, and set his back against it. "Are we expecting any other visitors tonight, my lord?" he asked with a touch of exasperation.

"I hope to God not." Scoville consulted his watch. "Two minutes past midnight. Are you finished packing?"

"Nearly. Another five minutes should do it."

"Excellent. You finish with that while I go throw myself on the mercy of the management. I need to get out of here."

The new suite was one floor higher, its second bedroom a little smaller, and the view, they were warned, was not so desirable. At this point, Jack didn't care. He would have happily dossed down in a broom closet. But though he knew he needed sleep, he had passed through the point of fatigue where he wanted it. Right now he was as keyed up as if he were going into battle, even though his brain was struggling through a thick London fog.

He didn't expect he'd be using the bed in this smaller room. But appearance was everything, and gossip was life and breath to chambermaids. Before he went about the little rituals of laying out their shaving gear and clothing for the next day, he took a moment to pull the covers down on his bed and climb under them, leaving the print of his body on the mattress and shoving the pillows around. He'd seen to Lord Robert's guest room often enough to recognize a bed that had been artfully rumpled but not slept in. It was so comfortable he had to struggle to drag himself out, but he managed. Just barely.

"Jack?" Lord Robert called from the next room. "Don't worry about unpacking again. That can wait for tomorrow."

"Yes, my lord. I'll just be a moment." Was that the proper thing to say, in this ambivalent situation? Hard to say. Hard to know what he should be doing, either, so he'd taken refuge in routine, retreating to his own room and setting their belongings to rights. Apparently he wasn't going to be allowed the distraction of domestic duties.

What had he gotten himself into? It was one thing to cherish a secret passion, however hopeless, quite another to face the reality. But he'd let the secret out. There was no going back.

No, what was he thinking? He didn't want to go back. It was only this morning—or last night, or technically the night before—that he'd wanted to climb into bed with Lord Robert. Well, he had the chance now, and in a much nicer bed than that narrow bunk on the train. What kind of fool would turn down that opportunity?

But he had to consider what might happen after tonight. Lord Robert had never shown any sign of wanting a permanent lover. He might just be curious.

Yes, that's all right. So am I. And after that incredible first kiss, more than curious. He had to know what the rest would be like.

And if he decides to send you away in the morning? He would at least be given a civilized space of time to deal with that necessity, if it became one. His lordship had never been an unfair man, and he certainly wasn't a cruel one. But he might, after a brief affair, prefer to resume their previous arrangement.

Jack wasn't sure he could do that. He didn't want a few nights; he wanted every night. It was mad to even hope for such a thing, but he wanted forever, and there was no guarantee of that. Having touched what he had been yearning for, he was now terrified of losing it.

He knew he could trust Lord Robert with his life. It was a hundred times harder to trust him with his heart.

He glanced in the mirror above the neatly ordered hairbrush, comb, and toiletries, looked himself in the eye. *Don't lie to yourself, old boy. He's had that since the day you met.*

"Jack?"

The object of his thoughts stood in the doorway, a hesitant smile on his face. He had changed out of his suit, and in his pajamas and dressing gown looked as young and even more handsome than he had all those years before. And for the first time Jack could remember, Lord Robert looked slightly uncertain.

Since he's got your heart, why not give him the rest?

119

"Yes, my lord?"

"No, Jack. I don't want to be your lord. I want to be your lover."

The simple sentence took his breath away, and words with it. Before he could find any they were in each other's arms, and words no longer mattered. His hands slipped down shimmering fabric, bringing what he'd dreamt of close enough to hold. Words and thought vanished under the onslaught of feeling. It shouldn't be possible for a kiss to be so utterly satisfying and at the same time completely insufficient. The only thing he could do was demand another, and another after that. Lord Robert clutched him like a drowning man, pressing even closer.

Even as he threw himself wholeheartedly into the embrace, he couldn't believe what was happening. Years of longing answered in the space of a few hours—it was too much. It couldn't be real.

He knew this dream. It was an old friend. He would wake in a moment and find himself alone in his bed, or on the floor of the railway coach, or even back at the townhouse in London. It was a wonderful dream, intense and vivid, but he would awaken.

Jack stumbled, and reality asserted itself when his back banged into the doorframe. He leaned back on it, pulling his—yes, his lover—tight against him. They were much the same height, and the brocade dressing gown had fallen open. Nothing stood between them save a few thin scraps of cloth. He couldn't reach his own trousers, but he was able to slip his hands up under the dressing gown and slide the pajama bottoms down.

When Jack's hands touched bare flesh, Lord Robert gasped and shifted just enough to reciprocate. The belt gave his lordship a little trouble, but in a moment Jack's trousers fell and they were skin-to-skin from waist to knees.

Maybe it wasn't a dream after all. This was nothing like his fantasies. It was foolish, undignified...irresistible. As their cocks met and slid together Jack felt like a lightning

120

rod in an electrical storm, and he dug his fingers into Lord Robert's arse, wanting only more of the breathtaking contact. And he got it. Even better, he felt lips brush his ear, and a whispered, "Yes, Jack. Yes. *Now!*"

His whole body shook with the climax. He couldn't hold back, and it didn't seem to matter. They were both thrusting and shivering together, and then sagging against the doorway, trying to keep their knees from folding under them. The corner of Jack's mind that normally gave him a shield of irony suggested that if he really was determined to shag above his station, it would have been sensible to lie down first.

As though reading his thoughts, Lord Robert said, "I think we should retire to the bed."

"Yes, my—" He caught himself just in time. He stared down at the garments puddled around his ankles, decided there was no point in pulling them back up, and stepped out of them. "Major, then—just how shall I address you?"

"Damned if I know, but I'm not one of those fretful sods who demands subservience in bed. I don't want that, never did. Naked, we're equals."

Jack could only stare. Did he really believe that? But Lord Robert had been raised in privilege. Perhaps that made it easier for him to disregard it, like a fish unaware of the water in which it swam. "But—"

"Jack, it's true."

He closed his eyes. A warm hand touched his cheek, and he turned toward it without thought; a thumb brushed across his lips. Jack knew he couldn't hide. He couldn't hide anything. He opened his eyes and met the clear blue gaze. "We're not—I'm not—*I don't even know my father's name!*"

Lord Robert met his anguish with a startled look. "I don't know his name either, Jack. And I don't care. I don't care if he was the King of England or a dustman! I don't want to sleep with your father!" He held Jack's face between his hands, kissed him tenderly. "Don't you see? If

121

it weren't for 'my lord' this and 'Major' that, we might have had this years ago. What good is a title that's done nothing but stand between us all this time?" He smiled, as though realizing how melodramatic that sounded. "At any rate, 'Major' seems a bit formal, don't you think?"

"'Robert' seems a bit..." Jack shook his head. The release had drained off all the tension that was keeping him upright, and he felt suddenly empty and slightly stupid, not able to hold his own in this debate. "A bit inadequate. I'd like to lie down now."

"Of course." Still holding one another, they made their way toward the bed, detouring around a wheeled cart that held a few covered dishes and a bottle of wine. "I ordered us a late supper while I was downstairs," Lord Robert said. "The cook's gone home, so there's just bread and cheese. It arrived while you were unpacking. Would you like a bite to eat, or would you rather have some sleep first?"

Jack pulled the coverlet down and sat heavily on the edge of the bed. He still felt as though he'd been dropped from a height and landed in an unfamiliar world. "Yes. I—if you'll give me a moment, I'll see to that."

"No, you will not. Get under the covers, Jack. I don't mean to pull rank, but you look dead on your feet. By my reckoning, you've had about four hours' sleep in the past two days."

Jack nodded dumbly. He took off his shirt, losing a collar button in the process. It seemed silly to go to bed in only a singlet, so he stripped that off as well. But as he lay back a frightening thought occurred to him. "The maid, in the morning—"

"I left orders at the desk not to disturb us until we rang. And there's a discreet tag on the door with the same instructions."

"Thank you. Sorry..."

Lord Robert was quiet for a minute or two, moving about the room. Then he turned off the light and climbed into bed on the opposite side. "Don't mean to make a nuisance of myself, Jack—but would you object if I were to hold you while you sleep?"

It was fatigue, Jack knew, but he felt tears well in his eyes. "Yes! That is, no—not at all." He went into those welcoming arms like a wanderer coming home. The faint scent of bay rum was only a trace of spice in the warm, musky fragrance of his lover's body. So good... too good. It couldn't last. But how could he bear to go on living if it did not?

His last waking memory was of a kiss brushed gently across his forehead.

Lord Robert Scoville lay awake for a few minutes, his face resting against the dark head cradled on his shoulder. He was awestruck. That had been the fastest and possibly least elegant sexual encounter of his entire life. A knee-trembler, for Christ's sake, and at his age!

But it had also been the most wonderful encounter he'd ever known. That hadn't been fucking. It hadn't been playing at sex, either, or scratching an itch. For the first time in his life he had genuinely been making love. How did the Welsh put it—"friendship set on fire"? He had been set on fire, a fire that had been banked for now but felt unquenchable. And he couldn't wait for Jack to wake up so they could continue their pyromania.

Scoville suppressed a mad desire to burst into song. It would have been unkind, given his singing voice and Jack's obvious exhaustion. But he wanted to. He wanted to do something to express the idiotic joy bubbling up within him, joy mixed with chagrin that it had taken him more than ten years to give Jack the chance to tell him what he wanted so badly to hear.

It's you, he thought, holding his lover close. *It's you, and I have been ten kinds of a fool. And so have you. For God's sake, Jack, why should I care where you came from, so long as you're here?*

Lying in his arms, trusting and utterly relaxed, Jack pulled in a long, slow breath and began to snore gently. Scoville thought it a very civilized, endearing snore. He could listen to it forever. And with any luck, he would.

For the second night in a row, Jack woke in a dark hour before dawn. Thankfully, the cause of his wakefulness this time was nothing more than his own body requesting a visit to the water closet, but it was still annoying.

He didn't want to move. He had rolled on his side while he slept, and the delicious warmth all along his back told him Lord Robert was curled up behind him, one arm thrown over his body. And—yes, that was his lordship's other arm beneath his head. Jack shifted experimentally, and the embrace tightened.

Jack sighed. Why did this sort of thing have to happen? Here he lay in his lover's arms, having attained his heart's desire, and his body was doing its damnedest to spoil things. Of course it was his own fault for diving into bed without attending to the necessities first. But that had been more a fall on his face than a dive, really. If not for his lordship's kindness—and supporting arm—he might not have made it to the bed at all.

Jack waited as long as he possibly could, then carefully disentangled himself, made his escape, and attended to his business. He crept back under the covers carefully, but not carefully enough.

"You're freezing," Lord Robert said. "Come here."

He didn't need to be asked twice. The bed was wonderfully warm and so was his lover. But he was too absorbed in enjoying the closeness and comfort to go back to sleep. It would be a sin to waste even a moment. He tried to keep still.

"Are you asleep?" his lordship whispered after a few minutes.

"No. Sorry—am I keeping you awake?"

"I don't mind at all. We're on holiday now, Jack. We can sleep in as late as we like. As far as I'm concerned, so long as we devote one day to the Conservatory and one evening to the opera, we can spend the rest of the fortnight here, under the covers."

Jack turned toward him and received a welcoming kiss. "This may not be the right time to ask," he said, rearranging himself comfortably on Lord Robert's shoulder, "but if you don't want to hear 'my lord' or 'Major,' what shall I call you?"

His lordship sighed. "My name, perhaps? It's nothing special, but I do answer to it."

Jack knew it was a foolish request, and he wished that it didn't bother him so much. Was it worth endangering all this to keep harping on a subject that was so obviously bothersome? But what use was the promise of equality if he had to hold his tongue? "I would rather not, sir. If I am to continue in your employ—"

"Jack, unless you truly want to leave, I wish you'd stop saying that. You can't desert me now. I'd never be able to replace you."

His heart full to overflowing, Jack wondered if he was just playing a game, seeking reassurance. He didn't think so. "Then I would rather keep to 'my lord,' or find some name that no one else uses. If I were to suffer a lapse of judgement and mention you by that name, it would seem I was referring to someone else."

He could not give Lord Robert his most genuine reason. If he were to say, "'Robert' is what *he* called you," he would sound like a jealous fool. And perhaps he was jealous, and a fool as well. Perhaps he was trying to set this liaison apart from all those others.

To his relief, Lord Robert said, "That's reasonable. I suppose I'm the lucky one—I can address you as Darling as often as I like, with no one the wiser. It does suit you."

Jack stopped this foolishness with his own mouth, and further discussion was delayed for several minutes.

"Unfortunately," Lord Robert said, pausing for breath, "If I were to change my own surname to Sweetheart, people would talk. It's too bad, but I don't like most of the nicknames—I don't much like my actual name, but there's no help for that. Bob cuts it too short. Rob is a criminal act, Robbie makes me think of Burns and his wee timorous beasties. Bert is my uncle. My grandfather used to call me Cock Robin—"

Jack laughed out loud and arched his hips forward.

"Not in that sense, you lout. But I admit it's the least objectionable. I shouldn't mind Robin."

"That puts me in mind of Sherwood Forest and merry men. I like it very much. Robin." Jack rolled the name around in his mind. It would take some practice. "Please forgive me if I address you with too much respect. I may not be able to change the habit of years in an instant."

"That's settled, then." Lord—no, Robin—lay back on the pillow, one arm around Jack's shoulders. "I don't mean to make things difficult for you, Jack. It may seem a foolish whim, but I've sent too many men to their deaths with my orders. If a man doesn't want to be in bed with me just for the fun of it, or the friendship, or whatever harmless reason—I don't want to think he might be there because of my rank or position. That's why I never went to bed with any man who wasn't free to tell me to go to hell if he chose."

"Is that why—" Jack caught himself as he realized how presumptuous the question might seem.

"Why I never approached you? Yes, indeed. You found Cecil's advances offensive, did you not? I had no reason to think you would see mine any differently. You did your very best to appear a ladies' man, my Darling." He reached up and ruffled Jack's hair. "You played your part too well. If you hadn't been so damnably decorous—if you'd so much as given me a hint—"

"And have you think I was some sort of conniving rent boy? You never looked twice at anything less than a

Captain or a Baronet. And you never kept—" The conversation was leading him into dangerous territory. Perhaps there were some things better left unsaid.

"Jack?"

"I don't imagine I'll tell you to go to hell, m—Robin. But if you begin to find my company a bore, I won't hold it against you if you tell me to pack my bags."

"What?" His lordship rolled over, leaning up on an elbow. "Jack, what in God's name are you talking about?"

Jack glanced away. "Men have habits," he said. "And I've observed over the years that your habit consists of brief liaisons with a variety of friends that you seldom see more than two or three times a year, as though you were deliberately avoiding attachment. I mean no criticism, my lord, and I apologize if I give offense. It's merely a pattern I've noticed, but it makes me think that you will wish for a change before too long."

Lord Robert was quiet for so long that Jack was afraid he'd wrecked it all. Finally he said, "So you think I'll tire of you after a month or two, and discard you without a second thought?"

"I did not mean to suggest you would be thoughtless," Jack said carefully. "I just—my lord—I'm sorry, Robin—I would not want you to keep me on out of pity. I think you might do that."

"Not thoughtless, merely a fickle fool." Lord Robert dropped back to the pillow. "I suppose it's good that we're both rational adults, not a couple of reckless pups, or we'd drive one another to distraction. But it's a relief to know you're human enough to make mistakes. Let me tell you this, now. As soon as we return to London, I'll set up a fund so you will draw your salary for the rest of your life, whether you stay or leave. You have my word."

"What?"

A hand sought his in the blankets, held tight. "I want you beside me, Jack, but only if you want to be here. You're free to stay or go. I hope you'll stay."

Jack felt as though all the air had been drawn out of his lungs. "I couldn't ask that of you."

"You could, but you wouldn't. I don't mean to insult your pride—you'd probably never need the money, you could give it to the old soldiers' home if you wanted. It's yours if you should need it, though, as much for my own peace of mind as your security."

"My lord—"

"In case you've forgotten, you saved my life. I'm here now because you risked your life for me. I can never forget that, even if you can."

Robert shifted again so he could look at Jack directly, and Jack noticed that the room was getting brighter. They had talked the sun up. "Bear with me, Jack. I must explain."

Jack shook his head, but his lover kissed him and continued. "A gentleman may have a wife. Some would even say he *must* have a wife. He may not have a lover, even a female lover, who shares his home. As for a male lover, the best of friends couldn't live together, much less share a bed, without exciting more social condemnation than I would be willing to face."

"Men frequently share lodgings," Jack objected.

"Not if they can afford to have an establishment of their own. I am not interested in making a public spectacle of my private life, Jack. I'd rather face Jezail bullets than Society on a witch-hunt."

"I understand."

"You discerned two of my personal rules—you called them pretty accurately. There's a third, but anyone would have missed it. Besides being equals, they had to be men that I could like but probably would not love, men I knew I could not possibly live with. I could do without that in the bedroom because I had you filling up the rest of my life. In a sense, they were taking on a chore that I thought you would find distasteful."

"And now?" Jack held his breath.

"I think we can deal with the first two. A man's home is

his castle, is it not? I hereby dub thee Sir Jack, Keeper of the Keys and Guardian of the Royal Bedchamber, and further elevate thee to peer of the realm."

"You have a strange sense of humor, my lord—though if you are my King, I should more properly call you 'Sire.'"

Lord Robert sighed. "I think 'my lord' will do, if you can't restrain yourself. We needn't worry about spending too much time under the same roof, either. If you could convince me that you were uninterested for twelve years, I think you can convince the world indefinitely. As for the third, it's already too late. I do want to live with you. In fact, I've no idea how I would live without you."

"How can you say that? We've only made love once, and it was—" Jack had no reservations about sex, but he felt shy about discussing the details. "It was delightful, but I can't imagine you'd be satisfied with nothing more than what we've done. What if you find I don't measure up?"

"I'd be astonished. But if you'd like to explore further possibilities, I am reasonably experienced and entirely at your service. You may observe the jar of facial cream conveniently located on the bedside table."

"My lord?"

"Not while we're in bed together, I'm not." Lord Robert administered a kiss that took the sharpness from his words. "Jack, we've spent too many years hiding from each other, denying our feelings because of an absurd misunderstanding, and now that we're finally naked together, we're building walls of words between us. I'm tired of talking. Show me what you want to do—and what you want from me. If I have any objections, I'll voice them."

Jack blinked. The room was quite bright now, and his lover was watching him expectantly. "Would you prefer—"

"I prefer you use your initiative, Sergeant." Lord Robert reached down between them and wrapped his fingers around Jack's cock, giving it a gentle squeeze that set his nerves afire. "I prefer we make love, not conversation."

"Very good, sir." Jack grinned, taking the lid off the conveniently located jar. Since kissing had been highly successful thus far, he started with that. Cradling his lordship's head in one hand, he tilted his face up and dropped a light kiss upon his lips, just the barest touch. He did it again, lingering a bit longer, and then again, repeating the teasing kisses until he could feel Lord Robert reaching up every time he came close. He stopped teasing and opened his mouth, inviting his lover's tongue out to play.

But that wasn't enough. And he was at something of a disadvantage, because the other gentleman had neglected to remove the top of his pajamas. Still administering kisses, Jack slid his hand down the front of the shirt, opening the buttons as he went, until he reached the highly agitated object at the bottom. Robin gasped when Jack's hand closed around his cock, but he was playing fair, not trying to take control.

Oh, what to do next... With ten years of wishful thinking and fantasy to choose from, he felt like the proverbial donkey starving between two piles of hay. But one thing he did want to do was feast his eyes. He flipped open the shirt front and gazed at the sculptural symmetry, from delicious collarbone all the way down to the foolishness of toes. He couldn't keep himself from touching, brushing his lips along jawline and throat, blowing cool air against the warm skin. He caressed the flat belly, scratching it lightly with his nails as he closed his mouth around a nipple. He teased it with his tongue while he pinched the other. Lord Robert moaned softly, tangling his fingers in Jack's hair.

Jack glanced over at the jar beside the bed, and hesitated. "Are you sure you want me to—"

Robert grabbed Jack by both shoulders and shook him. "Yes, I am sure! For God's sake, Jack, I don't think anything less would convince you I'm in earnest!" He pulled him down for a kiss, then fell back against the pillow, arching up in a way that drove Jack to distraction.

"And you ought to know," he added with a lazy, sensuous smile, "I really do enjoy it."

Was there a more beautiful man on the face of the earth? That was theoretically possible. But why look anywhere else with perfection before him? Jack had begun with a vague idea of making long, slow love, but he realized his own body wasn't going to cooperate. And judging by the way—he grinned—the way Robin's cock leapt when he touched it, there was no reason to delay.

It seemed rude to give orders to the lord of his heart, so he stroked gently down those muscled thighs before insinuating a hand between them, coaxing them apart. The face cream was indeed convenient, and he warmed it in his hand before putting it to the necessary use. "Is this all right?" he asked, guessing from the way his lover pushed down against his fingers—and the blissful look on his face—that it was perfectly all right.

"Yes. *Oh,* yes. Shall I turn over?"

"If you like."

"No. This would—oh!" His voice wavered. "Jack, I don't mean to rush you, but—"

"Not at all." He took his time, making certain that both of them were as ready as humanly possible, and then positioned himself between his lover's knees and lifted him slightly. "Tell me if you want me to stop." He pushed inside slowly, biting his lip against the intensity.

"If you stop, I'll do something we'll both regret," Robin said raggedly. "Could you lie down upon me? That would feel...oh, yes."

Jack was happy to oblige, but the feel of his lover's hot organ against his belly, the feel of his own moving within, the unbearable need to go deeper, took the last remnants of his self-control. When he felt his lover's legs wrap around his own, locking them together, the rhythm of thrust and response passed back and forth between them until they were moving as one being. The pleasure flowed, built, and finally peaked, leaving them lying panting, drenched in sweat and satisfaction.

"That's better than conversation," Lord Robert said drowsily.

"Infinitely." It felt good to lie here like this. So good...

Jack only realized he had fallen asleep at that point when he awoke some time later. The room was filled with a golden glow of full daylight filtered through the heavy draperies, and that same wonderful warmth once again enveloped him.

"Good morning, slug-a-bed," Lord Robert murmured in his ear

"Are you certain it isn't afternoon?"

"Still morning. Just past ten."

"Mm." He stretched against the body behind him. "Did you sleep well?"

"Like a babe in arms. The most comfortable arms I can remember."

"And did I pass muster?"

Lord Robert laughed. "If you think you can apply yourself, I believe fifteen or twenty years of diligent practice should make up for any minor deficiencies. Yes, of course. It was lovely."

Jack rolled over and stole a kiss. "I promise to practice every day, sir. I will be a credit to the regiment."

"The one thing that drives me to distraction is to think of all the years we've wasted," his lordship said, cradling Jack's face in his hand. "So many nights we've slept alone."

Jack felt free to touch in return, and caressed the long line of his lover's body from shoulder to hip. "Not entirely wasted. I think we may know one another better than if we'd spent all that time in bed."

"That's true. You've seen me at my worst without giving notice."

"The thought never crossed my mind. Except those times you had a lover stopping by—those times I felt sorely tried."

"I'm sorry, Jack. I never realized. I was just relieved

that you didn't seem to object to my illegal, immoral behavior. I was grateful for your loyalty and tolerance."

"My cowardice, more like."

"Never."

"Yes. It was my fault. I should've come to you and said, 'My lord, this job is splendid, I've never had more comfortable quarters, my pay is more than generous, but if you don't roger me right this minute I shall die of longing.'"

Robert smiled. "Is that a request?"

"Absolutely. But might we get a pot of tea or coffee up here and turn that late supper into a late breakfast? I'd like some sustenance first, if there's time."

"There's time," his lover said. "All the rest of our lives. We may not be able to retrieve the past, Jack, but now we've got the future."

Chapter Three

June, 1919
London

It was a gentleman's club like so many others in the better part of London—deep leather chairs, well-cooked meals, discreet servants who came and went on silent feet—a reserve of men, ladies permitted only in the Visitors Room and, on certain days, the dining room.

As Lord Robert Scoville, threw in his hand and bade his card-playing companions good night, he caught the attention of a pair of older gentlemen sitting near the fireplace in the front parlor. Glancing up, he said, "Colonel," sketched a salute, and continued on his way.

"Wasn't that Scoville?" asked the other gentleman.

"Yes, the younger son. Good man. Under my command in India—if it hadn't been for him I'd not be here today. And he pulled his weight in the late unpleasantness as well. He must be nearly sixty now, but you'd never guess it to look at him."

"Hm. My wife carries a mild grudge against that gent. She thought he'd be just the husband for our Penelope, but nothing ever came of it."

"Your Penny? Happy enough with Cooper, isn't she?"

"I've heard no complaints. They're starting my grandson at Eton next term. It surprises me a bit that

Scoville never married. No shortage of pretty girls thrown his way, but he's just holed up with his gardens, his manservant, and that pack of Springer Spaniels."

"Well, lucky him," said the Colonel. "He's bred some steady gun dogs—and they won't turn him old before his time. Did you hear what Phyffington's boy got up to last week? Ran his motor off the road, drunk as a lord, with a girl in the car—they're both in hospital, the girl's parents are fit to kill—Scoville's well out of all that, and that man of his keeps the place running well enough."

"Pity his lordship can't just marry the fellow," said his friend, probably grudging the lost connection to the Scoville fortune.

The Colonel frowned. "None of that, now. Darling's been with him through two wars, and I know for a fact you once tried to hire him away." He chuckled. "Half this club has tried—I did myself. Never been told off so politely. No, Lord Robert's an honest man." He leaned closer and lowered his voice. "See here, if he'd married your girl you'd have no chance to brag about your grandchildren. Scoville took a bullet at Maiwand..." He shrugged expressively. "Darling got him to the medic, but I never was certain the doctor did him any favors keeping him alive."

His companion winced. "Christ. Funny, though. You'd never know it to look at him."

"He's a brave man," the Colonel said sternly. "And you keep it to yourself, Carstairs, or I'll know where the whispers started."

Carstairs was suitably chastened. "God, yes. The poor bastard!"

In the vestibule just off the parlor, out of sight but not out of hearing, Jack Darling grinned and gave the Colonel a mental tip of the hat. He had long since discarded his jealousy of Robin's former lovers. Most of them were decent men, after all, and the Colonel, one of the few who knew their secret, was a positive angel. They'd have to invite him over for dinner one evening so he could regale

135

them with the story of spiking Carstairs' guns.

Still smiling, Jack went off to summon a cab to take them home.

The End

HARD AND FAST
ERASTES

Chapter One

In which I meet the young lady my father has meant for me and I deflect my father from spoiling his own endeavors.

There are certain things expected of a third son. That one will not put oneself forward, that one will join the army or the church or the bar. That one will not, in an attempt to inherit and whatever the provocation, murder one's elder brothers. And that one will, if at all possible in the circumstances of *being* a third son, marry well.

This is particularly important if one's family is wealthy (but not titled), and one's brothers have married ladies who have increased the financial aspects of the line, but who have disappointed one's father in being, like him, rich but ignobly born. One is taught that one does not talk of the origin of such income. One's ancestors may have their portraits on painted walls and may well have been forced by circumstances to work for their subsistence, but that same shameful toil enables their grandsons and further scions to live in comfort without ever having to mention such endeavors.

One is taught, from the nursery and all through one's schooldays, that one should be a gentleman above all things. To be a good shot, to honor one's parents, to do well for the school, and to be gallant to the fairer sex. One is schooled to deal kindly with staff, and otherwise with bullies and cads.

One is equipped for life.

But I have never been taught what I should do if I fell in love with someone of a sex that was not, as I expected it would be, opposite to my own.

To say that I was shaken to discover this about myself would be an understatement in the same vein as were I to airily state that the Taj Mahal was an attractive mausoleum or that Switzerland was a trifle undulating. The sight of a curving cheek, a chestnut curl, a well turned ankle, and a trim waist, these are all things that I expected to wake the first stirrings of Eros, and indeed they did; it is just that I did not think they would come from such a wholly unexpected direction.

You might, were I so injudicious to write this account down, raise an eyebrow, your quizzing glass, and your voice. You might order me out of the club—blacken my name and drive me out of England and onto the Continent— or you might ask me how this came to be. But would I answer you?

I might.

It was last spring, the first spring free of war—a soldier's spring—and London, though cold as h—, was still resplendent in red and white. It was, it seemed to me, as I drove through St James's with my father, as if London had draped itself in the colors of Victory, daring the Corsican to come again if he dared, to strike north and east—for London at least was ready for him should he dare. It was a glorious puff. I could not begrudge the city for its arrogance. We were all still living on borrowed glories.

We paused as a brougham pulled up beside us and my father, dressed in a jacket from an older bloodbath, raised his hat to the occupants. I followed suit.

"Colonel Chaloner." The lady within the carriage lowered her parasol and inclined her head in greeting.

"Lady Pelham. Wonderful morning, is it not? You

know of my youngest, of course. Did well under Wellesley. Very proud." My father laughed at his own pun. "Geoffrey, may I introduce Lady Pelham and the Honorable Miss Emily Pelham, of whom I have spoken." His voice was fraught with inference. He paused and addressed the third occupant of the brougham. "If I knew your name, sir, I forgot it."

My eyes traveled with the introductions. The mother was a ship of the line, impressively wide in dark lavender. She seemed as if her timbers would creak in the slightest breeze. The young lady, suitably pink about the ears and cheeks, was as pretty as any of a hundred ladies out in the sunshine, all of them armed with large nets to catch whatever suitors had limped home from France. In these less selective times, a suitor who may have been sure to be rejected by many a young lady might now find himself acceptable if he came blessed with the full compliment of arms, legs, and facial features. I knew of Miss Pelham from my father's recommendations, although due to circumstances, I had not met her before. My father had expressed his views, and I was under orders to fall in love where directed.

The dowager bent her head in response to my father and introduced the young man sitting beside her, dressed sombrely in black. "My nephew, Adam Heyward. After my brother of course." She sniffed into a black laced handkerchief. Her brother, I knew, had been gallantly crushed by his horse at Hougoumont.

The young man, given his curtain, rose and bowed, and as he did so I felt something stir within me. It seemed a little like concern—a similar lurch to the insides that I recalled feeling when my eldest brother's child rode his pony too fast. I was appreciative, I reasoned later, that perhaps that Lady Pelham's horses were restless and that by standing, the young man was in danger of being thrown out, for he did not seem at all steady on his feet. But I wondered at my approbation all the same and was only deflected in my reverie as I saw my father fairly bristling beside me. I should have been prepared for this, for as we had circled the park he had been making his usual tally of men not in uniform.

"Not all men had the opportunity..." I had said not ten minutes before, but it was as far as I had managed; my father's tirades on the slackness and abject cowardice (as he saw it) of a man who didn't offer himself up as cannon fodder was well known, particularly to me, as since my regiment had returned to the capital, I was the only son now left at home and the only audience to his lectures.

"Well, they should have!" he had declaimed, far too loudly and drawing the ear of all in the vicinity. "Don't see how they have the gall to live in a country they're afraid— afraid, do you hear me?—of fightin' to protect! We've rid France of Boney. Let 'em go and live there!"

Banishing someone to the wilderness of France was, to my father, who rarely set foot further south than Canterbury, the most revolting punishment. To consider anyone happy to live in such a place was beyond his comprehension, and should anyone dare suggest that France did in fact have some qualities that he might enjoy, he would go puce in the face and appear in some danger of apoplexy. I may have served my time under fire, but I was not as brave to be positively foolhardy.

It seemed that Lady Pelham knew his views as well as I, for she looked anxiously from her nephew to my father. I spoke before my father could say anything further, gaining myself a grateful smile from that lady, a blush from Miss Pelham, and a cool look from the young man in black. "I knew your brother well, Lady Pelham," I said. "A most gallant officer." In truth, Major Adam Heyward had been a drunkard and a bully, and his heroic charge into the French lines at Hougoumont had been caused by a bullet in his horse's rump. The matter had been hushed (the bullet rumored to have come from his own brigade), and Major Heyward had posthumously received honors he could never have hoped to attain in life.

Lady Pelham was suitably touched and, in consequence, invited us to their town house that evening to dine. My father was delighted, so much so that I was grateful to drop him at his club. His enthusiasm at the meeting, which I was soon to realise was hardly accidental, and his subsequent ebullience at the invitation was overwhelming, and without a word being spoken between myself and Miss Pelham, it appeared that I was already married and buying furniture for town and country.

Chapter Two

In which the circumstances of myself and others are explained, a visit is made, and the value of a pair of fine eyes is considered.

Now that you have met some of the principal players in this tale, a few sketches are needed to help you navigate the plot as it unfolds.

I am the child of my father's autumn. Ten years after having lost his first wife to influenza, my father married again.

I have no memory of my mother, and though, naturally curious as a youngster, I tried to glean some information about her, I found it impossible. "Your mother's name is never to be spoken in this house," my father had said and he had refused to discuss it further. Stubborn as any infant, I went to my brothers. I went first to Charles for enlightenment and thereafter to Edward, but they were both silent and referred only to father's instructions, both forbidden to speak of her, even in secret, and I grew to manhood as ignorant of her looks and her manner as I would be for a stranger of whom I had never heard. That she was alive, or had been when my father had divorced her, were the only two facts I ever learned, and there was no kindly aunt or favorite cousin who might have informed me further. I did not, heartless child that I was, follow the tradition of a little boy left alone in a masculine house bereft of feminine influences. I heartlessly declined to harbor any deep emotional need for her and my curiosity waned by degrees. My brothers had warned me to say, if my peers were to ask of her—and they did—that she was dead. I did not understand the import of this until I was much older, but I trusted my brothers and did as they bade me.

There was no thought of me not joining the army. England had been considerate enough to be at war for so long that she had trained, injured and killed Chaloners in every generation. I was raised in a nursery (and I can only assume that my nursery-maid must have been as war-like as my father) that had walls decorated with bloodstained flags and with stirring pictures of men dying gloriously. I rode a dappled rocking horse replete with fiery eye and flared nostril, and I was more adept with a wooden sword than ever I was with a quill. I should, of course, were this a novel, assure you that this conditioning did nothing but make me eschew the very thought of war, that I would march against my fellow-man only reluctantly, if at all. And if I did so, it was only to rescue my companions or other such nobility.

But of course this would be untrue. With such a rich tradition of soldiery in the family, I thought as little of going to war as I did of anything else I knew that I would be doing in life. I did not race to meet it, for I knew that when I was sixteen, there would be a war willing to welcome me. I never doubted for a moment, at a bloodthirsty seven, that when my brothers marched away, I would not eventually join them.

Wiser and more lucid minds than mine have discussed every aspect of the war against Napoleon, and I will not speak of it more than is necessary. This tale has little relevance to it. In fact I came out of it relatively unmarked, as did my brothers, and if my father was disappointed that the generation of Chaloners that he had provided had not sacrificed one of its number as was the custom, surprisingly he did not enlighten us on the point.

I was then, that spring, living back with my father after years of campaign. The necessity of living with my father was very real, for although at twenty-six I wished for the independence my own rooms would give me, a major's half pay did not make this possible.

As you may have already surmised, my father was a man of distinct opinions, and our close habitation was at times uneasy, for both of us were used to our own way. He had been of a bombastic nature all his life, and in my turn, I had long been used to the autonomy that the army provided. However, between my father's club and my administrative duties, it happened that we met rarely enough, breakfast and dinner being the times when such skirmishes were likely to take place.

Such encounters were eased, therefore, when we were invited out to dine, and I dressed that night with the satisfaction that, for all his forthright and frank exchange of views with me over many subjects, he did at least know how to behave in company. I could not help but think, as I slid into my dress uniform, that I was rather glad that I had it to wear; men's fashions, always a rather obscure and specialized subject to me, who had been in uniform for ten years, appeared, by the display in the park that day, to be spiraling into farce. Surely there must be a limit to how high a collar should be, or how many ruffles one could have at one's wrist without losing the use of one's fingers? The young man—Adam Heyward—had been the only young man I had seen who had not been dressed like a peacock, and it had pleased my eye to see him dressed soberly in neatly tailored black stuff, his chestnut hair cut fashionably short, if teased rakishly high at the crown.

My father, as usual, was ready before me, great-coated in anticipation and pacing in the hall when I appeared. I was rather hoping for a bracer before the fray, but he was impatient and waved away the manservant with a gloved hand.

"About time!" he barked at me. "Kept your men waiting like this, did you? Needed to look the dandy at Las Bras?" I suppressed an answer. It served no point and as all I had done was pull on my dress uniform, and had not, as my father had done, dressed painstakingly in the latest fashion, it would only make more of a disagreement. I climbed into the carriage behind him, and one of us sat in silence whilst the other complained of the state of the roads, the appallingly slow encroachment of the gas lighting, and the ruinous prices he was having to pay his equipage.

The carriage was dismissed at the door; my father, with his usual omnipotence, was certain of the weather and it was "no distance." I was as sure as if he had said the words aloud that he was thinking that it could be no distance for me in particular, for I had once admitted to him that I had often given my horse to a tired or wounded soldier and had walked the roads of Europe with my men. That my father would object to such coddling hardly needs to be stressed.

The Pelham house was lit with no seeming regard for economy or concerns of ostentation, quite contrary to my father's housekeeping, and had it not been for the Honorable Miss Pelham, no doubt lying in wait within, I would wonder what on earth my father could find in common with our hostess. We were relieved of our coats and announced into the drawing room. As I have said, I had visited the house once before, when Lord Pelham had been alive. He had been a man of serious tastes and had filled his life with the study of politics and philosophy. I remembered the visit clearly for I had trouble staying awake during the after-dinner discussion. Miss Pelham had been too young to attend, if I remember, and Lady Pelham, the only lady present when I dined there last, had retired and had not appeared again, no doubt well used to her husband's pursuit of the intellectual.

If I had expected more of the same, I was pleasantly surprised. Gone were the great and the gloomy, and it seemed that in their place Lady Pelham had filled her salon with a younger and much more lively set than ever her husband had entertained.

As I bowed low over the good lady's hand, I couldn't help but be aware of my father's reaction. With a speed that left me startled, he offered Lady Pelham his arm and led her to her seat, whereupon he sat beside her and was a man transformed; smiling and nodding at every word from her lips.

To save myself gawping like a landed trout at this miracle, I accepted a glass and stood solitary for a moment or two, appraising the company around me. Miss Pelham was seated on a settle by the windows, surrounded on one side by another young lady and on the other by a bluff old gentleman with great ornamental whiskers. I shrunk back to the fireplace and assumed a pose, wondering if the evening was going to be as dull as it already threatened to be. I was acquainted with no one in the room, and now that my hostess and her daughter were apparently occupied, was unlikely to be so. It was with some relief, then, that I spotted young Heyward making his way through the room, and I remember my feeling of very real surprise when I saw that he assisted his progress by use of a cane, and even with this support he limped quite badly. Here then, I realised, was the explanation why he had seemed so unsteady in the carriage that afternoon, for I had noticed no cane with him there.

I noticed, too, that he made little impression on others as he passed, that he was almost ignored. It was not that the guests were ill-bred enough to cut him, for he was the nephew of the hostess after all, but an atmosphere seemed to hang on him and infect the company so that he passed unseen by most and addressed by none.

I thought for a moment that he would pass me without acknowledgement and I felt for his solitude; he seemed to have noticed his isolation, as his face was set into a sulky scowl that, on a less attractive young man, would have seemed disfiguring, but with him, it merely dimmed his light a little. I stepped forward and held out my hand, blocking his path through to the window seat, happy to have an acquaintance, happy enough to put myself forward.

"Mr. Heyward. It has been a while since I have been here, but there have been some changes made, I think."

He stopped and with practiced grace swapped his cane to his other hand and shook mine with a warm, firm grip.

"And I don't know if it is for the better," he said. "Chaloner, isn't it?" His voice was as warm as his hand and his eyes, dark but sparkling like torchlit caves, seemed to laugh, even if his face did not.

I asserted the truth of being whom I could not help but be.

"I have met your brothers," he said. "They are both at my club. They have spoken of you." Each sentence was punctuated with a small pause, and he seemed to search my face with his eyes as if waiting for a reaction. I could think of little to say that would be of any merit to his ambiguity. "I have to be frank with you," he continued in a confiding manner, smiling for the first time since our introduction, "that before I met you in the park, I had it in my mind to dislike you a very great deal."

Again, he made me silent; I was not practiced in drawing room banter, but my surprise must have showed on my face.

"I see I have offended you, and yet I did not mean that for a moment." His mouth quirked up at one corner, as if he were permanently privy to secrets of which I was woefully unaware, and he was unsure of whether he would or should divulge them. It was an expression that I rather liked, and I found myself smiling in spite of the growing discombobulation.

"If you think that, Heyward," I countered, "you are mistaken, for you have given me no reason for offence. If my brothers have spoken of me, then I hold you in no malice for your intention. Siblings with such a disparity of age as we are cannot be expected to ever like each other. I am to them, I am certain, little more than the brat who broke their belongings."

His smile widened, and he pounded his free hand against the mantlepiece in applause. "Were you ever such a terror?"

"I imagine so," I said, wondering why I was speaking of something I'd not talked of before to a man I hardly knew. "I little remember, but I am certain there must be many instances when an infant can irritate the smooth passage of a young man's life." I was pricked and interested in why he had set against me, but his mocking and mildly smug behavior had determined me that I would not ask him. The annoyance that raged in my breast for his teasing would normally have had me striding away, but something kept me near him. It could have been one of many reasons; he was my host, although in lesser standing than Lady Pelham; my father's censure at causing a commotion would not be small; Heyward was a cripple, and it would have looked poorly had I given him a harsh word and stepped away, only to find myself ignored in another part of the room, but if I were to speak the truth, it was simply that I wanted to know his reasons, and in spite of my lack of pretty words, I wondered if I might be able to draw him out.

Chapter Three

In which I find myself at odds with the grain and the grape.

I found my new found aspiration denied as dinner was announced before we could speak another word to each other; and before I could rally my thoughts for another battle of wits, my father had arrived with Miss Pelham on his arm. I was duly attached, and I had no recourse but to bow deeply, support the girl, and follow my father and that young lady's mother through into the dining room.

I was seated at my hostess' right hand with Miss Pelham on my other side, as I had anticipated. The treadmill had begun; the great crushing wheel jolted slowly and moved another inch towards my impending betrothal. I could hardly have failed to realize my father's intention; all I needed to do now was find the girl unobjectionable and the matter, my father had assured me, was as good as settled. The good graces of the Pelham ladies had been his favored topic of conversation since my settling at his house, and his hints, never subtle and sugar-coated at the best of times, had become more leaden as each day passed.

Oh, he repeated daily, Miss Pelham was everything a man could desire in a wife. Accomplished and graceful. Her standing as a paragon of maidenly virtue and desirability was described to me so often that I was forming suspicions in my mind as to some hidden faults. The more my father praised her, the more my mind found reasons to set against her.

If she was said to be fair, then I felt that she must be plainer than my gunnery sergeant. If her figure was described as elegant, then I envisaged her as unattractively skinny as a pikestaff, or else a walrus draped in muslin. Even as I sat beside her, grateful that her resemblance to my sergeant, or indeed any walrus, was in fact rather remote—I wondered if perhaps she hid horrors in places that none but a husband might ever discover them.

She was not quite the Aphrodite that my father had taken such pains to describe, but she was unobjectionable and certainly, on first examination, I could find no obvious reasons why I should not obey my father, despite the fact that I found the idea of marriage entombing.

Her hair was a shade darker than her cousin's. I am a plain man of few words and am unable to compare it to the particular shade of a bird's wing or some such, but it was brown and it suited her well enough. Her features were regular, apart from her mouth, which was a trifle large. Her eyes were of a similar dark brown to her cousin's, dark enough to look ebony, but they seemed to lack Heyward's fire, and were indeed rarely lifted and so rarely seen. And as I waited for her to be seated, I surmised that, as to her manner of comportment, she was unlikely to be deformed in the various ways I had imagined.

"Did you enjoy your drive this afternoon, Miss Pelham?" I inquired, noting that her cheeks flared into color immediately as though I had asked her to accompany me to Ranelagh alone.

"Emily dislikes the brougham," Lady Pelham said, her voice cutting across the table, encouraging all others to listen and giving her daughter no chance to answer. "She says it gives her *mal-de-mer*." As I turned to listen, I was once again reminded of a ship in full sail, bearing down on its enemy with no manner of slowing before full cannons were discharged. It was rather disconcerting.

I tried again, directly addressing the young lady. "I understand that with these new springs that that malady is not uncommon. I have heard in fact that Lord Wellesley himself finds himself as unwell in a carriage than ever he is at sea."

"Stuff and nonsense," said her mamma. "It's just that she won't look up at the horizon. She convinces herself that she will be ill and so she becomes ill as a consequence. As for myself," she continued, as if addressing an entire theatre and not just a dinner table, "I don't allow myself such idle fancies. Too imaginative, these girls today—don't you think so, Colonel?"

My father agreed wholeheartedly and started to recount a tale of my childhood that I would not relate even here. I could feel the color rising in my face, and it was with not a little gratitude that I heard Heyward's voice interrupt my father's, proving him to be a braver man than I.

"I admit, Aunt, that your driver does not take the care he should, but I have suggested before that Emily needs to face forward. It is most disconcerting for her not to see where she is going, but only where she has gone." His eyes skimmed the table, smiling his encouragement at Emily, who smiled shyly back at him, unseen by her mamma. His eyes then met mine and remained fixed on mine as his aunt replied.

"I sit forward, Adam, as you well know. How would it look to others if I did not see them early enough to acknowledge them? Within a week I would have no friends at all." She gave a brittle laugh and continued to talk to my father.

Young Heyward lifted his soup spoon and spoke quietly as if to the dish in front of him, his eyes cast down. "Then Emily shall have my seat next to you, and I shall ride in her place." The table had begun to chatter and it seemed that I, alone of all the table, with the exception of Miss Pelham, who looked more discomfited than ever, and Lady Pelham, who had unaccountably gone white, was paying any attention.

Heyward's words, however, had deflected the general attention from my conversation with Miss Pelham, and as the conversation continued, I was able to lean down to her and reassure her, for she looked terrified at the sudden attention. "I think that will help," I said to her. "And your mother is right; you should look up when in motion."

She nodded, and after a long pause, when I was about to speak again, she said, "I'm obliged to you, sir."

It was about as much as I received from her for the entire meal. Her natural shyness made my incapacity for small talk appear that I was the most garrulous man alive, and trapped between Miss and Lady Pelham, I had no alternative but to persevere. My father's eye, too, was upon me for much of the time, so I struggled on, as lost in the morass of feminine small talk as ever I had been in my life.

From time to time I noticed Heyward's attention directed our way, but the one time I caught his eye, he looked away. He had a smirk on his face that fired my temper, and as he turned to the lady beside him and whispered in her ear, I was sure he was laughing at me and my pathetic attempts at gallantry.

I think the dinner in all took several years, and I was surprised, when I stood to acknowledge the ladies leaving and I caught sight of myself in the mantlepiece mirror, that I had not aged, that my hair was not graying around the temples. I felt exhausted with the effort of attempting to woo Miss Pelham, and as I slumped back into my chair, I felt that my endeavors had been in vain. It was quite obvious to me that the young lady had found my attentions positively unwelcome.

Heyward, my father, and myself were the only gentlemen left at our end of the table. I half expected my father to join me and to critique my progress or lack of it, but I adjudged that even he would not be so indelicate as that. I was pleased to be found correct, as he stood and joined a group of military sorts at the other end, including the elderly man with the impressive moustaches I had noticed earlier.

"That's my grandfather," a voice said, and I was pulled out of my reverie on how one grew moustaches of that luxury to find Heyward's attention focused once more upon me. "And Emily's, of course. You'll have him to impress if you are serious in your suit." He leaned forward a little, and I wondered again at the expression in his face. "There's not a penny in the Pelham name, as you no doubt are aware."

I didn't, and I felt myself coloring like a schoolboy. Was there anyone who did not know of my father's intentions? I clenched my teeth and fought for a glib answer, but nothing came.

"However," Heyward continued, "I can understand your sudden interest. You aren't the first. I doubt you have the stamina, to be frank, so I doubt you'll be the last." I had no idea as to his meaning. I was not minded to cross-examine him in public and I was almost grateful when he changed the subject.

"A truly appalling meal," he continued as he yawned and stretched. He drained the remainder of his wine and looked pointedly at the port, sitting untouched in front of me. I helped myself and pushed the decanter across to him. He gave me a mock salute and said, "My aunt outdid herself. The soup was made with fox, by the smell of it, the fish was hard, the veal undercooked, and the beef inedible. What say you? I would *most* value your opinion of the cook." He leaned forward and knitted his fingers together, resting his chin on the backs of his hands.

I hesitated. I knew this young man not at all, and he had already shown more than a propensity for challenging conversation. I had not found any of the courses to be any better or any worse than many other dinners had in large gatherings; certainly nothing I had eaten bore resemblance to his description. Was he attempting to make me slander the hostess? His teasing irritated me, and I was surprised at myself. I'd dealt with brash young subalterns and jumped-up lieutenants for years. It galled me to be so incommoded by this (and I found myself becoming my father as I thought the word)...*civilian.*

Swallowing my annoyance, I took a cigar, handed it to a footman to clip, took it back, lit it, and leant back, scowling. My father's voice drifted up the table, deep in discussion with Miss Pelham's grandfather, and I felt my future closing around me like a marble sepulcher.

The cigar smoke went deep into my lungs. In moments, I felt like the warmth was draining from my skin. A headache began to throb at my temple, and when the port arrived around with me again I pushed it toward young Heyward without taking any more of it, disgusted to notice that my right hand was shaking.

I took another pull on the cigar and felt my innards churn. I dropped the vile thing into the ashtray and poured my port over it. The stench of the sodden tobacco smelled like French mud. Gritting my jaw, I pushed my chair back and nodded tersely toward the elder Mr. Heyward. "If you'll excuse me, gentlemen," I said, hardly able to open my lips to speak, lest I disgrace myself, "I have a desire to see the garden."

"Use the pot, boy," my father said. "Don't go pissing into our hostess's roses." This, unsurprisingly, received an enormous guffaw from the young bucks around the table, and I kept my face immobile as I pushed past a footman holding out the blue and white china article. I could hear my father apologizing for me as I made my way out through the door and into the hall; some calumny about my always being delicate, unable to hold my drink. "Bad thing for a soldier, but a good sign for a prospective husband, eh?" I didn't hear Mr. Heyward's reply.

I was directed through the conservatory to the garden, and once alone, I gulped in the cool spring air and gradually came to myself, the nausea going more slowly than it had arrived. I was ashamed at my lack of control, but I should have remembered that whilst white wine had little effect on me, and indeed my fame to be able to drink the stuff by the pint was renowned within my regiment, large quantities of red combined with tobacco had often caused me unwarranted headache and illness. It had taken the distractions of the evening to make me forget how much I was consuming, and the white variety had been less in evidence than its red cousin.

I took advantage of the cool and the dark to fly in the face of my father's instructions, and I relieved myself in a dark corner of the garden, hidden from the house by myriad bushes. Thus lightened, I made my way back to the balcony only to find that I had been followed. The unmistakable slimness and cane-wielding silhouette of Adam Heyward waited for me at the top of the steps. A sense of something like irritation swept through my frame for being thusly pursued, but now, perhaps, I thought I might get to the bottom of his intense and sudden interest in me.

"Ill met by moonlight," he said, irritating me still further with his pretentiousness. He seemed intent on aggravating me, and I wondered if it was a ploy to deflect my suit, however feeble that might be. "I would have joined you, but I find the steps difficult."

I felt a further warmth at his words, and wondered at his ability to produce wave after wave of emotion in me; no man, other than my father, had been able to nettle me more. Now the wretch was making me feel somehow guilty that he had not been able to traverse the stairs. As I reached the top, I had half a mind to pitch him down to the bottom of them.

He propped his cane against the wall and leant heavily on the balustrade. I was torn between wanting to leave—for the gentlemen would have joined the ladies by now, I was sure, and my father would be expecting me to monopolise Miss Pelham—and wanting to find out why this man was being such an irritant.

I asked him the question I had been wanting to ask since almost our first exchange. "Why had you set yourself to disliking me?"

"A soldier's question," he said quietly, his face in shadow. I wanted to see his eyes to try and gauge his thoughts. "Sharp and hitting true. To the point. I engage. Put yourself in my shoes, Chaloner. Give me one good reason why on earth I *should* be predisposed to like you?"

Chapter Four

In which I learn nothing but what is expected of me.

I stared at him. In the light of the conservatory behind us, I could hardly see his face, but I could tell by the set of his eyebrows that his expression was unfriendly.

"Mr. Heyward," I said carefully. "You have me at a disadvantage. I am a guest in your aunt's house, and you have treated me in a way that has me at a loss." In another country, in another year, if he had been another man, I would have called him out. "I do not wish to cause you any further offence, so if you will excuse me, I will rejoin the ladies." His changing demeanor had me confused; he had begun our acquaintance on a more friendly basis, and he had swung so far in his manner as to be defensive and off-putting.

I went as to step past him, but he turned, putting his face full in the light and checked me with his cane. Another man—taller and more whole—I might have pushed to one side, but I was still trammeled by my father's expectations. "Kindly allow me to pass," I said, attempting to keep my voice under control. He had pushed me almost to the limits of my civility, damn him. "I will not quarrel with you, sir; particularly as I do not know what your quarrel with me might be."

I took hold of his cane and moved it gently, but with strength and without mercy, to one side. Our eyes met; I hope I gave him the impression that I was not a man to back down and that he could not rely on his infirmity to bully me. With a deft movement I twisted the cane in his hand and gained possession of it. As I opened the conservatory doors, I turned and threw the article back at him. I admit now, and am a little ashamed of it, that I took a perverse pleasure in seeing how he nearly fell as he attempted to catch it. I left him then, confident that, if he were to follow me into the ladies' withdrawing room, he would not now continue his harassment.

A servant found me wandering the corridors and led me into the ladies' company. All the party was now assembled together again and the conversation stilled somewhat as I entered. I knew I had a scowl on my face and I had to rearrange my features when my father waved from across the room. He was seated in a square with Lady Pelham and her daughter; and there was a convenient empty seat beside him. It was almost enough to make me go back to the balcony, but I had no choice but to march, back straight, hand on sword, into the dragon's den. Once, incidentally, I was called before Wellesley himself (hence the snippet of information about his aversion to over-sprung carriages), and I had felt less timorous then than I did as I sat beside my father. I assumed what I hoped was a bland but pleasant expression, but it was an expression difficult to maintain at any level when Heyward appeared not long after I had settled myself. I was listening to Lady Pelham telling a tale of her one voyage to India. It was meant to be extremely amusing, with anecdotes of the natives she had met and the substances she was expected to eat and drink and the conditions under which she was expected to live ("my dears, positively horrid") but I found it boring at best and, having spent a year there myself in T—'s regiment in '05, wildly inaccurate.

Heyward's expression was no lighter than mine, and he did not take any pains to make it more appropriate to the occasion. He limped through the throng, again ignoring all and being ignored, until he reached our party where Lady Pelham astounded me—having not shown much attentiveness to her nephew before this—by fairly leaping from her seat with a cry of concern.

"Adam, my dear boy. You look pale. Are you well? You are burning up, I do declare, you should go and rest. Where have you been?"

The young man pushed her solicitude aside with a grimace, and refusing the space between herself and Miss Pelham he sat between me and my father, there being ample space as we were of no inclination to sit closer than we were.

"I'm well enough, Aunt. I was outside on the terrace."

"In this weather? It's far too damp for you to be out." She turned to my father and spoke confidingly for all the good that would do in a crowded room, whilst young Heyward's face went from a scowl to a look of pure anger. "Sarah, his mother, was a Burroughs before she married. She was so delicate, never well enough for so many pursuits, but spent many years in bed—at one time the doctors thought she would never be able to walk again, but she recovered, although she was never strong. She was my dearest, dearest friend, and although she was never well enough for school, we were tutored together and our families were very close.

"I can't tell you what pleasure I felt when my brother asked for her hand. Can you believe that she hesitated? She considered that she wasn't strong enough to be a soldier's wife." She looked pointedly at Miss Pelham, who blushed hotly. "Of course I encouraged her, 'No-one,' I said to her, 'will be more solicitous of your health than my dear Adam.'"

"Perhaps she should have ignored your advice," Heyward said. Miss Pelham gave the smallest of gasps, but Lady Pelham just smiled indulgently.

"I for one am very glad she did not. She was proved right, of course, the traveling and, well..." she gazed fondly

161

at Heyward, "proved her undoing, but I do believe she was the happiest of wives."

"For ten months." The bitterness in Heyward's voice was unmistakable.

The older Heyward gave a gruff and very decisive cough. I knew the signs and had that noise come from my relation, I would be duly chastened. "That's enough," he said. "Not a fit subject for company." I was glad he interceded and considered that that would be the end of the matter but Adam Heyward proved himself less cowed by his elders than I. He pushed himself to his feet with a slight grunt of effort and walked out without another word to anyone, leaving a silence in his wake. As he left I couldn't help but notice his lame foot; one of his boots was specially made, with a thick raised sole. I felt a pang of empathy and a glimmer of why the young man was quite so prickly. He had a club foot.

The elder Heyward excused himself and stalked out after his grandson. The silence that ensued was thick and heavy, and in the end, it took my father with his usual sledgehammer precision to break it and to turn the conversation to his plans to visit Bath for a few weeks. Lady Pelham seemed quite discomfited by young Heyward's departure, and it took her a minute or two to be able to concentrate on what my father was saying.

"Are we? Oh... Yes," she said, her gaze flying to the door as if expecting it to open on her nephew and father.

To my great surprise, Miss Pelham turned to my father with complete composure and said, "We always go to Bath for the second two weeks in March, and then on to Wensom for the summer." She spoke as if I knew what Wensom was, but I was not given the opportunity to ask for such clarification.

"Capital!" my father replied. "We have rooms booked in George Street." He rose, surprising me, and I hurriedly joined him. "I trust we will see something of you whilst we are there?"

Lady Pelham smiled for the first time since her nephew had left the room, and said that she would be delighted; I was pleased to note that she did seem to mean it, as she appeared to be genuinely friendly with my bluff, unforgiving parent.

It was not late when we emerged onto the pavement, but the rain had started, a cold relentless drizzle. As tempting as home was, I told my father that I would go to my club. I was restless and annoyed in turns and would feel better perhaps after a glass or two of brandy and a round or two of fencing, should there be anyone around to spar with. "Let me find you a cab, sir," I said, turning away from him. There would be vehicles at the far end of the square, I knew.

"I'm not senile, Geoffrey," he growled. "I'll walk. Do me good. You'll likely be in at dawn and too drunk to converse sensibly before luncheon, so tell me now. What did you think of her? You'll take her, what? Of course you will." His voice echoed around the now damp pavements, and I shuddered inwardly at his inability to keep his voice down to anything less than a stentorian roar.

"Do you wish me to come home now, father?"

"Don't change the subject!" my father bellowed. "You can do as you like, you always do, damn you!"

I clenched my teeth at the injustice of *that* particular remark. "As for Miss Pelham, I find her pleasant enough. A little shy, but, Father— I'd really not discuss it on the street. We'll both go home and..."

"No no," my father said, changing mood as swiftly as a wind shifts direction. He was beaming—no doubt at my declaration that I found the girl pleasant. To my father that would be an assertion that I'd be buying a ring the next day. "Go and enjoy yourself, sow those oats." Again, I shrunk from his words bellowed in public. "Little enough time for that now—for you'll make your offer in Bath, yes yes, perfect for an autumn wedding, then. You'll make your offer in Bath."

He turned away, waving at me with a dismissive hand

163

and marched with surprising speed up the wet street and turned the corner, leaving me damp in body and damper in spirit.

Chapter Five

In which my brothers prove they never change and Heyward tests me in many different ways.

I had had no idea that my father was planning to relocate to Bath this late in the Season. He had been known to go before, but had usually been more than a little scathing in his disapprobation of the place. "Full of twittering quizzes and old men who take too much pleasure in their own bad health, and even more pleasure in describing it."

On the day that he'd made this now infamous statement in Bath itself, it had been as if no one else was speaking and the Pump Rooms stilled into a shocked silence. However, I have to say, it was probably one of the only times that I have thoroughly agreed with my father, as I was not overly fond of the place myself. I'd visited it many times during the war years and found the behavior of some soldiers—not all, for it would be unfair to tar all my fellows with the same disgraceful brush—to be, if not beyond the Pale, but firmly on its outskirts. There seemed to be something about the place, and I don't know what blend of circumstances brought it about, that encouraged an officer, who was probably of fairly solid stock away from Bath to lose his head when in that city, whether it be for the tables or for the girls, or both.

It baffled me as to why any self-respecting mother

would bring her daughter to such a place. Perhaps it was the possibility of the prizes on offer which made them think that running the gauntlet of the roués and the cads was a risk worth taking. And it has to be said, that many a dissolute son was the son of this Lord or that one, so perhaps that fact alone allowed certain imperfections to be overlooked.

I was soon to find, by the flurry of correspondence that my father entered into from the next day onwards that he had had in fact, no plans at all to go to that town, and that he had to pay the normal rate several times over to persuade a family to leave their lodgings early. There was little point me suggesting that he settle for a lesser address, as once my father had said something, he considered it done. George Street was the address he'd mentioned and, therefore, George Street was the only place that would do.

My brothers and their wives dined with us the night before we were to set off, and I couldn't help but notice the amused glances both Charles and Edward were exchanging every time my father mentioned Bath or the Pelhams. I had little opportunity to catch either of them out of the earshot of my all too astute parent until we were all in the parlour together, but I took Edward aside under cover of showing him some mementos I had brought back from Waterloo and quizzed him thoroughly.

"I'm afraid you have no recourse for mercy, my dear Geoff," he'd said, clapping me on the shoulder with a grin. "You are hooked and landed. I've met the girl once or twice. Cripplingly shy, of course, which is why she's not been the magnet she should be—with the title an' all."

I stared at him. "Title?"

Charles joined us, sitting down and pretending to show an interest in what we were pretending to inspect. It was a ruse we'd used over the years, to be circumspect under our father's eyes, far more effective than trying to be secret elsewhere in the house, for he always discovered us.

Edward leaned forward, a piece of shattered cannon in his hand, "Charles, our idiot brother says he didn't know about the fair Miss Pelham's rare prospects."

"Well, he *is* an idiot, so one shouldn't be surprised. If it's not a horse or a gun, he's not interested in it."

"Ride it, or shoot it, or both, eh?"

Our father called out to us to stop being unsociable and I spoke urgently, irritated by them treating me like an infant. "There's no time for this, and in case you both have not noticed, I am six years old no longer. What is it I don't know?"

Edward stood up and pretended to yawn. "Miss Pelham, as you probably know, has not a penny to her name to speak of."

"Yes. I knew that."

"So why," added Charles, "is father of all people, so very desperate to have you marry her?"

"To be allied to a titled family, of course; it's what he's always wanted."

"Tut tut, Minimus," Charles said, patting me patronisingly on the head. "Wrong. There are many Honorable young ladies who are blind enough to have you, incredible at that seems to the saner portion of the population. But no. The Pelham title was written by writ and not by patent."

I frowned at him. "Kindly pretend that I have little interest in the peerage, dear Charles, and am completely ignorant of the workings of the aristocracy."

"You do not stretch me, dear Minimus. But actually you are forgiven, and you have been busy. It's a very rare case. Only happened once to my knowledge before. Henrietta of Marlborough inherited her father's Dukedom and became the Second Duchess of Marlborough. And so it is with your filly. She inherits the title. Has done already, actually. Unlike Henrietta, she doesn't take the title herself of course, but if you marry..."

"When," interrupted Edward.

"Forgive me, of course," Charles continued with exquisite mock manners. "*When* you marry her..."

167

"I'll be a count?" I felt myself go pale.

"Of course not, idiot boy," Edward said.

"But your son..."

"Who no doubt will inherit the pug-face of his father."

"Will be a count..."

"And God have mercy on the Peers of England," laughed Edward.

"And so say all of us," agreed Charles. He rejoined the ladies, leaving me as stunned as the netted and landed fish he considered I was.

This, then, I surmised, was the reason for Heyward's antagonism. He must have thought that I knew—that I was after the shy girl with no fortune merely for the title. It was more galling for the fact that it was true. I caught Edward by the arm as he turned away.

"What do you know of her cousin?"

"Heyward?" Edward frowned. "Oddfish. Comes to the club but gets in his cups too often. The old lady and the young are both devoted to him, by all accounts. No accounting for taste—but then they *are* considering you for a husband. I've heard stories about young Heyward. Stories I'd rather not believe. I'd stay clear of him, if you'll take my advice. Although, I've heard that when it comes to Miss Pelham, Heyward's word is the one that matters."

"Her grandfather?"

"You would think that would be the case, wouldn't you? But for some reason, it's young Heyward that holds the power there."

The rest of the evening was more enjoyable, I am pleased to say, although I had plenty to ruminate upon; I revenged myself on my brothers by fleecing their pockets at whist, and we parted amicably enough, even if they cast me meaningful looks over father's shoulder as they said their goodbyes.

The next morning was crisp and cool and the wind was

bitter. We bundled up against the cold, and I for one was grateful for the stone warmers which, placed on the seats and under our boots, managed to alleviate a little of the chill. I had spent too many years in warmer climes; these freezing winds bit deep. I had suggested going by Post coach; it would be days faster, and the company would at least keep us warm, but my father would not hear of it. In this way then we crawled the distance and arrived, eventually, more sick of each other's company than I can bear to express.

Our rooms were better than I had stayed in before in Bath; and I took full advantage of the staff on hand, getting myself clean and sleeping from the afternoon of our arrival until the next morning, after which I felt human again.

The interminable Bath routine was adopted; we paddled, we bathed. We drank the vile waters. We lunched in the Pump Rooms. We visited in the afternoons. We were seen. I was bored. There were many officers in the town, as was usual, but after one too many evening redrawing the lines at Waterloo and dissecting every single one of Wellington's decisions, I found that I was actually looking forward to the Pelhams' arrival. It might be pleasant for once to discuss more than the recent past. I had kept away from the dancing in the evenings, not only because, as an eligible man with no obvious disfigurements, the Master of Ceremonies would have spread me thin around the young and not-so-young, but also that my father would have been infuriated to see my attention drawn to anyone else. He seemed, from his daily admonishments to me to keep away from temptation (which, it seemed, did not include cards or wine) to consider me some Lothario who would lay waste to the virgin hordes and do myself out of the opportunity he was planning. This surprised me, for I had never shown the slightest talent for seduction, and indeed had only lain with two women, both Spanish and both ruinously expensive and each a vacuous, damp disappointment. However, I did not disabuse his opinion of me. I yearned for some reputation, however untrue.

After a week, a card arrived by messenger to inform us that the Pelhams had settled in and that we might visit that afternoon. All our normal routine was cancelled, visits postponed, the lesser mortals we had planned to visit let down. My father himself supervised the brushing and polishing of my uniform until I feared the fabric would rend under his valet's enthusiastic hands. Thus shining and ready for the slaughter, I was led into the rooms that Lady Pelham had engaged (smaller than ours, my father noted with some delight). We were ushered into the drawing room to wait, and suddenly my father remembered he had left his glass in the carriage and dashed out to find a footman, leaving me alone.

I was not in that happy state for long, however, and I had not entirely expected to be. My father's tact is negligible, and I was expecting Miss Pelham to be ushered in under some pretext or other. My mouth was dry, and I paced the room feeling caged and helpless. It was of course too late for me to show my heels; the time for showing filial rebellion had been a long time ago and long past. To refuse to do my duty now would only lead to anger and a swift eviction from my father's favour. That I could not manage on my half-pay was plain, but following my father's wishes in this matter would mean a large settlement, and consequent freedom, or at the very least, a different order of captivity.

The door opened and I stopped pacing and stood at ease, with what I hoped was a not unattractive expression of interest on my face.

"It's all right, Chaloner," said Heyward as the door closed behind him, "you don't need waste the faux-lover on me." He limped across the room and sat down, waving for me to do the same. Perching on the edge of my seat, I gave him attention. He was dressed in somber colors as he had before, his only concession to dandy-ism were a few fobs; one holding a seal, and several others with stones the names of which I knew not. He was giving me the careful scrutiny I was affording him and neither of us, by the scowl which was adorning *his* features at least, was happy about it.

"I think we can be blunt about matters, Chaloner," he said at last. "You want to marry my cousin, and I think that all of England knows it by now. Correct?"

Embarrassed at his frankness, I stood and moved back to the fireplace to give myself a moment to consider. When I turned again to face him, he was standing, also, his expression dark.

I swallowed the irritation I was beginning to find normal in his presence, an irrational need to shake him like a terrier would a rat, and took a deep breath, affecting boredom. "Shall we then consider that we have already greeted each other like civilized men, Heyward. I have spoken, perhaps about the weather, the unseasonal chill and gloom of the season which should already be full of flowers and is not. You, I'm sure, have acquaintance in Bath and have relayed an amusing story of something that happened last season. We shall talk for awhile about horses, perhaps you'll," I looked scathingly at his infirmity, "ask me about the war, and I shall gloss modestly over any heroism I may have done. Eventually, over our second sherry," I looked down at my empty hand and gave a look of mock surprise, "we might, with some delicacy, move to more tender subjects."

I thought he was going to explode, and for a moment I wondered if I had gone too far. That thought lasted no more than a second; for if he was already persuaded to take against me, it was better that we knew where we stood. I was no dissembler; I could not solicit his good regard if he was determined not to give it, but I was going to find out why or be expelled in the attempt of it.

"For whatever reason you have for taking against me without making my acquaintance, Heyward, I wish you would explain it, for I am tired of being frowned at as if I were some quiz."

He moved closer, and to my surprise his expression was mild, almost curious. I wondered how many times he had been in this position—for I was now certain it was the fact he thought I was no more than a trophy hunter, and from a certain perspective, I was—even if I had only just discovered that fact for myself.

He was very close to me by the fireplace, so close I could feel his breath on my cheek. He looked a little flushed as if he had been drinking, but there was no scent of it that I could discern. He reached out and I thought for a moment that he was going to touch me. At the idea of it, my heart leapt in surprise and I felt a strange and not unpleasant warmth in my loins, which shook me to the core. Immediately afterwards I had that sensation of violence again; there was nothing I wanted more but to hold him by the shoulders and shake him until he lost that smug expression. However, he did not encourage me to manslaughter; all he did was to grasp the bell-pull, which I was blocking. A servant arrived, poured some Tokay and left. He raised his glass to me. "I think first blood then, goes to you."

"I have no quarrel with you, Heyward."

"Nor should you. But if you had a sister, would you not be as solicitous of her welfare?"

"I should hope to be, but my father would probably stand in for me in that instance—your grandfather..."

"Is easily persuadable," he finished. All trace of the scowl had left his face, and I noticed again how handsome he was. His face was long, and the curls of his fringe hung heavy over his wide forehead. His eyes were unsymmetrical, but their imperfection gave him a great deal of character, and their expression seemed to change constantly; he seemed incapable of being unable to disguise his emotion. But it was his mouth that seemed to define him, it was capable of much movement and whether he was aware of it, he used it well. Full lips, but not pouting, and a width which might look out of kilter on another man, but on him seemed to suit him perfectly well, giving him even more ammunition to express himself. I gauged that for a man unlikely to be able to defend himself by way of fists or weapons, for I guessed he was untrained in either, a ready wit was good artillery.

He didn't seem to mind my examining him, but paused a little, as if appraising me in return. "I have to say," he continued, showing no signs of moving away, "that my grandfather is impressed by rank, wealth, and stature. He would accept *you* in a heartbeat."

"I wasn't intending to propose to *him*," I said, almost without thought, and one edge of his extraordinary mouth quirked up. "I was under the impression that Miss Pelham was of age."

At this he smiled, the damnable man, but his eyes were still wary. "She is, indeed. But she listens to advice. She is—as you may have—as *many* predatory suitors have discerned—a little unworldly. My grandfather would have her married to Mr. Finbarr Thouless by now had I not stepped in."

At the mention of that most damnable rake, the scourge of many a family in the past few years, my blood ran cold. "Surely not?"

"Why not?" he said, putting his glass on the mantlepiece and idly stroking one of the ornaments there. "He may have no title, but he has an income of ten thousand, and estates in Ireland, even though he sells them as fast as he can." He seemed to be looking straight into my soul and knowing exactly how much I would be worth, should this marriage go through. I had a feeling he knew more than I did, although truth to say, that would not be difficult.

"He also has at least three women who thought they were wife to him."

"And many more who should be and were not even deceived into ceremony."

I took a breath; I did not like the way the conversation

was turning. I would not be so insulted as to be considered in the same breath as *Soulless* Finbarr, as he was becoming known. "I am in earnest, sir. Not titled, it is true." There was little point telling him that I had no idea of the young lady's status when I had met them the first two times, "and I don't insult your intelligence by telling you that I am in love, for I am sure it is a tale you have heard before. But I am in earnest." I hoped that my face would speak for me.

He stared hard into my eyes, and as he did, I felt that warmth again, but this time without the need to inflict violence upon him. The warmth spread, and my rod stirred in my breeches. I paled and drained my drink, wishing for another. Damnable time for such schoolboy inconvenience.

"You do not look a dissembler," he said slowly. "But then Thouless has fooled many with those angel eyes and silver tongue of his. Shall we not shake hands, sir?" He moved his cane over, and held out a hand. "I give you leave to woo, at least—and I look forward to your progress with some anticipation."

I smiled at him, probably for the first time since we'd met, and I saw his expression change once more, and his look was hard to describe. My batman, Porter, who had dragged himself across the Peninsula after me, was an avid collector of insect life and had, at all times, carried a case full of dead specimens he had picked up on our marches. The expression that Heyward had at that moment was so similar to Porter's as to be identical; it was as if he'd discovered a new species of butterfly. I took his hand, shook it soundly, and nearly fell backwards when Heyward drifted forward as if off balance. His cane fell to the floor and the damnable man kissed me full on the lips. The weight of his stumble forced us together for mere seconds and I was almost too startled to move, and then I found I could not push him away. The feel of another's lips on mine, the warmth, the slight dampness, and the incredible sensation of sight—impossible to describe—but I could *see* his mouth with my lips, and God help me, I wanted to crush him to

174

me, as strongly as I wanted to shove him away, to see him sprawled and helpless on the floor like a turtle on its back.

Instead I took him by the elbows and lifted him, easily—he was surprisingly slight—pushed him against the fire surround and bent down to get his cane. I found I was shaking, with what I thought was anger. "You continue to test me," I muttered, "although there are more gentlemanly ways to do it than trying to prove me unnatural." I wondered briefly if he had tested Thouless in the same way, and I felt an unwarranted stab of emotion at the very thought of it. Knowing what I did of Thouless, I wouldn't have imagined *he* would have pushed the handsome Heyward away with such anger and ease.

I strode toward the door and pulled it open, stopping in the doorway, now recovered in composure, even if my rod were misbehaving in a thoroughly atrocious manner. "Tell my father I shall see him at home."

It wasn't until I was out in the cool fresh air that the words of my brother returned to me.

Chapter Six

In which my father insists on results and I repeat a mistake.

I expected my father to be angry, and in that I was not at all disappointed. I kept my temper, listened to him rant and rave and said nothing in my defense. "I explained your actions by saying that you were taken ill," he said finally. "Young Heyward backed you up, by God, although why he should have done so I don't know."

"I am sure he had his reasons," I said, going cold. "He seems quite capable of doing whatever he likes."

"As do you, sir, as do you! One more performance— one more!—and you shall seek your fortune elsewhere. You'd find a livin' in India, I'm sure of it, if you can't stick the company here! And a wife more to your liking, what?"

"I have no objection to Miss Pelham, father. I've made myself more than plain on the matter."

"Then why the devil d'you keep runnin' out on her?"

I changed the subject, knowing I'd start to say things I'd regret. "Am I welcome, then, to visit her again?"

"Yes, you are, although why I can't imagine. That girl has offers coming from all directions, you may be sure of it."

I couldn't resist it. "I hear she has. Thouless for one."

He went puce, and I took not a little delight in it. "Damme, sir if her grandfather didn't tell me that he isn't now regretting turning him down! At least he was there, sir, kissing the hand and passing around the fine cakes, at least he was *there*, sir!"

He looked ready to explode into further admonition, so I bit the inside of my cheek to refrain from commenting further. Patricide is sometimes tempting, but I would have had to explain myself to my brothers.

I spent the day with some of my fellow officers losing what little money I had. I was mocked for my suit, and for the fact that I did not seem the happiest of lovers. It seemed that Heyward was right; all of England seemed to know of my lofty ambition, but rather than take heart from the cries of encouragement, all it did was sink me into further gloom. For all that my life was an open page to be read and critiqued by my peers, the shame of that forbidden kiss was all that I could think on, causing me to lose my concentration at cards and preventing me from applying myself to the pursuit of much needed inebriation.

My glass sat beside me, unemptied, as I lost myself in the memory of the immorality I had done. That I had, for a lost second, enjoyed. Relished. *Craved*. The recollection that, with my hands on his shoulders, I could have pulled him closer, crushed him to me, drove me to despair, and thereby I was a doomed man. I had not afforded him the reaction I should. A man would have struck him *immediately* and insisted on satisfaction. A man would not have waited one—maybe two—seconds before gently putting him away. A *man* would not have been gentle! And Heyward knew all this as well as I, and I was now under his damnable obligation; his disposal.

Why had he done it? Was it just to test me? And if so, was it only for his cousin's protection? Perhaps he thought I was the kind of man who would do whatever it took to get what he wanted. Why, when I should have knocked him down, could all I remember was the way his lips looked like after ours had parted? Why had I hardened then? Why was I hardening now? Why could I picture *his* face, but could hardly recall what Miss Pelham looked like? Fears that had pulled at me for many years, fears about myself that I had buried deep, working and living with men as I had all my life, raised their heads and chilled me to the bone.

"You brood on your fish, Chaloner?" Captain Byrne pulled a chair up, straddled it and smiled at me, his good humoured round face quite ruddy with drink. "You won't be the only one who's cast his line in those waters to land nothing. My brother tried. Fell at the first. The girl wouldn't even see him."

Considering Byrne's brother—rumor had it—had married an Indian princess in 1803, I wasn't entirely surprised. But Byrne's thoughts brought me to myself, that I had been sitting brooding over the wrong member of the family, and unless this endeavor was going to founder, it was about time I did something a little more positive than sulk like a poet with a broken quill.

"Give me some paper," I said. There was a cry of enthusiasm from the assorted officers and as a man they picked me up and carried me across the room to a small desk, all the while teasing in affected voices about matters they obviously knew nothing.

"My DEAR Miss Pelham, I love thee with all thy peerage"

"Miss Pelham, take me—and my fortune, and make me the happiest of counts," and other such ribaldry rang through the house as I wrote. First I wrote a long and formal letter to Lady Pelham, apologizing for my rudeness the day before and giving my intention of calling again in the morning.

"Perhaps," I wrote, "you and your daughter would grant me some assistance in buying gifts for my sisters-in-law." I wanted to portray myself as a kind brother who, used only to masculine company was incapable of buying anything with lace and ribbon, which was hardly artifice, it was completely true and the butt of my brothers' jokes more than once. "My father will join us for luncheon, and if you have not tired of my company by then, I hope you will join our party tonight at the Assembly Rooms?"

Then I scribbled the shortest of notes to Heyward.

Sir,

You doubt my suit, and you have me now at a further disadvantage. I would clear my name, or remove my intention before I take it further. I hope to collect your aunt and cousin in the morning, and I will call half an hour earlier, at which time I hope you will grant me the honor of your time.

I had to see him, before I saw Miss Pelham again; I wanted to be sure what I might face—whether he might have already spoken to her, persuaded her mind against me. I grew hot just imagining the injustice of that conversation between them. Perhaps he held her hand as he broke the news, held her close with a smile. What did he say to her? What did he *want* for her?

I walked home to clear my head and decided upon action. There was no point beginning the skirmish if I could not win it. Better to receive my father's banishment and take up active service again.

A few sleepless hours later, I was greeting him again, back in the same room where he'd kissed me. That alone was to unsettle me, but I had been pacing, and I was calm for a short while. It lasted less than a minute, as after he entered, my heart seemed to leap in its cage, and all the restlessness, fear and confusion of the day before returned.

He looked around the room as if expecting...whom? My father? My second? I had every reason to have one or other of them present, and it was not until that moment that I wondered at the sense in seeing him alone. He lowered himself gently onto a chair and raised challenging eyes to mine.

"I was surprised and pleased to receive your note, Chaloner," he said, putting both of his hands on his cane. I tried not to look at his fingers, which were slender, the nails long and well tended to. I could not imagine them wrapped around man's throat, covered in blood, or ripping a rifle from a dead man's hands. He made me feel large, loutish and uncomfortable in too many ways. "If we are to converse, then perhaps you could come down to my level?"

I sat opposite him, nettled that he was giving me orders.

"I would clear the air between us," I said.

"Oh, I think the air is perfectly clear." He smiled; a terrible, knowing smile that made me go cold.

"And yesterday...Miss Pelham has been told of that?"

"My dear Chaloner, do you think I would hurt my cousin in that way? She has spoken of you most favourably."

I started to breathe a little easier. "Then..."

"Exactly. Is that all you wished of me?"

"Of course."

"Then I'll take my leave." He stood up and I copied him. "If you are satisfied that I am kinder than you consider me," he continued, "then we are on equal footing again, I think. It was hardly worth my rising so early."

I walked beside him to the door while I tried to work out what he meant. I failed. I was wary of shaking his hand, but it seemed churlish not to. "Let us be friends, and hope to be closer," I said. It seemed a natural ending, as I hoped to be his cousin in a while. His reaction was so swift that I wonder now how he managed to move like that, he pulled himself towards me, using his cane in a complicated move, like a dancer I once saw in Spain. His left hand came up as if to strike me, but I could tell by his face that his intention was less than aggressive. My own hand rose to block him from touching me, and his palm met mine, his fingers threading through my own with such natural grace that it was as if our hands were created to intertwine in such an intimate manner.

With a deliberate movement and an angelic smile that

belied his actions, he pushed his cane away from him, leaving me his only support, and left me no recourse but to grab his waist to stop him falling. Then somehow, and as much as I relived the moment (and I did, over and over) in my mind I cannot fathom how, we were kissing. I know, for the clock was pressing against my back, that we kissed for perhaps twenty seconds and no more, but for those twenty seconds the world ground to a halt and all I could do was kiss him back as if commanded to do so. My kissing experience—or lack thereof—showed lamentably, not that I was trying to impress him. I wasn't trying to do anything. It simply felt more right than anything I'd ever done, save perhaps the first time I was put onto a real horse. He belonged in my arms; his lips warmed mine and when his tongue touched my mouth I opened it without a thought in my head. Instinct, need, want, vice, sin—call it what you will—all I know is that I wanted his tongue in my mouth more than I'd wanted anything before in my life, and I wanted mine in his.

It was, however, the catalyst to bring me back to my right mind, as some forgotten sense came to me, tapped me on the shoulder and reminded me that letting (and enjoying) a man slide his (admittedly sensuous and delicious) tongue into my mouth was probably one of the worst decisions I had ever made in my life. So I pulled away and looked him hard in the face.

"You... No. NO!" I stepped away, forcing him to use the door handle for support as my voice, my very body was hardly under my own control.

His face was unreadable, and his lips—oh God, his lips—were wet from my own mouth. I wanted to feel that body in my arms again. I wanted to kiss him until... He was more honest than me, at least. He glanced downwards to where my prick pushed against my breeches and gave a small smile, as if he were actually sorry for me, the blackguard.

"You appear to be in some confusion, Chaloner.

181

Wanting one thing and then another. Perhaps I should leave you to decide what it is you do want?"

"*You* want to ruin me," I muttered. "Not satisfied with ruining my suit, you will destroy everything. What have I done so heinous to warrant that?"

He bent down and picked up his cane. "You wrong me, again. I want whatever it is you want. Perhaps you'll come to realize that, one day."

"So this, all this, was all to dissuade my suit?" I found that I was angry with him again, and I was standing almost chest to chest with him in my fury.

"Did it seem like it? Did it *feel* like it?" His eyes were warm, overly bright and piercing into mine. I couldn't answer him. It had felt natural, and I was sure he had felt the same. I wanted to hold him again so hard it hurt, but I couldn't, I *couldn't*. "My inclinations are rarely wrong, Chaloner. I've chased off men with better claims than you. You strike me as someone who could make Emily happy— away from...Well, away."

I still didn't trust him, for what other reason had he just done what he did if it hadn't been to ruin me?

But he went, without another word. The interview had been short. I had plenty of time before Lady Pelham would come down, and I needed every second of it to convince my recalcitrant rod to soften.

Chapter Seven

In which I suffer the slings and arrows of haberdashery and I am driven to acting on my own worst impulses.

The ladies joined me (thankfully after I had control of myself), and we spent the morning in retail establishments the like of which I had not been in before, and hoped sincerely I would never enter again. Under my artifice, they helped me buy muslin and lace, shawls and parasols. I had brought gifts back from India as a much younger man, but I believe that anything exotic was welcome; the vagaries of fashion were always beyond me, as my uniform at least rarely changed.

At one point Miss Pelham found a shawl of some silvery-white stuff, festooned with patterns of birds and flowers. I have no doubt it was fashionable—the emporium modestly boasted of its own exquisite taste and the latest lines from Paris—but to me it looked no different to twenty others here and there about town. I said as much and was treated to a glare from the serving woman. Miss Pelham seemed extremely taken to it, however and I saw her return to it more than once during the time we spent there. I don't think she knew she was observed as she only revisited where it lay when her mother was elsewhere.

Once I saw the pair of them, their heads almost touching, examining a bolt of a fine grayish stuff that shone in the light. Miss Pelham pushed it back across the counter once, but Lady Pelham was nodding. I approached them, stepping gingerly around two dowagers who were, it seemed to me to be abusing a length of lace in altogether too rough a manner.

"Please," I said, "if there is something you like? Allow me the pleasure of making it a present to you" I knew that men bought fripperies for ladies, so I was confident in my offer.

Miss Pelham blushed deeply and the woman behind the counter laughed behind her hand. I had no idea what I said to cause such hilarity, and no one seemed willing to enlighten me.

"Not *this* fabric, I think." Lady Pelham said, but she did smile at me, which left me encouraged enough to play the dashing suitor for the rest of the day, and I left them at their door with promises to collect them later. If it hadn't been for the disturbing memory of Adam Heyward and the heat of his mouth against my lips, I would have had not a care in the world. In fact, as I ordered the carriage to return to Union Street so I could buy the shawl Miss Pelham was so admiring, I was the very image of the eager lover.

My father was positively bursting with pride that as we walked into the Rooms that evening. The buzz had most definitely traveled before us, and it was obvious that people were talking of the upstart with no pedigree who was daring to push himself up into a higher social sphere. My father was actually cut by one or two grander gentlemen, but if he noticed, he was sensible enough to ignore it.

We settled ourselves in a good position, and as was expected of me, I escorted Miss Pelham up to the first two sets. She looked fetching, if a little pale.

"Are you quite well?" I asked as we took our place, the music started and our conversation was limited to the times when we could easily speak together without being overheard. I was almost disturbed by the size of her gloved hand in mine; it was so small I felt it could slip away at any time, or that I would crush it in my fist. How awkward it felt, stiff and unyielding in comparison to the natural way that Heyward's hand had curled into mine.

She smiled, and for a second I was reminded of Heyward's smile. "I was rather chilled after our excursion," she said and colored prettily before she continued. "You must think I am rude for not thanking you for your gift before now, but I wanted to have you to myself before I did."

I was all confusion, as I was quite unused to buying lovers' tokens and so was unused to responding to thanks. I changed the subject. "Your cousin, he will not be joining you?"

"I do not expect him," she said, as I passed her down the promenade. "He does not dance and expresses distaste for such large gatherings. But you must allow me to be grateful, Major Chaloner, it was a thoughtful gift. I...would have worn it this evening but...I had this dress already arranged and it would not go."

The colors looked dashed similar to me, but I let it pass. I had no idea of such things, that was plain. I admit that I felt a pang of disappointment that Heyward was not in attendance, but the feeling passed as we danced on, and the evening went by without any incident more exciting than a dropped fan and the raised eyebrows and glasses as I accompanied Miss Pelham into a daring three sets (thereby sealing my intention, as far as Bath was concerned). I found that, away from her mother (who seemed unaware that her daughter had the capacity for speaking for herself), and once she seemed confident in my abilities as a partner, she was quite pleasant company.

If I were to be forced into marriage, I reasoned to myself as I handed her from the carriage and asked to see her on the morrow, I could do a lot worse in manner and agreeable conversation. Under it all, though, in the pit of my stomach, was a cold creeping guilt; I was the most pathetic lover, in truth. I had not once had the desire even to press her hand to my lips, had not thought even to catch a glimpse of ankle as she descended the carriage. Something had even prevented me from giving her hand the slightest encouraging pressure as I bade her goodbye. To her eyes, I was sure—although she knew well of my intention—I was not cutting much of a dash.

I was only grateful that such subtleties were not obvious to my father, for he would complain of their lack. I only assumed that these things, these...desires would come when, as there now seemed no obstacle, we were betrothed and were allowed some time to ourselves.

My father's voice broke on my reverie as we deposited our gloves and cloaks. "I assume from the lack of girlish vapors that you have not asked yet?"

"I have not."

"What's the matter with you, boy?"

I led the way into the study and poured us both brandies.

"Well, sir? What's your excuse? You've said you like the girl well enough. Gad, if you couldn't help but scandalize the Rooms tonight. You've as good as eloped, now, you know. And then you don't ask the girl!"

"I fully intend to. But I haven't asked Heyward for his permission," I said. It was an excuse, I knew that at the time, some sneaking cowardly reason I'd worked out during the evening. Although the man had given me permission to woo, I reasoned he had not yet actually said that I might have her, and that would mean another visit, another chance to see him, one last perhaps before I was bound to Miss Pelham irrevocably.

Wrong? Yes, of course I was—but I made sense to myself, my self-deceit masterful. Somehow I had brushed aside the act we had indulged in and had transmuted it into a bond of friendship, one that must be broken once I was tied to his cousin. It was an escape, and Miss Pelham would be my sanctuary.

The next morning, in my best dress uniform, I presented myself at the Pelhams' lodgings and requested an audience with young Heyward. I found him already in the drawing room and was shocked at his appearance. He was paler yet than his cousin had been the night before. Dark circles showed a lack of sleep and his appearance was less than immaculate.

"So, you are decided that you will have her?" he asked, almost before the door closed. "Despite your...inclinations?"

"Inclinations that I did not have," I lied, "until you attempted to pervert me. Be plain, Heyward, either you will let me have her or you will not. I could take her without your approval." It was a shallow threat and we both knew it.

"You might take her by force," he said carefully, "but to have her willingly still requires that I tell her I approve of you. And I don't. I don't trust that you are the open book you appear to be. I want assurances that your newly acquired activities will not make Emily unhappy."

"And if I refuse to give you such assurances?" I was becoming angry with him. We would not be having such a ridiculous conversation had he not used such a corrupted and corrupting manner of proving a man's nature.

"Then it might not only be Emily who learns of your inclinations."

The anger swelled around me. "I haven't got time for your riddles and nonsense, Heyward." His eyes were devilish and I kept my distance. I had learned my lesson well and I would not put myself in that position again. I felt my ears go pink as I remembered the feel of his hand on me, but I lost what color I had when I saw him smile at my discomfort. He had no proof of what we had done. It would be an officer's word...against a gentleman.

No proof. But the scandal by itself would be enough to ruin me. Just the allegation of such predilection would cost me my commission. What would follow after that was not a matter I wished to speculate upon.

His mouth quirked up at the edges. He walked back into the room and leant against the fireplace, resting his arm along the mantlepiece. I knew him well enough now to know his staging ways, that every move he made was deliberate. I noted that for all his apparent ease, his knuckles were white around the handle of his cane. I was learning to read him. I followed him, and for a moment I really thought I would strike him and damn the consequences. The wave of emotion surging through me at his statement was almost overwhelming. Anger at the base of it, the sting of injustice riding the crest. I took a deep breath and completely forgot what I was planning to say.

"You...I..." I spluttered. *Damn* the man. Somehow he always managed to turn the tables, leaving me floundering and somehow in the wrong. "You instigated this and then you threaten me with blackmail?"

"Did I?" he asked. "Or was it you who made me do something so *unnatural* to my nature?"

"Un...To *your* nature?" I couldn't remember being so angry—except maybe that rare pagan state that I'd learned to work myself up into before a charge, pacing the floor and turning myself into some sort of killing machine. My men had spoken of the way that my face drained of color, as I marched the lines after the time of attack had been announced. I heard from my batman, one drunken night in Madrid, that my men would follow me into h—, but they'd rather walk into that fiery pit alone than to interrupt me when I was pacing.

I stepped forward to him. "Your nature," I said, between gritted teeth, "has been nothing but unnatural since the first moment we met."

He didn't move a muscle, didn't take his eyes from mine; for all his apparent fragility, he certainly didn't appear to be intimidated by me.

"Perhaps," he said, almost idly, as if he weren't being towered over by a furious and insulted major, "it takes one to know one." It was as if our intimacy had not taken place and we were swapping insults in a card room.

I grabbed him then, with hands long schooled to denial; not to take what they wanted, not to fire at civilians, not to touch what it should *not* touch. I crushed him to me; I heard his cane fall to the floor and felt him waver in my arms as he struggled to support himself. All this in a moment, and all I had registered from him was the sudden intake of breath. No complaints, no barbed wit, no exultation—nothing that I had expected.

I felt nothing of the giddiness I had heard poets sing about. I felt like Hercules, his last task completed. I felt fierce and victorious, swept away with the madness of the moment. His hair was against my cheek, the scents that had haunted my dreams were more real and more delicious than I had remembered. He clung to me; his right arm around my neck for support, his left arm snaked around my waist. I shuddered in pleasure as he turned his face a little and his skin touched my face. Gooseflesh sprung around all over my body as he touched my cheek with his lips.

There was no thought in what happened next; I remember every second of it, but I remember most clearly of all that I made no decisions in my actions. Everything I did was ordained, or some deep held instinct to act only, not to think. I lifted him an inch above the ground, and he wrapped his arm further around me and murmured something I couldn't understand, buried his face in my neck. He was, and I find it difficult to make my meaning clear as to exactly how I felt—how *he* felt—like something alive within me. Perhaps it was the feel of his fingers at the back of my jacket, the fingertips moving in slow sensuous circles over the small of my back, perhaps it was because I had him entirely supported and he was willingly allowing me to hold him thusly. I don't know. But although we were separated by layers and layers of cloth, I could *feel* him. I could feel his heart beat, feel the warmth of his skin, his breath on my face.

From my description, it sounds like we were cleaved

together in this way for many minutes but it was not so, the process took seconds, but it held such a world of sensation that I would that it had continued for all that long afternoon. I loved the weight of him in my arms, loved that he was dependent on me and wasn't moving, loved the sweet stolen intimacy of it. I don't think I'd ever been as close to a living human being in my life before. My breath was coming shallow and fast as my body reacted to the warmth of his fingers on my back, and my blood, already fired up at his teasing, seemed like it would boil over.

I shook him backwards, my arm in the small of his back. He was boneless, it seemed, and had it not been for the rush of color to his face, the wide smile on that beautiful slanderous mouth, and the pressure of his fingers against my neck, I would have thought him insensible. His head lolled back and it wasn't until I found myself tearing at his cravat and then burying my lips in his neck that I wondered if he'd done that deliberately. His skin was rough with stubble and my tongue dried with the tang of the scent he used.

It came to me gradually that since the first time I'd seen him, I'd wanted him like this, helpless and mine to do with as I would. Every encounter we'd had he'd been master of, leaving me gasping for air, wordless and helpless. No more. I was the master of my fate and I was the master of him, at last.

I spun around and marched him towards the couch; he struggled a little. "Geoffrey," he said as I carried him, but I wasn't letting him go, not now. What he had coming, he'd asked for, even though I hardly knew what to do myself. I was in the grip of something primal, and instinct took over.

The only men I had ever undressed had been dead men, but I was fast and experienced at that. He lay still, the only movement the rise and fall of his chest and the glimmering brightness of his eyes. Perhaps if he'd said anything I might have stopped. Perhaps he knew that. In seconds I had wrenched his trousers from him, (I wanted to complain about the foppish items—I did later—but that was certainly not the time) and had pulled open his waistcoat and tugged his shirt over his head. All the while he lay there, acquiescent; shifting only when it aided his disrobing, but he gave such a sigh when my hands reached his skin that it sounded like he'd been waiting for me all his life.

Madness. It was madness, but I must have been mad. Possessed. We could have been disturbed at any time, and I had not even checked the door.

He was as slight as he had felt in my arms; almost a boyish physique, and I stared stupidly at him in wonder, stopped short from my bullish assault. His skin was a pale cream and without blemish. His shoulders were wide, though, his upper arms developed, due, I realized later, as I had little thought processes at the time, to his having to support his weight where his leg could not.

His legs were long and slender, one foot slim and perfect, the other twisted, the leg shorter than the other.

"Don't," he said, as my eyes devoured every inch of him, but in answer I leant down, and, without taking my eyes from his, I kissed the poor little foot. I did aright, I think, for Adam smiled at me. My hand was trembling as I touched him, just below his chest and above his navel and his eyes closed, finally, his head tipping back, as if just my touch was delirium for him. My eyes roved over his body, noting the slender hips, and a dark line of dark russet hair which led my eyes downwards to where his cock waved cheekily at me, as full of devilment as Adam himself.

"Oh...God..." I said. The enormity of what I was doing threatened to make me stand and run, but his eyes flashed open; urgent, imperious. His hand caught mine and pulled it down to grasp his cock, which I did automatically, then willingly, so very willingly. The heat of it startled me, more slender than mine, but as long and so beautiful. I lost any self-will at the moment. I was his and he was mine to do with what I would. Gently I stroked him in the way I did myself, light on the downstroke, firmer on the upstroke, my thumb brushing over the engorged vein and teasing the rim when I passed it. His eyes fluttered and he pushed his hips up to meet every stroke. The noises coming from his mouth was muffled but so sensuous I thought I would spend myself just listening to him.

"Harder," he ordered, "harder." I obeyed him, watching first his face as it twisted in pleasure and then his body as he writhed as I changed strength and rhythm, lost in the joy of making someone that aroused. My own cock had hardened from the first moment I had grabbed him and it pushed against my breeches, demanding attention. Clumsily, with my left hand, I undid the buttons and released it, taking hold and matching both strokes together. His eyes opened and he watched me, with eyes greedy for every movement.

"Beautiful," he said, gasping. "I wanted this—right from the first moment." I wondered at his capacity for speech and longed to kiss him silent, but to move at that moment would have been impossible.

I felt the familiar pleasure heating, then a rush of heaven as my seed rose in a surge. I tried to fight to co-ordinate my work but I need not have worried, for as I spent, each spurt heavenly agony, Adam sat up sharply, and his seed gushed out over my fist. His cry of "Oh, God!" was muffled only by his fist pushed against his mouth.

Swiftly, as if we had been lovers for years instead of moments, he pulled himself forward, damp and naked and slid into my arms. The kiss was everything I remembered and nothing I expected, sensual and with so much feeling behind it, a heartfelt gift that I could almost hear him saying that he loved me, and I tried to kiss him back the same.

Chapter Eight

In which I accept my life changing with an unaccustomed joy.

I sat up, dazed, with the terrible realization of how much my life had just changed. He was smiling, just a little. He lay there, looking so delightfully debauched, his lips swollen from my mouth's assaults, his eyes huge and so dark as to be almost black, that my heart twisted with emotion for him. He reached down and took my hand, still resting on his thighs, caught it in his hand and brought it up to his mouth. With slow, deliberate movements of his tongue, he licked my fingers clean, then turned my hand over and kissed my palm, his eyes closing as he did. It was such a simple and heartfelt declaration of love without words that I was unable to do anything but swallow hard.

Our situation and the danger of it came to us both as the madness receded. We had already been too long closeted together; we could not afford much more time. But our preparations to appear to the others of the house and his gradual re-dressing were delayed again and again by tenderness and kisses as he came to me, again and again.

"One more," he said, pushing himself against the door and myself. "For I'll have to live on this moment for who knows how long." I, too, saw the future stretching away from me with nothing more than circumspect glances, unendurable social contact and nights spent lonely, hard, and longing.

How my life had reversed in so short a time. From being determined to grant him no quarter, to stand against him in every endeavor, now I was his to command. Just a pressure behind my neck brought my lips down to his; the smallest of his touches had tamed me, just as I fooled myself that I had mastered his recalcitrant nature. I brushed the back of his hair with my fingers, curling it where it had been flattened, and I wanted to say how my heart felt but he had confounded me—as ever.

I tried, knowing that something was needed of me. We could not open that door and resume our lives without some declaration of our intent. And yet, I thought—rational in spite of the glow of new found love—what intents could there be? This madness could never happen again, not in his aunt's house, and would, inevitably sink to degradation, hidden away in the class of houses that such...tastes were enjoyed, becoming as vile as it was rumored.

I was not sure we had escaped scandal as it was, but to repeat the experience (although every inch of my body wanted to repeat and repeat and repeat) would be insanity of immense proportions.

"Heyward..."

His eyes hooded in a sensuous manner and he leaned against me, his hands almost kneading my chest, like a cat does. "I think, my dear Geoffrey, that now perhaps we might be a little more intimate than that? At least in private."

He brought my hand to his lips again, stirring my blood and my loins as he sucked my naked thumb into his mouth. I groaned in frustration, and gently took my hand from his.

"We cannot now go back to the haven of that couch," I said as firmly as I could, my insides melting as he raised an eyebrow. "Although, Heywa...Adam. Know this—I—you spin my head around with words I cannot say. I would take you back there and keep you there a lifetime, if it were at all possible so to do."

He touched my chin with his finger, trailing it up and over my mouth. "La, is that a declaration, Major?"

"God damn you," I hissed at him. "You'll unman me yet more, will you? I *will* say it then. I love you, want you. How that is—what that even *means*—I don't know. But if love means want and need and an almost overwhelming desire to keep you here in my arms forever, than that's what it is. You dared me to do it, and I have, but know this," I said, pulling him tight to me again, so tight that I reveled in the gasp he made as I crushed him against me. "Know this." I covered his mouth with mine, and kissed him briefly but harder than I ever had. My member, fresh with interest, pressed eagerly against his hip. "You woke me, Adam Heyward. You must deal with the consequences of that."

For a second he looked unsure of himself as if he had, indeed, woken something in me he was not expecting, but it was veiled in a heartbeat and the teasing and spoiled child was back in his eyes, dancing with mischief. "Just so," was all he'd say and I got no more from him. He pulled the door open, and as if nothing had happened between us, he began to talk of some country house or other of the family's and what the shooting was like. I hardly listened, but followed him back to the others.

We joined the ladies in the morning room and I was invited to stay with them for breakfast. It was clear by the significant looks between mother and daughter and cousin and cousin that all was arranged—it just needed my word to make it final, but my stomach churned, for after my acceptance of my true nature, I was more uncertain now than I ever had been. I glanced at Adam from time to time, sure that I must have the brands of his kisses on my cheek, on my forehead. Surely the marks of my hands must show on his skin? But he looked no different, acted no different; playing the wit and the fool, making his aunt smile indulgently and his cousin color the next. Nothing, it seemed, had turned his world upside down and no one would guess how he'd been clinging to me only minutes before. I only hoped I was half the dissembler he was.

After breakfast I engaged with the Pelhams for the next afternoon and arranged to drive them out, weather permitting, and then I walked back around to our lodgings, my mind in a whirl. I had no doubt that Adam—how easily his name had changed in my mind—would accompany the ladies, even though I had not, and deliberately not, included him in the invitation. How would we be together? What would we do? What could we do? I had a thousand answers and none. I was more in a dilemma that I had been, for as much as I could have taken my reluctance to marry at *all* to Charles or Edward, I could hardly take this to them. At the worst they would be scandalized, at the very best they would treat it as some kind of peccadillo. I could just hear Charles, and see Edward's slightly patronizing grin. "It's something most of us try at school, Geoff. But then of course you missed out on boarding school... But one grows out of it."

So that was out of the question; I could expect no help there.

Perhaps then, I thought, that's all it was? Something that a man needed to get out of his system? A rite of passage, if you like. If many men tried it, many men also left it behind them. If I had given in to the many urges I'd felt and had hardly understood in the army, perhaps I would not be in my current predicament. There had been many a man who had stirred my blood and my imagination, but I kept it under control, even though I knew that some others did not.

Then there had been Captain Sidell. Ice-cool and aloof from everyone. I had wondered about him. He was well respected, but never let himself get friendly with very many. Once he had surprised me by asking me to join him for a drink in his tent, and I had said no automatically for no other reason that had been planning a devilishly tricky skirmish the next day. Now I wonder if that had been an invitation to more than it seemed. I'd never know that now. He had been killed at Toulouse.

I thought as I stopped outside my father's lodgings and looked up. *Well, if there was only one way to exorcise these feelings, and that way was to...exercise them, then so be it.* My prick was stirring in my breeches at the thought of Adam, his warmth, his mouth, his scent. The house seemed to frown down at me, as if it knew what I was planning. I gave it a cheery salute and went to face my father's inquisition.

Chapter Nine

In which a journey takes a dangerous path and performance means more than effort.

The weather the next day was overcast and cool, but dry enough to consider a drive to Prior Park, so I sent a boy to hire a barouche for our excursion. To my very great annoyance, my father insisted on accompanying me, even though I complained that, should young Heyward come—which I hoped very fervently he would, I had great hopes of him pressed next to me on the seat—it would be rather cramped, and to take two carriages would be difficult to arrange for I could hardly yet drive alone with Miss Pelham even if I had wanted to. I pointed out the extravagance of such an adventure, but he was adamant that one equipage would do, and no more and "Young Heyward can dashed stay behind if he don't like bein' squashed."

I said that perhaps it was the ladies who would not like to be so incommoded, but I may as well not have spoken at all. I positively glowered all the way around to our destination, but when the ladies came out, my father, contrary as ever, waylaid Lady Pelham at the door and suggested she accompany him for an afternoon at Lord D—'s.

"The young people can enjoy themselves the more without us," he said, almost winking at me, "and your nephy's shoulders might not fit a uniform, but the office of chaperone suits him well enough, what?"

The insult made us all color and I went hot and angry in Adam's defense. What had my father expected him to do, limp across the Peninsula with a rifle in his hand? I turned away, opened the door of the barouche and helped Miss Pelham into the carriage, facing forward, which earned me the sweetest smile she had yet bestowed upon me. It was with relief that I was able to order our departure, and it was with some delight that I found that Adam was where I hoped he would be, his leg pressed up against my leg and jolting delightfully against me with every wonderful bump in the road. I hoped there were many hundreds of such imperfections between now and our destination. Such tender friction soon removed every thought of my father.

We were cozy enough then—but less than two streets away from our departure point, Miss Pelham gave a cry. "Oh, please stop. Please?" and I urged the coachman to do as she asked.

"Are you well?" I asked her. "Should I ask him to turn around?"

"No. It's an acquaintance of mine, Miss Clynes. I have not seen her for some time."

Adam raised an eyebrow. "That might be because you are forbidden to see her, of course."

Miss Pelham surprised me by rounding on Adam. "And you are forbidden to see that Thouless...creature...but I know you do! So if you say a word..."

"My dear girl, I wouldn't dare cross you."

"Rightly so." She turned her attention to me. "Forgive me, Major, but I must speak with her." She fixed her attention to the pavement and after a few moments, a young lady with light brown hair, accompanied by a female companion approached the carriage. Miss Pelham sat at the edge and held out her hand for her friend to take, which she did gratefully and they exchanged fond words whilst I sat there and tried not to be jealous at the casual mention that

Adam was apparently well acquainted with Thouless. In the few moments it took for Miss Pelham to remember us, I cannot say that I did particularly well.

"Major Chaloner, I am happy to present Mrs. Clynes and Miss Clynes. Isobel was my dearest friend at school. Isobel, my dear Mrs. Clynes—this is Major Chaloner of the —th, and of course you both know the dreadful Adam Heyward."

Curtsies were given and hats were doffed. I stepped out of the carriage and offered them a ride to their destination, but Mrs. Clynes declined, saying, "We are at the end of this row here, but thank you."

"Then, perhaps you would consider accompanying us?" I said, wondering where my gallantry was coming from and trying to ignore the quirked and amused eyebrow under Adam's hat.

"It is most kind of you, Major," Mrs. Clynes said, "but I have much to arrange. We leave Bath in a few days. But Isobel? You would enjoy it, I'm sure?"

"No, mamma, I would not hear of going whilst you remained behind."

Miss Pelham grasped Miss Clynes' hand. "Please do, Isobel."

It took but a second for Miss Clynes to be persuaded, and she stepped into the carriage with a small smile. The driver ensured their comfort and we set off again, with Miss Clynes' arm entangled with Miss Pelham's and I am sure that I do us no injustice when I say that we made quite a fashionable quartet as the barouche clattered down the street toward the country. As the young ladies renewed their acquaintance and forgot us temporarily in catching up with their news, Adam leaned towards me a little and gave the merest pressure with his left thigh.

"Beautifully done, Chaloner," he said, pretending to point to a monument as we passed it. "You are obviously a natural at this. You will lose a little of my aunt's affection, of course, but have gone a long way in winning the heart of my cousin. Just be careful with it."

I felt the familiar irritation he had caused before our mad interlude. If he had not pushed me quite so far, I would not now be in danger of hurting those feelings of hers of which he was so solicitous. I had many questions, and not one of them could be asked in our mixed company.

It was no distance to Prior Park, less than two miles, and the road was less bumpy than I would have liked, but there was a little neighborly friction between Adam's leg and my own. The sun made a watery appearance and by the time we arrived at the park and I helped the ladies out of the carriage, the weather seemed to smile on us, and some sun had filtered through the ever-present clouds.

The ladies walked ahead of us down the incline towards the lakes and the Palladian bridge and Adam caught my arm to slow me a little, his fingers rubbing sensuously behind my elbow. "You have hardly smiled once in half an hour's time, I swear."

"The grass is slick," I said, not looking at him, "I am concerned for the ladies' stability."

"You should worry more for mine," he said, his voice almost a whisper. "I nearly walked to your house last night to throw stones up at your window like a lust-driven poet."

I laughed at that vision, imagining my father demanding an explanation in the middle of the night. He joined me in my laughter, and I felt my groin warm for him. "That's better, you are less forbidding when you smile."

"Forbidding or not, you are hardly put off by it."

"I could have been, when I see the same scowl on your father's face as on his youngest son..."

"My father needs to hear your wit," I said dryly, "he seems to think that your lack of uniform leaves you without weapons."

He grinned at that and we reached the bridge and caught up with the ladies, who were looking out over the lake.

I found myself beside Miss Clynes. "Are you often in Bath?"

"Every year since I came out," she said. "I trust you do not regret abducting me from the town."

"There was no question of it not being done," I said. "Miss Pelham wished it so and therefore I obey. I see nothing to regret."

She was silent for a moment as she took her parasol down as the sun went behind a cloud. "I am surprised, sir, that you appear not to know me." She cast a slightly furtive look at Miss Pelham who was now walking towards the far end of the bridge with Adam. "I imagined that you would."

"I hope I would not listen to conversations about a lady," I lied.

"It was a scandal that never truly happened," she said, "so perhaps it is less discussed. But if you don't know, you should."

"Please do not say anything to me that would distress you."

She laughed. "I have passed that particular emotion a long time ago, Major Chaloner. As I say, it was something that never happened but it has affected my friendships, which I regret. Two years ago, fresh from school I formed an...unsuitable attachment and I had planned to elope, but I was intercepted before I even reached our assignation."

"Please," I said, unnerved and embarrassed by her frankness, "you don't need to speak of it."

"I merely tell you so that you are forearmed in case Lady Pelham blames you for the excursion."

"I would hardly let Miss Pelham take the blame."

She inclined her head. "Then I shall talk no more on a subject that has little merit," she said. "I heard you laughing with Mr. Heyward, and you impress me. I have rarely heard him laugh out loud with anyone except Emily before."

"If truth be told, it is often more *at* than *with*." I colored a little to think that we may have been further overheard. "I am an amusement to him, I have found."

"I comprehend you perfectly. I have spent a lot of time at Wenson House in times past, and Adam takes much personal entertainment from the world."

"Miss Clynes, you wrong me, as usual," Adam said, returning with Miss Pelham on his arm. "And I would be grateful if you would not scare our new friend away, he looks positively ready to bolt. Your reputation has terrified him beyond words, I'm sure."

This brought a shocked reprimand from Miss Pelham, who drew Miss Clynes away from us both. "Adam Heyward, if I could tell mamma what you just said..."

"But you won't, of course."

She rewarded him with a furious expression, and I was grateful at that point that it began to rain a little, for I would have had to say something I might have regretted. There were black clouds sweeping across from the west, and I felt we were in for a downpour. We moved under the protection of the bridge whilst we waited for the driver to appear with the barouche, but after a few minutes there was no sign of him.

"I will have to go and find him," I said and strode off, ignoring the ladies' cries of concern for my welfare. I was half way up the slope when I realised that Adam was behind me. "Damn you, Heyward, you were supposed to stay with the ladies!"

"Really? I must have missed the dispatch—did you give out those orders, Major?" His cane slipped on the wet grass and I caught him by the elbow before he went down. The rain began in earnest, gray sheets which made our progress all but impossible as the slope turned to a river. I was minded for a moment to march him back down to the bridge but the gothic temple was nearer, so I half pulled, half supported him through the growing murk until we reached it and were under shelter. He was laughing, and his hair was stuck in delightful Romanesque curls to his forehead.

I was furious with him. "You left them alone down there!"

"Geoffrey, my dear fellow, this isn't Spain. Two young ladies in an English park under a covered bridge are as likely to come to harm as if they were in the arcade in Bath. They will be dryer than we two, and this affords them the opportunity of some much missed gossip which I assure you they will be indulging in as we speak. You, I am quite certain, are first in the categories for discussion." He shook his head, like a dog, and his curls sprang away from his face. "Don't deny them this time together, Geoff. They've been a long time apart. Don't deny it to us, too."

The rain worsened, making it almost impossible to see the bottom of the hill. I peered out, hopeful in case I might see the barouche arriving at the bridge but could make out nothing with certainty. Then Adam was behind me, his arms snaking around my waist, and in the shelter and privacy of the temple, I turned and kissed him. His face was wet and cold but his mouth was warm, and he clung hard to me, his fingers digging hard into my hips before encircling me and cupping my arse. I could feel the familiar prickle and heat as my passion rose, and only once did I make some half-hearted demurral that this was hardly the time, nor the place, but my words were almost habit; we would never have the time and the place—and we must take them when we found them.

I pushed him back into the shadows of the shallow temple, biting at my gloves and throwing them aside. As before, he was acquiescent to my hurry; unbuttoning himself as he saw me do the same whilst we both attempted to kiss as if we would never have the chance again in this life. I was hard when he touched me, and he was growing so as I pulled his manhood out into the cold and rubbed it vigorously, and I found myself groaning into his mouth as he throbbed under my rough palm.

His breeches slid down his thighs, leaving his arse open to the elements and my free hand sought his buttocks. He staggered a little and I turned, sat myself down on the bench against the wall and gasped as the ice-cold marble hit my fundament. Then I pulled him down backwards onto my lap. He opened his legs and my cock was welcomed into his cleft. In spite of the cool and the rain, I found myself sweating. He pushed back against me.

"Now, Geoffrey."

"Not here," I muttered, fighting the urge to bury myself in him.

"What are you waiting for?" He was tossing himself, his head leaning back against my shoulder. My lips were close against his ear. "A scented boudoir with rose petals? Spit and have done."

He thrust back and forth as if he were swiving a maid himself and the friction he caused made me bite down on his shoulder and brought me such feelings of delight that I forgot all else. I did what he said, oiled my pole as best I could. It was leaking from the end and I took the tip and rubbed it against his hole.

"It's impossible," I said, as I pushed a little.

"Not at all," he said. He breathed out, widened his legs still further and to my amazement I slid inside him. I felt the head push through, gripped in a way that was almost painful. I found I was shaking; my whole body seemed to shudder with pleasure.

"Oh, God." I said. "Oh GOD." I couldn't thrust in the position I was in, so I did the only thing I could think of to do. I took him by his hips and pulled him back still further until I was so fully a part of him that I could not see that I had a prick at all. He was breathing shallowly, almost hissing through his teeth,

He rocked back and forth, which was exquisite agony, so I took hold of him again and pushed him forward a little, then slid him back, then I could not control myself—and to my shame my cock fired off as if I were a schoolboy, and all I could do was cling to him as he brought himself to completion.

He pulled himself from me without a word, and there was a terrible silence between us as we cleaned ourselves up and arranged our clothing. I could only imagine what he must think of me, although it could not have been worse

205

than how I thought of myself. As he was fiddling with the buttons on his breeches, I left him; I strode out into the rain and ran up the wet slope to where the carriage waited. My face was red with embarrassment, and I imagined the rain fairly sizzled when it hit my cheeks.

I was sure that Adam had had lovers before me, and I could imagine *one* at least, with his urbane grace and devilish smile whose rod would not erupt at the first touch of another's skin. I could not see that my clumsy efforts would ever be required again. I felt as gray as the sky and my heart felt heavy in my chest.

The driver had already raised the canopy and within minutes, we collected both Adam from the temple, where he emerged looking hardly dishevelled, and the ladies from under the covered bridge.

How different was our mood for the journey back. Adam did not look at me or speak to me, and even the sweet touch of his leg was taken from me as he sat as far from me as he could, staring into space as if the world had offended him. I escorted Miss Clynes to her door and we rode the remainder of the journey in an icy silence.

Miss Pelham looked cold and pale, and not a little concerned at the change in atmosphere between us, but as I handed her out of the carriage, she said, "You will come in, Major?" The front door had opened, but Adam had paused at the doorway, as if he was going to turn and speak.

"I'm afraid not," I said, partly to her, and partly to his back. "My father will be expecting me, and I have taken up too much of your time as it is. Perhaps tomorrow?"

Adam moved into the house without a word, and it took all my strength to stop myself from following him.

"Of course," she said, with a curtsey. "You are always welcome."

I stood on the pavement for a second, staring at the house as if it had wronged me, before getting into the carriage and finishing that day in the blackest mood I'd had for many years.

Chapter Ten

In which Heyward makes his feelings plain and I am forced to be a reluctant Samaritan.

There was nothing for it but to proceed with my father's plan, no matter that my more private life was almost out of control. From the bristling eyebrows over the breakfast table the next morning, I was left with no doubt as to his growing impatience.

When I stood up, excusing myself, he reached into his pocket and removed a small case which he slid across the table to me.

"Take this," he said, "and make some use of it."

I opened the little box to find a ring of elegant beauty; a slim band of rose-pink gold with a single diamond with the same tinge.

"Was this my mother's?"

"No, it blasted well isn't," he said, going as red as my jacket. "It was *my* mother's. Get out of my sight, boy and bring me back a daughter-in-law." I fled, but with dignity.

The reluctant suitor (and the spurned lover) made his way to the Pelham house after breakfast and was ushered into the drawing room where Lady Pelham greeted me.

"I should be extremely angry with you, Major," she said as we settled down. "I heard what naughty thing you did."

For one second I went cold, until I realized that what I

had done to Adam would hardly be considered *naughty*, and wasn't something to be brought into any conversation. I must have showed my confusion as she continued, patting my arm.

"I don't consider you to be at blame; my daughter can be extremely willful, and for some reason she will not shake off the most unfortunate of acquaintances."

"It was at my insistence that Miss Clynes joined the party," I said, "Miss Pelham was aware of your prohibition, I am sure. I can only apologize..."

She gave me a small smile as she sipped her drink. "Please, Major Chaloner, I know my daughter. She would go out yesterday in spite of the fact that I said it would rain, and now she is suffering the consequences. Both she and Adam have dreadful colds, and Adam has such a weak chest that I am fearful that it may turn to influenza, or something much worse."

My emotion at that moment was so violent that all I could was to stand up and face the fireplace. Was every plan I had destined to bring ruin on others? "I am to blame for this," I said, "and I take the full responsibility. Is he—I mean—is Miss Pelham and your nephew... Are they being tended to? My father has a physician that he relies on utterly here in Bath. Allow me to fetch him. It is the very least that I can do."

"They have seen a doctor this morning, and he says that it is next-to-nothing, merely a chill, but what do they know?"

"You are quite right to worry," I agreed, ringing the bell for a servant. "Allow me to send for Dr. King. My father is plagued with cold in the winter, and he comes to Bath for the sole reason that the man practices here."

She nodded and the little line of worry between her eyes faded. "Adam is much more delicate than he would have you think," she said. "Emily has the constitution of an ox, and she will shrug this off in a day. Perhaps it would be better not to bother your doctor with her, but Adam..."

"He will see them *both*," I insisted. I scribbled a quick note addressed to my father's doctor and sent the servant off.

It seemed an age before the doctor appeared, and then there was a small altercation, although polite, between myself and Lady Pelham as to whom he should see first, but as I was the one who would be settling the physician's account, she eventually demurred to me that Miss Pelham should be attended to before her cousin.

Eventually he returned. "There is no danger to either of them," he said, "although they should be kept warm and not venture out until there is a sunny day. The young lady has a slight fever and I have left a supply of powders."

"And for my nephew, a further supply?" Lady Pelham sounded positively panicked.

"I'm afraid that the young man would not allow me to examine him," he said. "That does not mean that I will not be sending my bill for both." He shook my hand. "He was rather vehement that I go nowhere near him. However, he sounded in good voice, and his throwing arm seemed not to be suffering from any chill. Good day, Lady Pelham, Major. I shall call on your father in the morning."

After he was shown out, Lady Pelham turned to me and took my hand in hers. "Please, go up and see him. Tell him that he must see the doctor. If this chill goes to his chest, he'll be terribly ill—last year he was in bed for weeks. I thought his life was in danger." She looked so desperate that I was vanquished and let the servant lead me up to the second floor. It was hardly necessary to point out Adam's room because the noise he was making could be heard quite clearly as soon as I cleared the first flight of stairs.

His words were indistinguishable, but it was clear he had not run out of ammunition as regular crashes could be heard. I was not concerned for my life; vases and books and suchlike were not dangerous shrapnel, so I pushed open the door and ducked to one side sharply as a chamber pot (thankfully empty) crashed into the wall beside me.

Adam was sitting up in bed, his hair beautifully mussed, his charm rather spoiled with a look of black fury. He didn't look at all unwell, I have to admit, but his color drained a little at seeing me.

"If you're here to make me see that quack," he growled. "I have my own doctor."

"And he is in London," I said, attempting to be reasonable. "Your aunt is concerned—rather too concerned if you will excuse me saying—of your welfare. Although she is right to be concerned for Miss Pelham."

"Oh," his voice was suddenly sarcastic, "and you swooped in like the white knight you are. Knowing that she may have been displeased with you, you find a ruse to sweeten my aunt to you again. Well done." He lay back down with an exaggerated flourish and pulled the blankets over his head, muttering something I didn't catch.

I moved over the bed. I was seething with a dozen emotions, and his childish behavior was doing nothing to calm me down. "What did you say?"

There was no response. So I repeated my demand, grasping the sheets and attempting to pull them from him.

He struggled childishly and refused to be uncovered. "Go away, Chaloner. That's one thing you *are* good at."

I wanted to apologize for my pitiful performance the day before. I wanted to tell him that it had been his body that set me alight, the reason I shot my seed like a nervous virgin, because that's what I was. I wanted him to tell me how he seemed so confident, to confess that Thouless—damn him—had been nothing to him.

I wanted him to swear to me that he'd never see Thouless again.

But I didn't. My damnable sense took control and far too late, some might say. His moods and desires were obviously as transient as smoke—one moment I was what he wanted, and now he wanted me out of his life. I stared at the blankets and my hands itched to pull them from his face.

But I have never forced myself on anyone, no matter

how provoked; it was clear he had changed his mind regarding me. Regarding us, and for the lack of complication that would bring, I was almost relieved. I felt numb as I turned away, feeling like I was leaving something of myself behind, warm and hidden in the blankets with the man who wanted something more than I could give him, or something less. Something more sophisticated than a clumsy soldier. Someone else.

When I reached the door, he called me but I didn't turn around. It was better this way, I said to myself. It was all too dangerous, all too complicated and to stop it now, before it had really started, was best for all three of us. All the same, I don't know how I had the strength to turn the door handle. I heard the sheets rustle and I knew he was sitting up again, but he didn't say anything other than my name.

"I'm sorry to have troubled you," I said without turning around. "I only wished to be of service." I stepped out into the corridor and shut the door.

The noise that he made after I left was greater, if anything, than he had before I had entered and more valuable items—by the sound of shattering glass and china—were destroyed. I stormed downstairs, and my expression must have been terrible for the footman fairly cringed to the side to avoid me.

My mind was made up. What I wanted, I could not have. What I could have, I did not want. When Miss Pelham was well enough to be told, I would apologize to her—as best as I could—and get out of the country. Some damnable place with flies and heat and horses. Some place on some forgotten border where I could do what I was trained to do, not this brittle life of chandeliers and lies. I would tell Miss Pelham first, for it was she whom I had wronged by my forced suit.

Then I would tell my father, and I would take the consequences thereafter. It was not a pleasant prospect, for I would not be welcome back in England until at least after my father died, and the thought of not seeing my brothers

211

again, perhaps never if they took his side, although I hoped they would relent at last, hurt me badly. One thing I could be certain of was that my father's fortune would not be divided three ways, but two.

I asked to see Lady Pelham before I left the house. "You are not to worry," I said, taking her hand in farewell, "Heyward will, I am sure, be up and about in no time. He certainly seems strong enough."

"I have no faith in medicine," she said, "but I trust your father's judgment. And yours." She looked seriously distraught and I felt sorry for her until she spoke again, explaining much of what I'd seen of her solicitude. "I promised his mother I would look after him."

I bit my tongue on the promises a mother should make for her own daughter and said my goodbyes. It was quite clear to me that I could not withdraw my suit until Miss Pelham was quite recovered, and I promised to call daily, for what else could I do?

Chapter Eleven

In which the birds have flown, my father gets a shock, and a solution comes from the unlikeliest of sources.

The next morning I had some business to undertake for my father and it was not until after luncheon that I was able to make my way to Lady Pelham's residence. A footman greeted me at the door, but when, in the hall, I offered him my hat and gloves, he looked embarrassed.

"I take it then, sir, that you did not receive the message that was sent to George Street this morning?"

"I have not been at home since seven of the clock," I said, fearing that the occupants of the house were worse. "What message was this?"

"I don't know what the message said itself, sir," the man replied, "but I would surmise that it was a farewell, seeing as how the family decamped for London."

I stared at him. "Gone?"

"Gone, sir."

"But...The young lady...Miss Pelham, she was quite unwell. The doctor said she should not be moved!"

His face was professionally blank. "It was the young gentleman's orders, sir. The coach took them off at about ten o' clock. The doctor called just afterwards. I believe he expressed his concern, also, sir."

"I'll bet he did," I growled. The footman was perfect, I

would have liked to have him as my valet for his sang-froid if nothing else, but there was nothing to be achieved by staying in an empty house. I tipped him for his professionalism and returned to George Street, expecting—and not being disappointed—to find my father in a high temper. So bad was it, that he began roaring when I had barely entered the hall, and it went on for so long that I had a sudden sense memory of the only time he'd been quite so angry, and I had been very young. I remembered my hands gripping the curved balustrade and feeling that whatever he was angry about, it must be my fault.

However, as a grown man, I knew exactly where fault lay in this case. I listened to him rant and rave until my temper broke and long years of his bullying tore apart my shields.

"But WHY did the boy drag them from Bath, especially if the gel was unwell?"

"Heyward is nothing but a spoiled brat." My voice rose against my father with every sentence, as my frustration and anger worked its way out. "He's been coddled by his aunt since the day he was born—he considers the whole world to be his enemy. He's made it very plain that he did not welcome the suit you forced me to press, and he accused me of only wanting the girl for her title—which," I said, accusingly, "is the source of your interest, after all, isn't it?" By the end of my speech I was matching him for volume.

To my very great amazement, my father's color went from a deep puce to something like normal, and he stared at me. He seemed to shrink before my eyes and I realized, perhaps for the first time, that I was taller than he. "It's not for me, Geoffrey, you understand."

I nearly apologized. To see my father back down on anything at all was a shock, but this... With sudden clarity I realised that it was because he wanted it so much. "It's damned well not for me. What do I get out of your bargain?"

"What do you get? How about a pretty wife? How

about a country estate, that I'll pour money into to
refurbish? How about the chance for your children to live
on that estate—as noblemen? Don't say you ain't ambitious,
Geoffrey. You wouldn't be my son if you weren't. It
weren't just my money pushed you up all the way to major,
and don't forget it."

It was the first time—other than the occasions when he
showed me off to others—that he'd ever come close to
hinting that he was proud of me, to my face. I hesitated and
that was enough to put us back on a more familiar footing.

"That's right!" he shouted. "Don't tell me that you
wouldn't want the best for your children."

"It's not that..."

"Then what? Can't say anythin' much. You've been
paying her a decent amount of attention. Whole town's
buzzin' with it."

I gave up. We'd be going in circles repeating the same
old arguments soon and my father didn't have the
imagination to see what might really be wrong.

"Nothing, father."

"So what you going to do? Chase her! Of course you
are! Nothing shows keenness like a good chase across the
country!" At that he launched into action, as if breaking
bivouac, shouting for servants to pack, the carriage got
ready. For all that it took us a while to depart and although
we made good time, we never caught up, and my gallant
pursuit seemed likely not even to be noticed and a pointless
exercise.

My father sent his solicitations to the Pelhams the
moment we arrived back in London, after which we retired
to the study to recover.

There was no word from Lady Pelham until the next
morning, but when it came, addressed to my father. It was
not a rebuff and my father was pleased.

My dear Colonel,

My impulsive boy insisted on rushing us home, and although I was quite concerned for his health, the journey seems to have done him no harm. The kind boy immediately insisted that our own doctor attend Emily, and they will both be well enough for the ball on Saturday at Lord D—'s, I am certain. It speaks volumes for your son, that he insisted on following us so closely, his concern for Emily touches me greatly and if you will call for us at six, we can attend the ball together. I hope that Adam will be strong enough. He won't dance, of course, but he seems so out of sorts that I fear that his cold will return.

Etc.

With our subtly changed relationship I had the nerve to raise an eyebrow at my father over the mention of my pressing concern, and he had the good grace to look embarrassed.

After our argument, I had slipped back towards the idea of marriage to Emily Pelham somehow. After all, she was a pleasant enough girl; I could not see that we would disagree on a great deal, and many marriages had been started on far less acquaintance. So, pushing the thought of Adam's beautiful mouth and Adam's alabaster skin and Adam's temptation away from me and burying it as deep in my mind as I could, I sent flowers and fruit, a singing bird, and other such gewgaws as a besotted lover might send.

All too soon, it was the night itself and dressed in my stiffest dress uniform I led Emily up the stairs of Lord D—'s keeping my eyes firmly in front of me. Adam had not accompanied the ladies—although Lady Pelham assured me that he had known that I was collecting them—and that in itself was proof to me that he had, after all, only been dallying with me. A game that had turned too serious, and a lover who didn't match his expectations.

My father's face was granite as we were led in, and I felt nothing. The tomb was closing around me and there was nothing I could do to prevent it. The ballroom glittered with life, and it seemed to mock me. "This", it said, "is to be your life, Chaloner. Your life will be a ballroom filled with people you can't understand, and your father's ambition will rip away the last vestiges of your self-respect."

We reached our allocated seats and my father led Lady Pelham away while I secured Emily for the first set. My future was now running in two paths. Either I should come out of this evening an engaged man, or a disinherited one.

The expression in Emily's eyes surprised me not a little; for whilst she was as gentle and compliant as ever, and I knew the dances to be two of her favorites, her eyes held a hardness that I had not seen in them before. She looked more like her cousin than ever, and my heart hurt at the reminder of the look on Adam's face at our last meeting. It did not bode well for my chances of further acceptance and the brightness of the evening dimmed a little more in my eyes.

What a couple we were, and how ridiculous I imagined we looked. I could almost feel the room quivering with the expectation of my proposal, all eyes upon us as if I were going to drop to my knees at any moment. My father was standing behind Lady Pelham and the smile on his face could not have been wider, the look in his eyes as he fixed me from across the floor could not have been more clear. The music began and we were engaged in movement, trapped for at least the half hour.

"I am glad to see you in such good health, Miss Pelham."

"You flatter me, sir."

"Not at all," I said, although I ached with an almost irresistible urge to run, for all the good that would have done. "I was quite concerned, for yourself and for your cousin's health. I am glad that Dr. King did not hear that I allowed you to flee Bath when he had been so solicitous. It gives me joy to see your color high and your eyes so lively. I owe your doctor my gratitude." I was an ass, and I knew I sounded like one.

"Perhaps," the dance brought us to rest, side by side,

"my high color is merely brought on by how very displeased I am with you at this moment."

I almost missed my cue and almost had to skip to keep my place as she moved off. When we came together again I murmured, "If there is some disservice I have done you, please let me know, for I would do anything to undo it." I searched my memory for some insult or slight I may have given her, but could think of none. Even tonight I had made sure that flowers were delivered to her house before she set out. I had been happy to see (what I assumed to be) one of my blooms, something pink and frilly, on her shoulder.

"You have done nothing to me personally, Major Chaloner. But by implication you have hurt me as you have hurt another. You forget, I think, how very close, and how fond of each other my cousin and I have always been."

How could I forget? This sorry mess had come about because of Adam's protectiveness towards her, but I gleaned from the unusual arch of her brow that she meant a little more than she had said. I had no chance, indeed, if I had have had, I would have not been able to speak, as my thoughts were as tangled cobwebs. "You and he have had a falling out, I understand," she continued. "Is there no way you can become friends again?"

I knew I was flushing, and everything I feared would happen was just about to fall on me. Did she know? Had Adam really told her everything? "Oh, we grew up together," he'd said in Bath, "we've always confided in each other."

"I don't know what your cousin has said," I said carefully. It was hard to concentrate on the complicated turns and the conversation as it spiraled out of control, let alone attempting to keep a smile on my face.

As she put her hand in mine for the promenade, she squeezed it and smiled for the first time that evening.

"He has said nothing to me of his present unhappiness," she said, and she frowned a little. "He refuses to speak to me at all, and I've never been so excluded before. But he

218

has said much to me recently." She paused as we separated and as we came back to together for the rest she said, "Of his great, *great* happiness." Her look and the repeated squeeze of her hand let me know what she meant. "He means a very great deal to me." We moved diagonally over the set, and when we came back, she said with a full and meaningful glance. "*Too.*"

My world seemed to tip sideways a little, as I took in what she was saying. Adam still loved me? He was miserable that we were separated? It seemed too much to understand. "Thouless..." It was the one word that had tortured me.

"Oh—that monster," she said. "Adam owns a horse with him, Major." She paused and I could see her phrasing her answer, for we were in public, no matter how little likely we were to be overheard. "My cousin has a little more sense than that. And a *great* deal better taste."

It took an entire chorus for me to form any kind of response. When I had to opportunity to speak, I merely said that we should speak more when the set was over. Somehow we reached the end, and, avoiding my father's eyes I swept Miss Pelham outside without the least care for propriety or the wagging tongues.

Once in the moonlit gardens, I slowed and attempted to give the impression of a young man sauntering along with his betrothed.

"I find you hard to answer," I said. "It is completely outside my experience."

We had reached a fountain and she stood and looked into the water for a moment in silence. "I hope you think no worse of me, sir. And my experience is no more extensive than your own. But Adam has been my closest friend for all of my life and his happiness is bound up in mine as I know that mine has always been safe in his care." That much was true and I nodded, numbly. "I understand the conflict between Adam's world and the rest of society, but I've always known, and been privy to, his secrets. We were so young; we didn't knew it was wrong when first he began to speak of it."

She was more eloquent in this indelicate matter than ever she had been on any other before and I was startled, impressed; a warm feeling of friendship flooded through me.

"Still no answer?" She put her hand on my arm and we continued around the fountain. "I wonder what your silence means. Is it that you are stubborn as Adam attests, (which is quite as stubborn as he is himself), or the simple fact that neither of you silly men realise that the answer lies in your hands, Major Chaloner, yours and yours alone."

"Mine?"

"The answer is as simple as it can be."

"It is?" I really didn't understand her.

"Perhaps you didn't know, and there's no reason why you should, that Adam and myself had long decided that when I marry and move to Wenson House—with my *husband*—that Adam, who has no settled home or income of his own, would always have a home with me."

There was a deafening ringing in my ears as if every bell in London were sounding at the same time. It couldn't be that simple. It couldn't. The girl couldn't mean what she was saying. "But... you..." was all I could manage. I needed to speak to Adam, I felt that if I could just speak to him, he could decipher this all for me.

"I have been raised to marry, Major Chaloner. That is my role in life. I like you a very great deal, and that is more than I expected. When your father first called on us last winter I thought that perhaps my mother intended me for him." Her voice had not a little vigor in it. "But that was luckily not the case, although should you not..." We walked for a while longer in silence while I took this in and then she said. "I think, unless you object strongly, we should go back in and face the congratulations? That is, unless you refuse me, Major Chaloner?"

"Yes—yes, I mean no! I don't know what to say."

She laughed then, went up onto tiptoe and kissed my cheek. "I think that's what we like best about you, Geoffrey. Adam should be here by now. I made him promise to come. He didn't want to but I insisted. I think you should ask him for my hand in marriage now, don't you?"

"Again?" I said, aghast and we laughed together for the first time. We were still laughing when we re-entered the ballroom.

I found him in a side-room, gambling and drinking, a look of pure misery on his face. Unseen by him, I watched the play from the doorway, and I imagined how it would be when we would sit in our home together, perhaps us three, perhaps just he and I and be friends, brothers, lovers. As it should be. I was still reeling that it *could* be.

One of the players finally called to me, "Chaloner, isn't it? In or out, man, the noise from that infernal orchestra sets me teeth on edge."

"Miss Pelham has sent me to fetch her cousin," I said, not taking my eyes from the object of my desire.

Adam had started like a deer at the first syllable of my name and was glaring at me with a look not dissimilar to the one he'd had for me early on in our acquaintance. He stood and excused himself, throwing some coins onto the table with a casual grace. I held the door open as he stalked past, and I led him into an empty room that I'd found whilst looking for him and locked the door behind me. It was dark and I lit the candles on the sconces by the fireplace, then turned to find him scowling. I was so happy to see him, I didn't care if he scowled at me from now until Doomsday.

"From the look of your idiotic grin, I'm assuming this is some childish, military prank. And since my cousin is conspicuous by her absence, I'll return to my game." He turned to go.

"Don't go. Adam. Don't go." He turned back, slowly, leaning heavily on his cane. Then I said the wrong thing.

"You were losing, anyway, weren't you?"

He sneered at me. "That's what I wanted them to think. Don't you know the expression about being lucky with cards, Chaloner?" He sat down, as if grateful to take the weight off his leg. "All right. It's not like I can run away from you. What is it?"

I moved closer to him, so I was standing over him. "I want to marry Emily."

He tried to stand, but I was too close. I pushed him back down.

"Let me go," he growled. "You don't need to prove to me how much stronger you are." His voice was full of bitterness. "You made that very plain."

"I'm not going, and I'm not going to let you go either. Or Emily. I want you both. *She* wants us... both."

"What are you saying?" He looked revolted.

"I'm asking your permission to marry Emily," I said. "Where were you going to live when Emily married? Or is she not telling me the truth?"

His face contorted as he processed the information. "She said... she told you... she wants..."

"Yes. Yes and yes." I was delighted to see him lost for words for once and that made me laugh out loud. "Will you...?" I couldn't ask him the question; that would never be possible for us. I wanted him, loved him. I touched his hair and told him just that.

"But. How? What? She?" I could see the questions lining up in his agile mind, hard and fast, one after another, so I leaned forward and kissed him silent, feeling him relax as I pushed him back onto the settle. He didn't need to answer me—it was a solution, and not one we ever could have anticipated.

There were a thousand problems in front of us, all of us, but I knew that between Emily's courage and Adam's fearlessness, we'd all get what we deserved.

I certainly had, in fact, a lot more than I deserved.

The End

About the Authors:

Charlie Cochrane's ideal day would be a morning walking along a beach, an afternoon spent watching rugby, and a church service in the evening, with her husband and daughters tagging along, naturally. She loves reading, theatre, good food, and watching sport.

She started writing relatively late in life but draws on all the experiences she's hoarded up to try to give a depth and richness to her stories.

Coming November 2008 by Charlie Cochrane

Lessons in Love
Book One of The Cambridge Fellow Mystery Series
Solving crime isn't their only passion...

Lee Rowan has been writing since a second-grade nun explained that fiction lets you tell stories without being scolded for lying. She didn't keep much of the dogma from those early days, but retained the concepts of "love one another" and "do unto others".

Lee believes that loving and being loved is one of the finest things about being human, but after a difficult first marriage and a few short-term disappointments, she decided that humans were more trouble than they were worth. Eventually, a couple of cats and a big-hearted dog taught her enough about love to melt her cynicism, and romance started creeping into her writing. When she started writing love into her stories, it came into her life, and she is now happier than she ever hoped to be in her second—and final—marriage.

Lee thinks fiction lets a person try out new ideas before tackling them in real life—whether it's traveling to a distant place or taking an emotional chance—because before anything can happen in reality, it first has to happen in the imagination, where dreams are born.

When not tossing fictional people into mad, passionate embraces or doing research for same with her sweetie, Lee likes to garden, haunt garage sales, and take care of the four-legged fur family.

Also by Lee Rowan

Ransom
Winds of Change
Trilogy No. 109: Sail Away
Walking Wounded

Erastes lives on the Norfolk Broads and is the director of the Erotic Authors' Association and a member of the Historical Novel Society. He's had over 20 short stories published as well as a gay regency novel, *Standish*. His second novel, Transgressions, based around the English Civil War, will be published by Perseus Books in 2009. Erastes' aim in life is to make the gay historical novel as mainstream a genre as the heterosexual kind.

Coming November 2008 by Erastes

Frost Fair
Come in from the cold and let us melt your heart...

This is a publication of

Linden Bay Romance

WWW.LINDENBAYROMANCE.COM